Reckless Hunger

Reckless Billionaires

Maxine Henri

"Whatever our souls are made of,
his and mine are the same."
Wuthering Heights, Emily Bronte

Chapter 1

Ivory

"Hurry, Ivy, we're going to miss the best part." Julianna grabs my wrist and drags me up the stairs from the subway.

I wobble, almost spraining my ankle. "If you didn't force me into these inhumane heels, I'd be faster." We rush across the road.

I'm like a newborn giraffe in my bright yellow romper and the impossible platform shoes. Give it to my best friend to ensure we both draw attention wherever we go. Julianna in her skimpy red dress at least carries her part with grace.

Ever since I became the tallest person—not girl, person—in my class a few years back, I understand first-hand how an elephant in a porcelain shop feels.

"We're almost there. I'm so excited. Cassi is so hot—"

I roll my eyes. "And he hasn't had a show in years... you've only said that like a hundred times." I pull the strap of my loose top up my shoulder.

I'm sweating, and my thong is digging into my ass as I stagger down the path to Violet Mathison's gallery in SoHo. "Are you even sure we can get in?"

"I was until now." She stops suddenly and I'm propelled forward, unable to halt quickly enough. I avoid a close encounter with the pavement because she grabs my elbow to steady me.

I follow Julianna's gaze to a group of people in front of the exhibition space. The light from the gallery glows onto the street through large glass windows. Andrea Cassinetti hasn't publicly exhibited in years, but it doesn't seem people have forgotten him.

We might as well be attending a rock star concert. "Holy shit. Why do they all want to go in?" I step from one foot to another, seeking relief for my soles.

Laughter and animated conversations echo through the night. Inside, people push through the space like it's a nightclub. A sea of bodies spills out onto the street, forming a vibrant crowd of enthusiasts.

My heart races, the idea of immersing myself in this fervor filling me with trepidation. I don't go out as often as other people my age, but when I sneak out, I want to spend my time being reasonably crazy. This just might be a little too crazy.

"How are we even going to see the art? If we get in, that is?"

"Shut up." Julianna beams. "We came to see the artist. Come on, Cassi is waiting." She takes my hand and yanks me forward, acting like we actually have an invitation. "Excuse me." She smiles at a group of young people smoking by the door.

They assess us with glassy eyes and return to their muted conversation.

But somehow this non-existent exchange gets us closer to the door. When Julianna wants something, she gets it. And tonight, she wants a glimpse of the man of the hour.

We push in, and a collective murmur of voices and the smell of bodies immediately assaults us.

Julianna taps my shoulder. "Let's find him."

She makes her way through the room and I try to keep up, stumbling, colliding with people and apologizing. Stupid shoes. I glimpse her red dress disappearing into the next room.

"Hello, beautiful," a deep voice whispers into my ear. "Let's find a quiet corner."

Goosebumps—and not the pleasant type—cover my skin. I try to step aside, but there is nowhere to move. Breathing through my mouth, I hope to escape the rancid breath of the man beside me. Our eyes meet and I recoil. He's high as a kite and probably drunk.

I point to where Julianna has gone. "My boyfriend is waiting for me."

He shrugs and sways away. Jesus. I should have just stayed home.

My eyes land on a large canvas and I freeze. The crowd fades out as I'm drawn to the beauty on the wall. The painting's abstract layers of colors create a vibrant dance, and yet they also evoke pain and struggle. They touch me with familiarity.

Like every morning, when I step into my mother's room, hoping to see the kind face from my childhood. The painting, with its vivid strokes, could easily be a memory of her. A beauty that is no longer there.

I don't know how the artist depicted sorrow in a piece that shines with bright colors, but I can't tear my eyes away from it.

I stand there, mesmerized, ignoring the bumps and shoves of people around me. They disappear into the avalanche of emotions that seep through me as I try to understand why I'm drawn to this particular painting. Do others see the same suffering?

In the realm of art and emotions, where boundaries blur and possibilities swell, my world collides and oddly intertwines with this work of art.

My eyes finally find another piece and I shake my head, but the profound feeling remains. The strokes of this artist, whoever he is, touch me on the deepest personal level, leaving me breathless and yearning for more.

Frankly, it's unnerving. Like someone took a deep dive into my soul. I want to leave, overwhelmed by it all.

My life. My father. My mother. My cage. My chains.

I need to leave.

Making my way through the crowd, I finally find the red dress among a group of enthusiasts ogling a man who is talking in a small circle.

The mischief in his eyes doesn't run deep. It's a mask. I know, because I've been pretending for most of my life. Playing a role scripted by my parents.

I'm not sure what or why the man is hiding, but I'm strangely drawn to his mask, wanting to rip it off. Bare him.

I must have gotten a contact high by breathing the air in here, because it can't be the art that has me this unraveled and interested in the dark corners of some strange dude.

Everyone is staring at him. And it hits me. He is the artist. He created the moving pieces that scraped me raw, making me feel all the feels I've bottled up inside.

He scratches his chin. His pianist-like long fingers are rough, yet elegant.

He cups the face of a woman beside him and crashes his lips against hers.

Geez. I don't need to see that. I move to reach Julianna when a collective gasp silences the room around me.

Before I figure out what's happening, someone yanks at me. The platform shoe tilts and I lose my footing, hauled down by the force of another body.

Pain zaps through me as my ass hits the floor. I hiss, swimming in the darkness for a moment. The heaviness on my chest barely lets me breathe.

I open my eyes, and the need to breathe becomes a distant memory.

I'm on the floor, pinned by him.

The artist.

A rich blend of warm sandalwood and subtle hints of spicy cardamom help me breathe. His skin carries an underlying note of fresh earth.

The scent is confident, captivating, and undeniably masculine. But it's his eyes that draw me in, making me forget about the discomfort, and my probably bruised ass.

His perceptive eyes seem to see beyond the surface, delving into the depths of my being. Or I've hit my head and am hallucinating.

Because in his gaze, I find an inexplicable comfort,

as if he could unravel the complexities of my existence with a single glance.

Dark brown with hints of green, his eyes are as enigmatic as their owner, sheathed in some internal struggle.

It's like looking into a mirror. I don't want to do that. It's all a lie. I blink.

He pushes up on to his elbows, but doesn't move further. I more feel than see the lean muscles of his arms, bracketing my face.

His thigh presses against my center, and to my shock, I want to grind against his leg. Jesus, the man has just kissed someone else, and I want to dry hump him?

Well, I do.

His breath smells of alcohol, and I wonder why I'm not as repulsed as I was moments before when the other dude assaulted me. It must be the lack of oxygen. He's heavy.

"You're hurting me," I croak, even though I don't want him to move.

What's wrong with me?

"You're beautiful." His voice is like a melody to my ears, but it's his words that hitch my breath.

He thinks I'm beautiful? Perhaps he's more drunk than I thought.

My body is crushed beneath him and yet experiencing all sorts of pleasant reactions. The most embarrassing is the tingling in my core.

My eyes drop to the lips that spoke the words of praise. I crave more of it. I want to kiss him. I've never felt this uninhibited. I dare him with my gaze to lower his lips on to mine. I want to experience it with every cell in my body.

I'm sure he's thinking the same, but instead his weight lifts and he is dragged up. Away from me.

"Are you okay?" A woman helps me to my feet. I only vaguely register her, because I can't look away from him.

The intensity of my emotions is surprising, the irrational pull I feel toward him. It's as if an invisible thread connected us, drawing me irresistibly closer to his magnetic presence. The thread is fragile but vital. If we look away, it will burst.

"I'm okay," I finally remember to function like a half-human.

My ass is bruised, my ankle hurts, my generally wild hair is probably in disarray, and yet the only thing I'm focused on is the man who thinks I'm beautiful.

"I'm sorry," he rasps.

People fuss around us, but we keep staring at each other, as if the world ceased to exist the minute he took me down with him.

As if sculpted by some masterful force, his every movement captivates me.

I want everyone to leave us alone, to disappear so I can spend some time in the shadows of this man. I'm completely intoxicated by him. By his art. If he even is the creator. It's completely irrational. Dangerous.

Save yourself, Ivy. Run while you still can.

I stutter, "I have to go."

I can't run in my shoes, so I try to exit as graciously as possible, making my way through the crowd that parts for me miraculously.

The warm evening air sobers me, but my poor heart gallops around. I see the woman who my artist kissed earlier in an embrace with another man.

My artist?

"What the hell was that?" Julianna jumps from somewhere and hooks her arm through mine. "You lucky bitch." She jerks her shoulders up in glee.

"Who was that?" I want her to confirm my assumption.

"Cassi!" she squeals, looking at me like I'm an idiot. "Andrea Cassinetti practically assaulted you in front of everyone. I'm so jealous." She sighs.

"Of my bruised behind, and the most embarrassing moment the gallery experienced?" I feel a bit guilty. She's been dreaming about meeting him for weeks now.

"Are you for real? Most of those people won't even remember it tomorrow. He probably won't. Let's get a drink."

"I have to go home. It's late."

It's irritating that she thinks Andrea won't remember me tomorrow. Also disappointing that she's probably right. I need to go home to lick my wounds. The real one—because my tailbone hurts—but mostly the ones on my ego and my fragile soul.

Julianna protests for a moment, but then she relents and we take the subway. Daydreaming, I only half listen to her blabbering.

Would I have been this impacted by our weird encounter if I wasn't already moved by his work?

Was it his art that primed my senses to experience the man himself in a deeper, unexpected way?

What's wrong with me?

We didn't even talk, regardless of the messages he tried to portray through the colors on his canvases. His presence, the artistic one, left me feeling both vulnerable and empowered.

I don't know what this inexplicable connection with Andrea or his art is, but it defies reason. Yet it feels like destiny.

Like I don't want to carry only sorrow, the burden of expectations my parents bestow on me. I want to break free. I want to embrace the world.

"Have you told your dad yet?" Julianna's question catches my attention.

"I'm going to tell him tomorrow." Just the idea weighs me down with fatigue, but I can't postpone it any longer.

"What if he doesn't let you?" She lowers her head to my shoulder.

The subway tunnel blurs behind the window, and I fidget on the plastic seat. "He probably won't."

"I have an idea." She perks up. "Tell him you want to take a year studying art. That you'll go back to Columbia next year. It's not like you progressed there much anyway. He might be more amiable to you taking a gap year of sorts."

She is not wrong. I don't know what's worse: telling my father I want to study art instead of economics or him finding out I'm failing miserably at the major he believes is my future.

"And then what?" I lean back to look at her.

"*Then* is a year away. We'll figure it out." She winks, and I envy her carefree solutions to everything.

She grew up as a princess in her family, and unlike me she always got what she wanted, being the only daughter with three brothers.

I'm an only child, but the level of responsibility in my house would be hard to meet, even by three children.

"I'll see how it goes."

But my mind is far from the looming potential conversation with Papa. The colorful canvases I admired tonight hijacked all mental imagery.

And if I'm honest, the artist did as well. Just a little.

Chapter 2

Ivory

It's only ten o'clock, but the street is deserted by the time we get to Julianna's place.

"Oh, girls, you're home. Did you have a good time? Come and eat something." Mrs. Biachi, Julianna's mom, ushers us inside.

She's the most elegant woman in our neighborhood. Probably in the whole of Brooklyn. My mom is a beauty, but she lost her spark a long time ago. Agatha Biachi ignites the entire block with her kindness and generosity.

"We're not hungry, Mama." Julianna rolls her eyes.

My mother has never cared about my food. We have a cook now, but when I was younger she'd often forgotten about my meals. It's funny how some things are a nuisance to some but a treasure to others.

"I'll eat." I smile at her, finally getting rid of the stupid shoes.

Later, we listen to all the neighborhood gossip while I inhale the best plate of pasta I've ever had.

"How was the exhibition?" Agatha pours herself some limoncello and takes a sip.

"Cassi, the artist, has a crush on Ivy." Julianna laughs.

I roll my eyes, but heat spreads across my cheeks. "Well, more like he almost crushed me. I have a bruise like a melon on my butt." I pout.

"Oh my, sweetheart, let me give you an ointment." Agatha leaves.

"You have to stop this." I glare at Julianna.

"Not unless you admit you liked him."

"Who do you like? The artist?" Agatha returns with a tube and gives it to me. "Massage that into your skin and the bruising disappears faster. And don't fight the attraction. Love can spark out of unexpected circumstances. When I met—"

"We've heard the story a million times." Julianna makes a gagging sound and drags me out of the kitchen.

She isn't wrong. The insta-love story of Mr. and Mrs. Biachi has been shared many times. I'm sure she exaggerates bits and pieces, because the story is as sappy as the Hallmark channel. And while their marriage seems grossly happy, I know that's an exception.

The bigger the love, the larger the sacrifice. And at the end of the day, it's all for nothing. Just pain and suffering. Case in point, my parents, Eden and Cecil Harrington.

Upstairs in Julianna's room, I change back into my regular clothes and hang my yellow romper in the corner of her walk-in. My most inspired and favorite possessions reside in Julianna's closet.

In my simple black dress, I hug my friend and call my driver.

Oliver has been my best friend and protector since I was allowed to venture out by myself. If my father ever catches us, Oliver stands to lose his livelihood and probably the ability to ever get employed again on this planet. Despite that, he helps me out where my father sees no sense.

Like tonight, when he stayed behind so I could go out with Julianna like a normal person. Not like a gilded princess.

"Your father has arrived early." Oliver opens the door for me in front of the Biachis' house.

He's been my only gateway to some sort of freedom. On occasion. He trusts Julianna and her family—a sentiment possibly related to Agatha's cooking—so he lets me out of his sight when I'm here.

"How do you know?" I slide into the back seat, and he shuts the door behind me.

"Martha warned me," he says once he's settled behind the wheel. Our housekeeper isn't the warmest person in the world, but she likes Oliver, which helps me by association.

I sigh. "Mother was sleeping when I left, so let's hope everything is all right."

While I hated the idea of studying economics, I hoped staying on the campus would bring my parents closer. Instead, my father arranged with the school that I'd live at home. He couldn't leave Mother alone. I couldn't either. He hardly ever stays. I try as much as possible.

I sneak into the house and tiptoe upstairs. Peeking into Mother's room, I confirm she's indeed fast asleep. Slowly, I make my way along the hallway.

Light glows from my father's office, and I catch the angry rumble of his voice.

"I said I'll have it ready for you by the end of this month."

Ice clinks, followed by liquid being poured.

"I don't care about that," he snaps. "This business in South Africa will get resolved soon, and then you don't have to worry anymore."

Father's voice is colored with impatience, and I

rush along to make sure he doesn't catch a glimpse of me. The last thing I want is his wrath.

I get into my room, change into a nightgown and climb into my bed. Before I succumb to sleep, the colorful strokes of a brush continue to flash in my mind, along with the mysterious eyes of Andrea Cassinetti.

* * *

Mother cries when I make my way to her room in the morning. I don't bother asking her what's wrong. The reasons for her dismay haven't changed in years.

"Good morning. Did you take your medication?" I kiss the crown of her head.

Seated at the vanity, she stares at her reflection in the mirror. I guess I should be happy she made it out of bed.

"Your Papa is home. I wanted to look my best for him." Her glassy gaze focuses nowhere in particular.

"Let me do your hair." I smile and she lifts her eyes, meeting mine in the mirror's reflection.

"Don't you have to go to school?"

"It's Saturday, Mommy." I pick up a brush and gently stroke her hair.

"Oh, is it already? Where did the week go? Have you seen him?"

She never asks about me. It's all about the man who doesn't deserve her attention, but I can't hold it against her. The love of her life broke her, which has left very little room for me in her shattered heart.

And yet I hope. For her. For me. For the little girl who still remembers almost losing her.

"No, I haven't seen him yet. I came to you first." I separate her hair and twist the two sides into a high chignon. "This looks beautiful on you."

A ghost of a smile passes across her face as she slowly retreats into the world where we can't really access her. At least I know she took her pills.

"I went to an art gallery last night." I pin her fine hair to hold the updo.

"Oh, isn't that nice, chérie? Your Papa used to take me to every important opening in the city."

Her memories of my father are so remote from the man I know, I sometimes believe she's making it up. But she has photos to prove their beautiful love affair.

My mother's inability to conceive created distance between them. And their love fizzled out quickly after my father got full access to her inheritance.

When she finally had a baby—me—at thirty-eight, my father lost it completely.

I'm not an heir after all.

I continue styling her hair, and don't tell her that the paintings, and their creator in particular, unraveled something primal and alive in me. That it reflected all my dormant, hidden feelings.

It makes no sense anyway. My mother has been gone in her own world of self-loathing for way too long to exhibit any compassion.

My father broke any kindness she had left.

I finish her hairdo and we head downstairs together. Breakfast is laid out in the formal dining room. When Papa is at home, we pretend to run on some sort of schedule, like a normal family.

The air is always tense with his brooding presence, and Mother's fleeting attempts to capture his attention.

He sits at the head of the table, reading on his tablet. He looks up and almost smiles at my mother.

"Eden, I see you got up this morning. Good on you."

My mother smiles as if that was an actual compliment. At that moment, I resent my father even more than usual.

For mocking her. For making her weak. For enabling her madness.

"Good morning, Papa." I pour myself a glass of orange juice and plop down across from Mother.

"Is that all you're having? You are too skinny." He doesn't even look at me.

"You should eat some toast," Mother says weakly, always eager to please the lord of the manor.

I reach for the toast and tear a piece with my teeth, the crumbs scattering.

"Ivory, that's not the way a lady eats," she berates me.

Somehow, finding faults in my behavior is something that always perks her up. A bonding moment with my father.

I drop the toast to my plate and put a linen napkin on my lap.

When I'm home, it's like all my courage and rebellion leaves. Squashed by the iron rule of my father. Or perhaps I spend it all outside of my cage and none of it remains for here.

For when it matters.

For where it matters.

"Would you make my coffee, chérie? No one makes my coffee better than you." Mother smiles at me.

I stand up and pour her a cup with three spoonfuls of sugar, and a generous serving of cream.

My father puts down his tablet and observes me. I brace for his vicious comments because I'm used to them by now.

When I sit down and he remains silent, I know trouble is coming. When Cecil Harrington sets his eyes on someone, they are his prey. And only rarely do they escape.

My phone vibrates in my pocket, and I check it

under the table while Mother tries, and mostly fails, to pull my father into a conversation.

JULIANNA:

Have you told him yet?

I'm about to respond to her that this morning doesn't seem the best time for that conversation. But then, no morning, no time of day, is good for this conversation with my parents.

"I've decided to take a year to study at the Celestial Art Institute in Chelsea," I announce, my voice confident, but my heart thumps in my temples.

Mother drops the cup, spilling the coffee, and Father chuckles. He chuckles as if we were not talking about my future. But he says nothing. His silence fills me with more dread than his words would have.

"Darling, art is not something you should pursue. Only talented people succeed in that field, and the rest are just starving wannabes. You already study at one of the best schools in the country." Mother kills my ambitions with her sweet tone of well-meaning. She's always completely insensitive when in his presence.

Why do I even want to stay nearby? Because I'm a glutton for suffering. I can't leave her alone with him. Not that he's around much.

"Perhaps it's a good idea."

The words come out of my father's mouth, but

their meaning is too positive to make sense. I whip around to face him.

"You think?" My voice is just a whisper.

"But focus on art history. I don't need you to embarrass us in the more creative fields."

I lick my lips, my head spinning with possibilities. What just happened? My father allowed me to study art? At a prestigious school, but still...

"Besides, you won't be there for long."

He wipes the corners of his mouth and stands up, taking a few long strides out of the room. At the open double doors, he turns. "You will get married before Christmas."

Chapter 3

Andrea

"Really? No one else was available?"

I roll my eyes, but a part of me is grateful Gio is the one who came to pick me up. My brother is one of the people who deserves my apology, after all.

"Yeah, asshole, I drew the short stick." Gio gives me a half-hug and throws my bag onto the hood of his Lamborghini.

"And all the less ostentatious cars were in use already?" I smirk and climb into the passenger seat.

"You can always take a bus," he deadpans. "How are you?" He roars the beast to life and glides onto the road.

In the side mirror, the castle-like property of the rehab clinic disappears slowly from my view. Let's forget the place right now, shall we?

"I'm fantastic." Fake it until you fucking make it. "Does Mother know?"

Gio looks at me unimpressed. "You were there for over three months. What do you think?"

I drag my hand over my face. "Fuck."

"We told her you were in Europe." The bastard laughs.

"Thank you." Why my siblings have been covering my ass for years is beyond me. "And I'm sorry."

He taps his fingers on the steering wheel but says nothing.

The countryside unfolds with vibrant shades of green, dotted with red and white farmhouses and picturesque barns. In a few months, nature will change into a thousand fall colors.

It would be great to come here for inspiration. But I don't need that anymore.

Four hours later, the landscape gives way to the bustling energy and towering skyline of Manhattan. "I shouldn't have kissed your fiancée," I continue, like we haven't driven hundreds of miles in silence.

Gio gives me another unimpressed glare and returns his focus to the traffic.

"How was the wedding?"

As our destination approaches, I desperately try to keep the conversation going. To distract myself. To fucking delay the inevitable of facing my new life.

"There was no wedding," Gio finally speaks.

"Shit. I'm sorry, man. Is that because of me?"

"Don't flatter yourself, asshole. Mila broke up with me, but we're back together."

"What happened?"

"She deserved better. But for some outlandish reason, she gave me one more chance, so I'm trying to be worthy of her. It's fucking exhausting. And the most rewarding challenge I've ever had."

"Holy shit, bro, you fell. You fell hard. I'm happy for you." And I am happy for him. I think. My feelings have been numbed over the last few months.

"You should try to find someone who grounds you. I'm not driving ten hours back and forth again. Get your shit together."

"You could have sent a helicopter
or a plane."

"And have the media on your ass the minute you land? Fuck that. You're going to lie low in your home for a week and then slowly return to society like a functioning, productive citizen. You need to smooth things over with Violet Mathison."

"You could have just told Mother about this if you're going to parent me." He's not wrong, but that doesn't mean I have to like it.

The fucker clicks on his phone and Mother's number flashes on the dashboard, the dial tone filling the space. I stare at the screen, trying to figure out how to stop the disaster while Gio smirks.

"Gio, darling, how are you?" My mother's voice echoes in the small interior.

"I'm great. Guess what, Mom, I just picked up Andrea from…" He looks at me, amusement coloring his face. My stomach constricts. The last thing I want is to talk to the woman I keep disappointing the most. "The airport," he finishes, flipping me the bird. "Say hi, bro."

"Andrea, you're back finally. How are you, my boy?"

This is the problem with my mother. Even after all the disappointment I've caused her in my thirty-one years, she sounds genuinely happy to hear me.

"I'm not a boy anymore." *But I am an asshole.*

"Okay, Mom, I have another call. You can catch up with *your boy* at the family get-together this weekend. Ciao." Gio hangs up. "Seriously, the woman hasn't seen you since God knows when and you argue her pet name for you?"

I look out of the window on my side. "I didn't need her in my face right now."

"You never need anyone in your face. The woman has been supporting you throughout all the shit you put her through. The least you can do is fake your gratitude. You were on the way to your grave three months ago—"

"Shut up. I know I'm a fuck-up. I don't need your constant reminders. The well-meant older brother shit will drive me to drink." I fist my hair. This stupid car is too small.

Finally, we come to a stop in front of my townhouse in Chelsea and I open the door, but Gio's hand on my shoulder stops me.

"Have you ever considered that your family loves you? Unconditionally. Not that you make it easy, but fucking accept it."

I stare at him. His words make sense, but that doesn't make them a comprehensible concept. Or believable. More like they put up with me because they don't have a choice.

"You're getting sappy now that you're in a relationship," I snarl, and get out of the car.

The door of my house opens and my sister, Paris, beams at me.

"Oh yeah, asshole, surprise." Gio snickers. "Paris volunteered to be your roommate for the next few days." He gives me a thumbs-up and pops the hood open so I can get my bag.

"Thank you for the ride," I murmur, and bang the door of his car harder than necessary. At least I can fuck with his precious ride. My brother flips me off again and revs the engine.

I take the few stairs to my place. Paris, to her credit, doesn't talk, just follows me inside like a shadow.

It's my home, but it feels foreign. The air carries the scent of freshly polished wood, mingling with the strong aroma of coffee. I get to the kitchen, kind of lost, unsure of what to do. I'm exhausted, which is ironic since I have done nothing to tire me.

I reach out and trace my fingertips along the cool, smooth marble countertop. I itch to grab a pencil, but what's the point? I won't draw or paint.

"I'm going to lie down." I pass Paris without looking at her.

"Okay. I'll cook us something for later." She sounds fucking deflated.

I'm disappointing someone right off the bat. What was she expecting? A game of Monopoly, or cozying up on a sofa to watch soap operas?

I trudge upstairs to my room. Once a sanctuary, it now feels like an enigma. I navigate to the bathroom and wash my face.

The fragments of familiarity linger in the air, but I don't quite know what to do here. I plop on my bed and stare at the ceiling.

How am I to start anew? To give up my only

passion? The one that keeps me alive but kills me slowly?

* * *

"You didn't come down for dinner last night." Paris smiles at me from the sofa in the sitting room.

I stop my descent. She seems genuinely relieved to see me. What did she think? That I would slit my wrists in the bathtub?

"It would be nice to start the day without a guilt trip." I lean against the banister, glaring at her.

She stands up and licks her lip, her eyes pleading while her face turns crimson. "I'm sorry. I didn't—"

"Just fucking stop tiptoeing around me like I'm going to shatter. I probably fucking will anyway, so can you just treat me like I deserve?" I get to the kitchen and start the espresso machine.

"And what is it you deserve, Andrea? Enlighten me." Her voice behind me rings with hurt. I lower my head.

If they thought having a sitter here would work wonders for me, they were wrong. This is worse than the thoughts in my head.

"What should I be treating you like?" she urges.

"Like the fucking disappointment I've been. A

loser." I face her now and wish I hadn't. She has tears in her eyes.

Bring it on. I'll have a dose of pity with my coffee this morning. Just mix it up with the guilt and all the other fucked-up things roaming in my head.

Paris shakes her head like she wants to physically recover from my words. Sometimes I try to do that too. It doesn't work.

"Fine, go ahead and label yourself as such." She folds her arms across her chest. "But don't you dare force us to use those labels. There is no evidence to support them. You're an extremely talented and successful artist. For whatever reason, you're throwing it all away, but that's on you."

I down the espresso and throw the small cup into the sink. It splits in two. "You don't know what you're talking about. The pressure. The constant need to outperform."

I walk across the kitchen, through the double-door into my sitting room. I sit on the sofa, but immediately stand up and march to the window.

"I don't know what I'm talking about?" Paris yells. "At least you're putting yourself out there."

Fuck. I didn't mean to hurt her. Paris is an interior designer, and she is as talented as me—if not more—but she shies away from creating her own pieces.

I want to take the hurt back, but I don't turn

around. In the kitchen dishes clank. She is probably channeling her frustration into some unnecessary chore. "*You* put the pressure on yourself. *You* need to accept your talent."

Is she for real? "Like you? Have you accepted your talent, Paris?" Without making a conscious decision, I'm moving back to the kitchen.

She is leaning over the dishwasher, stacking plates inside. I kick its door closed, making her jump away.

We glare at each other, our chests heaving. What am I doing?

I sigh, lowering my head. "Any minute someone will discover I'm a fraud." The words cause me physical pain. I need to numb it. Fuck.

"So you'd rather behave like one? To save them the surprise? Are you even listening to yourself?"

And now it's there, the hint of heaviness on a soft exhalation. Her words carry a subtle undertone of resignation, a gentle deflation. I know it well. That subdued sigh conveying a sense of letdown.

Mrs. Smiroyevski had it in my art class when I was six. When instead of fall leaves, I painted something that did not look like leaves at all.

Or my mother, when at fourteen I ran away from school and spent the night in a rundown drug cave, spraying graffiti on public property.

Or my first gallerist when she found out my stepsister, London, purchased all my drawings.

The sound of my life.

"Let's have breakfast." I smile at Paris. If nothing else, I can fake my interest in survival. I have honed that skill for years.

"Okay, but you make the pancake batter." A smile ghosts her face.

We make a feast for a family of six, and as we sit down at my breakfast nook a sense of calm descends on me. Maybe I can do this. If I focus on simple, everyday tasks, I can exist.

"So, what are you planning to do?" Paris breaks apart a freshly baked roll, the steam infusing the air with a delicious smell.

"I accepted a position at the Celestial Art Institute." I cut a chunk of my pancakes.

She widens her eyes. "Oh my God, Andrea, that's one of the most prestigious art schools in the world."

I nod. My stomach churns. I'm pretty sure it's not food-related. "The therapist at the clinic suggested a sense of order and regularity would be good for me."

A cup in her hand, she stops it mid-way to her mouth. "What does it mean for your art?"

"I'm taking a break from that."

"A break?" She drops the cup, spilling the coffee. "For how long?"

This is the first time I've voiced my decision out loud, and it feels... I don't know, but it doesn't feel like the end of the world. Maybe it is the right move.

"You should be supporting me," I say drolly.

She stares at me like I've just grown a new head.

"Indefinitely, Paris. Indefinitely."

Chapter 4

Andrea

"We are honored to have you join the staff." Dean Wiggins purses her lips. The pretend enthusiasm of her words doesn't reach her eyes, or her tone.

In her fifties, the woman has silver hair cut in a stylish bob. She is tall and slender and could pass for a classy New Yorker. And perhaps she is. I don't know. Or care. I do know, however, that she is not thrilled to have me here.

I guess she isn't as important as she believed she was. Several board members begged me over the years to become a guest professor here, and I doubt she voted for that decision.

"I'm grateful for the opportunity." I kiss her hand. Charm has always been one of my go-to currencies.

She pulls her hand from me like I spit acid on it

and clutches it to her chest. "About your reputation, Mr. Cassinetti..."

And here we go. She couldn't stop the board from hiring me, but she will unleash her power trip to feel better.

"Yes, Dean Wiggins?" I challenge.

"This is a prestigious institution, and we pride ourselves on creating a safe and healthy environment. Alcohol, drugs and sex are not allowed on the campus."

"I shall make sure not to bring any." I smile.

Her nostrils flare.

"Alcohol and drugs, I mean." I continue.

"And stay away from female students, Mr. Cassinetti. You might be a talented artist, but I will hold you to very high standards when it comes to your conduct here."

Throwing my ass out of here at the first opportunity she gets, is what she means.

"I feel very welcome, Dean Wiggins. And inspired to work with an authority such as yourself."

A former art historian, Mary-Anne Wiggins has made her mark on the art world as a bitter critic and reasonably successful school administrator.

Her next achievement would probably be serving my ass to the board. Game on, lady. I'm staying. If for nothing else than for the lack of other sources of adventure.

"Make sure you follow the syllabus. Virginia Fox has been covering your classes in the first two weeks. Let me walk you to the professors' lounge. She will help you get settled and show you the campus."

It only takes Fox half an hour to give me an overview of the syllabus and the campus before we walk through the corridor toward my first class. Unlike my boss, my new colleague doesn't look at me like I'm carrying a contagious disease.

In her late thirties, probably, Virginia is short and curvy with an outrageous laugh. She offers the sound freely. Its sharp, jarring notes grate against my senses. I cringe and simultaneously marvel at the unfiltered expression of joy. And probably madness.

Maybe this new gig is something my soul has needed all along.

Though as groups of students rush around us, my palms sweat. I'm used to my studio, and the hours of solitude that I usually compensate with partying. Being around other people all day might be a trigger I don't need in my life right now. Especially since my pressure release strategies are off the table.

"It might be intimidating at first, but don't worry. These students are talented, and they respect your work, so you're off to a great start." Virginia picks up on my internal turmoil. "In the annex, you can find creative spaces. Usually, students use them for their assignments if they don't have opportunities to complete them at home. But there is enough room to find tranquility and solace after a long day."

Fuck. Is she a mind reader? "I have a studio at home. I'm going to be fine."

She stops and assesses me with a raised eyebrow. All students have withdrawn into their classrooms and the hallway is silent. It makes Virginia's scrutiny much louder.

"Look, I'm pretty sure you're not here because you need a job, or money, for that matter. The Cassinettis are rich, and your work is valued at hundreds of thousands. Whatever you came here for is your own problem, but if you need to talk, I'm here."

Just like that, a stranger wants to talk to me. Bullshit. Has Wiggins assigned her to spy on me?

"Thank you, Virginia, I appreciate it." *And never plan to take you up on that offer.*

She observes me silently again. "Okay." She smiles. "Friday afternoon, after school, some students host a creative workshop for children in the courtyard here. I'm a professor guarantor to oversee the project and usually we end up in a bar down the street, pretending we don't see their fake IDs. Why don't you join us?"

Is this a test? "I have a feeling Wiggins doesn't want me to fraternize with students."

Virginia utters one of her scary laughs. Its peculiar

cadence pierces the air, a cacophony of sharp cackles and shrill bursts. I shake my head, chuckling myself.

"Just keep your head down," she says, mirth lacing her tone. "Wiggins is tough, but fair. She's worried you'd be a bad influence on the students, but I can't blame her." She winks. I guess my life is an open book for everyone.

Well, everyone but me. I don't understand myself half the time.

"Fair enough." I shrug.

Virginia cocks her head, smiling. "You have trouble written all over your face, Andrea, but I'm happy our students have you coaching them."

We walk toward my first class. "You'll start with drawing basics to warm you up. I've covered hands and faces with them. It's mostly anatomy for this semester. Today, you're starting with live models. The school usually pays a small fee to student volunteers."

"Sounds good. Thank you, Virginia. Anything else before I enter the lion's den?"

She laughs again and I swear it's infectious. I'm in a better mood just from judging the deafening sound.

"No worries. They will adore you. Keep them focused on their sketches, not your pretty face."

She dashes toward another class, but before she disappears inside it, she turns. "And Andrea, there is no need to dress up here." She snickers.

I straighten my four-hundred-dollar tie. Okay, I might have overdressed.

Staring at the white door frame, I absorb the silence behind it. My new life. Observing the art of creation instead of conceiving it.

I used to consider teachers as mediocre losers. Like they couldn't be good enough in their field to succeed so they had to teach, trying to manifest their failed dreams through their students.

Now I'm one of them. Fitting my own theory.

I take in a deep breath and open the door. Several pairs of eyes turn to me. Students are scattered around the room. Some sit on sofas with sketching pads in their laps. Some stand behind easels.

In the middle of the room, on a circular podium, shines the most alluring tawny skin. Loosely sheathed in a voile fabric, the woman sits on a high stool.

Frozen, I stare at the perfect curve of her shoulders and the long neck. Someone clears their throat and I blink a few times, taking in the awkwardness of my ogling.

Good job, Cassinetti. What an entrance.

The woman in the center turns and our eyes lock. She's as vibrant and radiant as I remember. Warmth and boldness glimmer through her eyes as recognition passes through her features.

God, I dreamed about her more than I care to admit.

Vivid.

Moments stretch as we stare at each other. The flimsy fabric slides from her shoulder and she clutches it tighter. My eyes fall to the swell of her breast, and before I can think—because when have I ever done that —I move to her.

I yank her from the podium with one hand, while simultaneously trying to keep the see-through layers of fabric in place with my other hand. Dragging her to the door, I register a few gasps and murmurs. I'll fail the fucker who dared to whistle.

I kick the door closed and push her against the wall. Her heaving chest brushes against my jacket.

I'm mildly aware of the possible consequences of my actions, but the awareness is muted by the anger and inexplicable need to protect my muse.

"What the fuck are you doing?" I growl.

Her eyes widen. "Shouldn't that be my line?"

She's right. I'm a fucking lunatic, but for God's sake, those horny dicks were staring at her. I'm sure half of them signed up for the class just to jerk off to her image.

Not that I, a hypocrite, haven't done the same countless times.

"You can't do that. You're practically naked." The

reasoning behind my words is less than sound. Fuck the logic.

"I can, and I will." She spits the words, but she doesn't try to get away from me.

Not that I'm giving her much choice. Pinned between me and the wall, her body is molded against mine and—fuck, I want to hoist her legs to my waist and fuck her until we both scream.

I should never have become a teacher. I'm too fucked-up to be a mentor for these young people.

That thought is fleeting. Inconsequential.

We glare at each other. When I met her the first time, I was so mesmerized by her eyes I didn't notice her mouth.

Full, caramel, completely edible.

What's wrong with me? She licks her lips and my cock stirs. The electricity zaps, charged with tension and, at least on my part, with desire I should not feel.

I can't feel.

I'm a professor here.

It's been only an hour.

I can resign.

She swallows hard. "Are you going to bruise me every time we meet?"

I drop the wrist I've been squeezing too hard without realizing. "Sorry."

I shake off my jacket and drape it around her shoulders. She pushes her arms through the sleeves and wraps them around her mid-section.

She is tall and slender, and it hangs on her but somehow still fits. This woman is too sexy for her own good. And too young for me to even think in those terms.

Great, Cassinetti, from drugs and alcohol to sexual depravation.

We continue staring at each other. So, I dragged her out in the name of decency, and now what? I don't care, as long as she isn't naked there.

"Go get dressed." My voice is hoarse. Out of all the possible volunteers for my class, what are the odds this woman—this girl—ends up here? Fucking naked. Another wave of anger sweeps through me.

"No." She almost stomps her foot.

Oh, and she has a personality. A spark. That's just great. "What do you mean no?"

"I need money. I'm going to model." She narrows her eyes and folds her arms across her chest. "You have no say in that."

"Don't I?" I yank the door open. "Watch me."

If I'm lucky—and that's the largest *if* in fucking history—no one will report me to the dean as I utter my first words as a professor to my students:

"Class dismissed."

Chapter 5

Ivory

The little girl covers almost the entire paper with a black crayon. Black house, black tree, black clouds.

"What's your name?" I sit down cross-legged beside her. "I'm Ivory."

"I'm Emily." She looks at me through hooded eyes.

The beautifully landscaped courtyard of the school is sprinkled with colorful art supplies. Carefree kids lie on picnic blankets or sit at the benches around the wooden tables.

The air is alive with the gentle rustle of leaves from tall oaks shading us from the unexpectedly warm day in the middle of September. I still can't believe I'm a part of this beautiful atmosphere. I merely existed at Columbia for two years and this is like a dream.

Especially after the dreadful summer. Every day

I've feared my father will present me with my future husband. Or change his mind about the "gap" year. And my mother has swayed between complete desolation and the high from the occasional attention Father awards her.

To make things worse, Papa has been spending more time at home, growing paranoid about all his business associates, half-waiting for someone to steal from him.

The whole gloomy situation has one benefit, though. At the end of the summer, he's been so distracted by some deal that he didn't have time to discuss my school. In fact, I don't think he noticed where I've been studying.

At twenty-one I might be the oldest in all my classes, but I love every minute of it. If I never see another interest rate chart or taxation policy, I'll be the happiest person.

Thanks to Julianna's father, I was able to secure a student loan, so my tuition here is covered. Father has been skimping on my allowance, but I don't really have any expenses and I can make enough money to cover what little I need. Which would be easier if a certain professor didn't act like a jerk.

"Is black your favorite color, Emily?" It used to be mine when I was growing up. I couldn't see things in other colors, so I drew in a monochromatic fashion.

When my teacher in the second grade suggested my parents should take me to a therapist, my father got upset and yelled at my mother. I started using colors after that, afraid I'd push her to do something horrible again.

"I don't know. I think it's Mom's favorite. But when she looks at my black pictures, she says it's concerting." Emily doesn't look up but continues covering the paper with blackness.

"Do you mean concerning?" I reach for a sketch pad beside her and start doodling with a red crayon.

"I guess. Mom is really busy, and the only time she looks at my drawing is when it's black. So I like drawing in black." Emily meets my eyes, full of expectation.

"I think you're doing a fine job with that black color." Her face lights up with a beautiful smile.

We continue working beside each other. The afternoon passes in languid contentment as I talk to the little girl and doodle in all the colors of the rainbow.

After a while, I put the sketch down and lean back on my hands. Julianna is helping a group of boys tame a slab of clay.

Timothy, who is in his third year like my friend, is splashing colors on a large canvas in the middle of the lawn, and a group of kids is running through it squealing.

Other students are assisting children with different art projects. I smile as I observe the scene, wishing I could bring some of this atmosphere home.

When my eyes settle on Professor Fox, I freeze. She speaks with the man who has been stealing my attention since that night at the gallery. I didn't expect him to be here. I haven't seen him since the incident two days ago.

What was that all about? Who does he think he is? Acting like he has any right over my life. I have a man like that at home, and frankly that's more than enough.

Though, to be honest, his caveman routine stirred something inside me. Something I haven't felt before. It's beyond attraction. When he pressed his body against mine, parts of me I didn't know I had came alive.

Next day, Julianna confirmed her class was back to full body models. Male. Apparently, Cassi gave them an explanation why it is better to learn on a male form.

It's sexist. It's arrogant. It's bullshit.

Not that the measly fee for modeling would help me gain financial freedom from my father, but it was something. I can still get assigned to other classes. Sculpting with Fox is possible later in the semester.

But I need to find a job. Unlike my classmates who have had summer jobs before and have probably helped at home, I can't possibly imagine what I might do. I'm a privileged brat, and if I'm honest I've been enjoying my lifestyle.

Time to grow up, though.

"Your bodyguard has been glaring at you." Julianna drops down beside me.

I roll my eyes. "He's not my bodyguard." I chance a look and, sure enough, our eyes meet.

Cassi is alone now, sitting on a bench with his back to the table. Leaning on his elbow, with his long lean legs stretched and crossed at the ankles, he gawks at me.

If I didn't know better, I'd think he owns this place. His presence consumes the air between us. His attention on me spawns all sorts of reactions.

My heart races. My mind melts. I swallow and force myself to look away.

I don't know what it is about him, but the mere idea of him brings a flutter to my stomach—an anticipation that fills every corner of my being. I'm drawn to him with an undeniable force, and I can't help but wonder if he feels it, too.

Even if he did, he's a teacher here, it's not like... What? Where did that thought come from? I've been fantasizing about Andrea Cassinetti, but it's almost like dreaming about a movie star or a famous athlete. Yes, he's within reach in my stratosphere at the moment, but that doesn't mean I should allow myself to hope.

At least he behaves with inexplicable crassness, so I don't have to worry about falling for him.

"He certainly behaved like one in class. It was the hottest thing ever," Julianna says dreamily.

I face her, glaring. "Do *you* have a crush on him?"

"Have you seen the man? Everybody has a crush on Cassi." She shakes her head. "The more pertinent question is, why couldn't he stand anyone seeing you naked?" She is looking at him now, daring him to come over with her eyes.

Heat spreads over my cheeks. "Some outlandish need for modesty?" My voice is weak.

She laughs. "Yeah. You're a lucky bitch. He's into you, which begs another question. What are you going to do about it?" She moves her gaze to me.

"Nothing, of course. First, it's just a figment of your imagination. Second, he's a professor here—"

"Ah ha!" She points her finger at me. "And if he wasn't?"

I bite my lip. "There is no point to that theory."

"Well"—she stands up, dusting off her jeans—"you'd better act quickly, because the competition is fierce." She beckons toward his bench. "I'm going to check on the clay disaster project."

Sure enough, two girls are talking to Andrea now. I think they're two or three years older than me, certainly more experienced in flirting.

He shields his eyes with his hand as he looks up at them from his seat. They are all animated with the full female arsenal ready—batting lashes, hair flipping, giggles. Their behavior is pathetic. And so is my desire to swap with them.

Relaxed and perfectly comfortable, Andrea says something and they laugh. He smiles. I think this is the first time I've seen his face light up, and I wish I didn't.

As his features soften with whatever is so funny, he looks almost boyish, approachable. Someone I could talk to.

"You don't like your drawing?" Emily's voice startles me.

Without realizing, I've been squeezing the paper, dampening it with my sweat and wringing it between my palms.

"I'm going to start over, I guess." I smile at the little girl, who progresses to another black drawing.

When I look up, the two are marching away. One of them is shaking her head and the other glowers. They don't seem pleased with the turn of the conversation.

Before I can stop myself, I jump to my feet. *He's into you.* Julianna's words boost me with unwarranted courage as I walk across the lawn.

When I step in front of him, I realize I don't quite know what to say. He doesn't move or speak. Squinting against the sun, he cocks his head, amusement quirking up his lips. And he stares.

I lick my lips.

I ball my hands into fists.

I inhale.

My body keeps circling between these small reactions to his proximity.

To my inability to form a sentence or find any semblance of sass. Or wit. Or charm.

The longer we silently observe each other, the more uncomfortable I feel, sweat covering my nape.

"I still have your suit jacket." That's what I come up with after endless moments of charged silence. I could have just started with *I'm an idiot.*

He drags his eyes lazily down my red T-shirt and washed-out jeans, a smirk on his face. It's not the smile he gave those two before, which hits me with jealousy. I didn't know I was the jealous type.

I never cared about anyone enough until now. Wait? What? I care? That's preposterous.

"I'm aware." His velvet voice shoves my heart into overdrive. His eyes rest on my lips and my breath hitches. Jesus.

It's surreal. He's sitting on a wooden bench. I'm towering above him, yet he holds a strange power over me. In my mind, at least.

For all I know, he's indulging me out of pity. I have "crushing hard" written all over my face.

"I'll bring it on Monday?" I stutter. I freaking stutter.

All our encounters combined haven't amounted to half an hour, in which I've found myself under him, pinned against him half-naked, and now completely bared to his charisma. I guess moved by his art is also in the mix.

His actions have been embarrassing, but here we are, with me being the one mortified.

He purses his lips, trailing his gaze down my body again like I'm edible. "Keep it." He shrugs.

My eyelids move rapidly as I try to grasp what he said. "I can't. It's expensive. You can't just give me a Brioni. Besides, I don't wear men's clothes." Can I be more absurd?

He hums with an intense expression, like he's seriously considering how to solve this. Or just messing with me. The blood pumps in my cheeks.

"Pawn it." He licks his lips, and I swear it's in slow motion. Maybe it's too hot today and I should have worn a hat. And drunk more water based on the desert in my mouth. "You said you need money."

The nonchalance in his tone is confusing. Is he seriously suggesting I keep his expensive suit jacket? Or is he taunting me?

"I won't sell your suit jacket." I throw my arms in the air, huffing with exasperation.

He, on the other hand, seems amused by our exchange. Or annoyed. I'm not sure. He regards me like I'm a puzzle he's not sure he wants to waste his time with.

"Why not?" It's unnerving how serious he sounds. "I gave it to you. You don't want it. Apparently it's expensive. You need money." He stands up. "I'm not letting you strip in front of the class again. So take it as compensation for the lost income."

He's too close, his scent of sandalwood and earthiness swallowing me. His body heat robs me of reasonable brain function.

But, thank God, a smidge of reason prevails.

"Who are you to decide what I can and cannot do?" I step back.

We're on school grounds. At an event full of people. But that's not the reason I distanced myself. I need to save myself from him.

Maybe he's teasing me for the fun of it. It's appalling, but for some stupid reason I'm drawn to him even more when he acts like an asshole.

And I'm strangely thrilled we have witnesses. Like they're an invisible barrier between us. Protecting me from him.

He stares at me, his jaw ticking. He drums his

fingers on his outer thigh. Who does he think he is? His deep eyes—today more green than brown—devour me, though I'm not sure if he even likes what he sees. He is definitely battling something I can't understand.

"What is it you study here, Vivid?"

His question throws me off. "Vivid?"

He steps forward and I want to retreat, but I won't give him the satisfaction. He takes another small step and now our bodies are flush.

I should step back. But he shouldn't have stepped closer, so I won't blame myself.

Yeah, he started it.

Really mature.

It's rare I find someone matching my height, but Andrea—with his lean, firm body—seems to tower above me. Not by much, but enough.

"I asked you a question." His breath fans my face. God help me.

He sucks all my energy away. "Art history," I croak.

"Good." He steps back. "I won't have you in my class."

If he'd slapped me, it would have hurt less.

He turns and walks—no, prowls—away.

Chapter 6

Ivory

"What are you doing this weekend?" Timothy asks me.

I've been sulking over Cassinetti's remark, over his behavior, since we left campus.

The bar is as packed as they come on Friday evening. We had a reservation, and it feels like half of the crowd here is from the school.

On the other side of the long wooden table, Julianna is chirping away with Cassi. The traitor.

Okay, to be fair, most of the female population is hanging on his every word. What can be so riveting?

Why did he even come?

Teachers join us here at times, treating us like equals. Drinking, talking about art, debating politics. But Cassi feels foreign here.

I turn to him and force a smile. "Not much. Just helping my mother. I'm going to get another drink."

"Let me get it for you. Another beer?" He stands up.

I chance a glance, and of course it's when Andrea looks at me. I wish I didn't have all these conflicting feelings. I'm drawn to and repelled by him at the same time. He treats everyone with more... I don't know more of what, just better than me.

"Let's do shots." I smile at Tim.

My classmate's eyes light up before he rushes to the bar. I sigh and play with my empty bottle. Annoyed and deflated.

Everyone is having a good time. I was looking forward to this outing. Father is away on business, and I needed to let loose. And now I'm sitting here, stealing glances at a professor who acts like a caveman, and at the same time treats me like a child.

Tim returns with a full tray of shots and everybody around the table cheers. "These are for us." He swats everyone away and winks at me.

Julianna makes her way over to us. "Oh my God, he's so dreamy. Why don't you talk to him?"

"I'm not interested." I down my first shot.

She raises her eyebrow and snorts. "I see." She grabs a shot and hands me another one. We finish two more before my head starts spinning.

Cassi sits by himself, his flock of admirers probably retouching their makeup.

He rakes his fingers through his hair, some of it escaping into his eyes. He has one ankle crossed over his knee and a sketchpad propped against his shin.

He holds his pencil in a weird way between his thumb and ring finger. Like a child who is just discovering how to use it. It makes me want to help him.

I don't know what's forming on the paper, but it captivates me. With the lightest touch, he sketches and shades, the tip of the pencil scratching across the white paper in a beautiful flow.

It's like watching a dance performance. I can't take my eyes off it.

Tim pushes another shot into my hand, whispering something in my ear, but I'm completely entranced.

Either Andrea doesn't notice I'm staring or he doesn't mind. I don't know, but I wish I could witness this kind of effortless creation for longer.

An artist focused on his work. Immersed in creating.

A sloppy kiss lands on my cheek and I push Tim away. "Stop it."

When I look back, Andrea's chair is empty. I glimpse his lean form heading toward the exit. Without thinking, I jump to my feet.

"Hey, Ivory, come on, let's have some fun." Tim

pulls me into his lap, the alcohol on his breath mingling with the shots in my stomach and making me sick.

"Get off me. You're drunk." I push up to standing, the floor swaying a bit.

Andrea opens the front door and steps into the street. I'm struck with a pang of loss and disappointment, which makes no sense.

As I reach for my bag, I notice the sketchpad lies on the chair Andrea vacated. I round the table, my heart racing.

I pick up what he's left behind and gasp.

I'm slightly nauseated, my head swimming with the effects of too many shots. And yet my heart blooms as I take in the portrait.

A halo of hair fills the paper, smoothly turning the curls into flowers, flowing around a face.

My face.

It's like looking into a mirror that reflects me in high resolution while showing all my imperfections. He drew my untamable curls like a beautiful garden.

My slightly crooked nose like a dominant feature of my face, awarding it a prominent place.

The swollen lips that I find too large for the rest of my face fill a perfect heart shape on the page.

It's like he knew everything I hate about myself and proved me wrong.

I rush outside, pushing through the clusters of

people. It seems everyone is trying to block me, but I finally make it out.

Clutching the drawing to my chest, I desperately look left and right, but I don't see him.

Crestfallen, I sigh and fish out my phone from my pocket. I aim the camera at the paper. It's dark, but I still want to make sure that I have this drawing forever.

"What are you doing with that?"

I whip around, almost dropping my phone. Cassi stands a few feet from me, one foot propped against the wall casually, cigarette in his hand.

"You smoke?" I hold the sketchpad tight. It's white and large, covering my torso, but I still hope he won't focus on it.

"Why do you insist on ignoring my questions, Vivid?" He takes a drag, pinning me with his hooded eyes.

Why is every conversation with him so difficult? I step toward him, close enough to get burned. "Why did you leave that drawing behind?"

"Isn't your boyfriend looking for you?" He flicks the butt to the ground and straightens up, stealing the air and space between us.

"Why don't you want me in your class?" The alcohol makes me feel invincible. Okay, it gives me the courage I so desperately lack when I'm around this man.

"This conversation is a dead end if we keep asking questions without answering."

I swallow and open my mouth, but my drunken mind is blank. Andrea lifts his hand and traces my cheek, his long fingers like feathers. I don't want him to stop, and I need him to stop at the same time.

"Okay, girl, I'll start. I only smoke occasionally. I left the drawing behind because I don't want it. I don't want you in my class because one look at you drives me crazy."

Oh, my poor heart. It swells and races like a spooked horse. My brain grasps his words, trying to make sense of them. Stupid shots. Why did I drink so much?

"Your turn, Vivid." He continues dusting my face with his touch like he's trying to memorize it.

"Why do you call me that?"

He shakes his head and drops his hand. The loss is staggering. "Go home, little girl."

"I'm not a little girl." I huff, proving I'm a petulant child.

He drags his hand down his face. "Okay, go back to your boyfriend." He turns and walks away.

Like I'm possessed, I rush behind him and grab his arm, forcing him to face me. "I don't have a boyfriend."

He raises his eyebrows, unimpressed. "Well, the

Varsity boy in there didn't buy all those shots for nothing."

He glances at my hand, squeezing his jacket. I let go and he continues walking.

I follow.

That's how desperate I am.

Or drunk. Or just plain stupid.

"What are you talking about?" Why do I need to prove anything to him? Why is he dismissing me like that? It brings out the worst in me. I don't like this needy girl.

"He's been eating you up with his eyes all night and getting you drunk. What do you think he's after?"

I stop. This is too much. Have I been leading Tim on? Is Cassi jealous? Why is he having this conversation with me? Why am I insisting on it?

The wave of nausea comes unexpectedly, and I gag. That finally stops my professor.

"Jesus fucking Christ," he murmurs as I dash to the corner, double over and empty my stomach.

I almost fall on my face because I'm trying to protect the sketch, but a firm hand snakes around my waist while he holds my hair. More like fists it to keep it out of the way, but still the gesture is comforting.

Not enough to overwrite the shame. Please God, this would be a great time to send me a time machine, or eliminate the entire planet.

I stay bent over, hoping he'll just leave me here, but he stands patiently. I take a fortifying breath and straighten up.

Andrea doesn't let go of me. He turns me gently, pushing me against the wall. "Don't move."

I close my eyes, considering different ways to live this down, but the only option is to quit school and move to another continent.

"Drink." The order brings me back to my bleak reality.

I don't want to open my eyes. For one, the world spins less in the darkness. But mostly because I can't face him.

"Take the water, Vivid." The dominance in his voice hits close to home. Quite literally, in my case.

"Stop ordering me around." I yank the bottle from him and gulp it down.

"Slowly." He shakes his head. "You're going to retch again."

As soon as he says it and my brain is about to snarl at him, my stomach heaves again. I fight the wave of nausea with deep breathing and a few more sips of water.

"Thank you," I whisper.

"Are you returning to the Varsity boy, or should I get you a cab?" He hands me a piece of gum.

"He's not my boyfriend, and I don't sleep around." I don't know why I chose to make that point.

He narrows his eyes and takes me in. "I'll get you a cab."

"You don't need to take care of me. I'm not a little girl." I huff. Apparently my arsenal for exasperated sounds is limited. Which sucks given the level of irritation this man causes.

He growls, cups my chin and turns my face to him. We're inches apart. I'm painfully aware that the gum might not be enough to mask the rancid feeling in my mouth. But that concern disappears when he speaks.

"Make no mistake, little vixen, under different circumstances I *would* be taking care of you, and you would love every minute of it."

Chapter 7

Andrea

I'm fucked.

I'm royally fucked.

I'm screwed... like a-cactus-up-my-ass fucked.

Goddammit.

I tried to avoid her. And I succeeded. In a literal sense, at least. Because in my fantasies I can't stop thinking about those dark eyes with golden sparkles and her tawny skin.

Or those tiny freckles peppering her cheeks. I hadn't noticed those before. It's like each time I see her I discover a new beautifully flawed thing about her.

I tried to avoid her. Until yesterday. When I saw her at the children's workshop, I should have made an excuse and left. I didn't, and then Fox saw us sparking with sexual tension during that ridiculous exchange about my jacket.

I stretch and check my clock. Six o'clock. Fuck me sideways. I've barely slept. When have I ever tossed and turned over a chick? Over a work in progress, yes, many times. But a woman? A girl, for fuck's sake.

Somehow I got lucky, and my caveman routine from the first day in school didn't get reported. So there I went and pushed my luck. Of course, Fox noticed. Only a blind person would miss my drooling every time her slender, tall figure hits my line of vision. Which is fucking always.

Fox warned me on the way to the bar. That should have been my clue to go home. Because I'm a recovering addict to begin with. Yeah, that would have been the smart choice. Never have I leaned into those.

Nursing my water, I couldn't stomach seeing her getting drunk with that bulky asshole who was clearly planning to make a move.

Over my dead body.

And that's where I'm wrong. I have no claim on that girl. She's a fucking girl. I smile at the memory of her exasperation when I called her that.

I groan and swing my legs over the edge to push off the bed. I had noble intentions when I stormed out of that bar, because she's becoming a trigger for me. At least I squelched it with a cigarette.

When she ran out, looking all lost and vulnerable, I couldn't help but speak. She clutched that sketch to her chest like it was a treasure.

That's another issue about Vivid—she inspires me. I swore off art, and there I was, sketching in the middle of a bar.

Fuck. I drag my hand down my face and trudge to the bathroom. After a shower, I get downstairs and sneak into my backyard. Inhaling the fresh air, I close my eyes and let myself glide on the wings of imagination.

Just under the corner of her eye, the freckles form a little star shape. A tiny caramel star. The same color as her lips. My cock stirs in my slacks. I open my eyes, forcing my focus from Vivid to the two tall chestnuts dominating my miniature oasis.

Pulling out a lighter, I play with a cigarette between my fingers. I take a long drag.

"You went out last night." Paris leans against the glass door.

"Jesus, you move like a ghost. Why aren't you sleeping?"

"Why aren't you?"

Have all women decided to drive me crazy with their questions?

"I have a lot on my mind." Shut up, idiot.

"Did something happen last night?"

I take another drag, studying the chestnut's broad crown, weighed down with heavy branches.

"Nothing happened last night." Well, aside from my completely inappropriate conduct with a student. "I was out with a colleague and some students. I drank water. I left early."

"Because you can't have fun without alcohol or weed?"

"Fuck, Paris, it's too early for this shit." Though I appreciate she's stopped tiptoeing around me, the candid version isn't necessarily a welcome intrusion. "I'm still clean. You haven't failed."

Her shoulders slouch. "Sorry. Do you want coffee? The last thing we need is Mother's three-sixty while tired."

"Now I need a drink." I sigh.

Paris's eyes widen and I chuckle.

"Hold your horses, sis. I'm just kidding." I toss the butt in an empty plant pot. "Though a good inch of whiskey to begin the day..." I push her through the door.

She swats at me. "You're such an asshole."

I laugh, despite the toll of the sleepless night. "I wouldn't want to disappoint you."

We make coffee and eat breakfast. I must admit that while I hate the reasons that Paris is here, I'm enjoying her company. It keeps me out of my head, which is a good thing.

She tells me about a new client and shows me some of her ideas on her tablet. "I'm trying to find the perfect painting to place here, but I can't find any."

"We have to stop at Violet's gallery today, so you can pick something up or have her search for you." I shrug and move to the sitting room.

Plopping onto the sofa, I turn on the TV. I don't think I've done that in years. A part of me wants to go upstairs and shut myself in the studio. But I can't do that.

"You want to go there before we visit the parents?" Paris asks, walking to the stairs.

"Yes. I need to..." I scratch my neck. "Apologize. And I'm too chicken to go by myself."

She smiles. "I'll hold your hand."

She takes two steps at a time to get to her—my—guest room. If I took those steps, I would be only a flight away from my studio. The smell of turpentine fills my nostrils, though I know it's my imagination. The room is sealed.

I turn to the television and flip the channels. With no idea of what I'm watching, my mind circles between a certain vivid muse and the reality of all the time I have on my hands. If I don't paint or party, what do I do?

* * *

"Well, well, well, if it isn't my worst client." Violet greets us with her arms folded across her chest.

I study the floor for a moment and then turn around, but Paris blocks the entrance. Trapped between the two women in the vast space of the gallery, I sigh.

"Can we talk, Vi?" Not sure why I ask since that's what I came for, but this journey of penance is excruciating.

Whose idea was it to put me through a triggering situation on my way to sobriety? Fuck me.

"Unless you're here to admire the art, which I doubt, I'm assuming we're going to talk. Shall we go to my office?" She doesn't wait and turns to the door in the room's corner. "Rory, please mind the floor and come to find me if someone comes," she instructs her assistant, a young gawky girl.

Vi pushes the door open and waits for me and Paris to enter. If it wasn't embarrassing, I'd turn around. But I force myself to act like a reasonable adult. A concept I'm familiar with only by observation.

"Look, Vi, I'm sorry about the opening night." I deliver my words to the floor.

"Are you, though?" She leans against her desk, folding her arms once more.

I meet her eyes. "I'm sorry I ever agreed to exhibit." That is true. What happened afterward was just a casualty of my lack of judgment in the first place. "You pursued me long enough to wear me down, but now we know I was right to keep refusing."

Paris sighs. Okay, probably not the best apology. But a fucking truth.

"So you're saying it's my fault? My mistake to have spent years building a reputation and then having you jeopardize it because you can't face attention or, God forbid, success?"

Her words land like a punch in my stomach. "Let's go." I turn to Paris, who fucking sighs again.

"Apology accepted." Vi stops me in tracks. "You're an asshole, but all that well-hidden insecurity comes across in your work, and it moves people." She rounds her table and opens a drawer. "Here. You weren't answering your phone and I wasn't sure where to send your check. Your infamous exhibition sold out."

She hands me an envelope. I reach, but she snatches it back. "I took a higher cut because I had to work extra hard to get people to come back to look at those pieces."

She flips the hand again, so I can take the check. I stare at it for a moment as if it was burning. "Thank you." I open the envelope.

"Well done, bro," Paris mutters when she glimpses six digits over my shoulder.

"I'm not throwing an exhibition for you ever again, but I'm happy to broker deals whenever you have a piece to sell." Vi extends her hand and I shake it.

"Don't hold your breath."

"So after all the trouble, you'd go to my competitors?" She shakes her head and opens the door to see me out.

"Don't be so dramatic, Vi, I'm taking a break."

She bangs the door closed. "A break? Why?"

I let out a long breath through my cheeks. "I'm seeking regularity in my life, so I started teaching."

She narrows her eyes. "While I applaud your efforts to raise a new generation of artists, holy shit, Andrea, you'll die of boredom. You don't do ordinary."

Paris clears her throat. "I think it'll be good for him. To focus on himself."

Vi opens her mouth and closes it again, but then speaks anyway. "You have a gift, Andrea. A unique, beautiful ability to layer emotions and opinions on canvas. You can't give that up."

"I can and I will." I open the door and walk out, the check burning a hole in my pocket.

"Wait." Paris stops me at the door. She makes quick arrangements with Vi about her client and catches up with me.

"You sold out." She bounces beside me and trips. I grab her arm to steady her.

"Give me a moment." I cross the street and enter a branch of my bank. I deposit the check and immediately transfer all the money.

Paris is leaning against her car, typing on her phone. "Maybe you should take me shopping." She wiggles her shoulders before she gets behind the wheel.

"You have your own money to do that," I mumble, and fold myself into her stupid electric car.

"To celebrate. I mean, you can't drink, so shopping seems like a blast."

"To you, maybe. Besides, I don't have the money anymore." I start playing Fruit Ninja on my phone.

"What do you mean? You've just deposited the check. Oh my God, Andrea, are you in debt? Have you spent all of your trust fund? Are you in—?"

"Shut up, Paris. For fuck's sake, I gave it to a charity."

"Oh, that's nice. Still, you must be pleased you sold out," she chirps.

Her words whirlpool in my mind, creating a thick fog. The air is suffocating. The car's interior spins, blurring at the edges. My right hand trembles.

Paris turns on the music, but even the silent hum of the air-conditioning is already too loud. Desperately trying to ground myself in my inner chaos, I grab my quivering hand. Fuck.

"Why doesn't anybody understand?" I yell. "I don't want people owning my paintings. If they look too close, they'll discover what a fraud I am."

Chapter 8

Andrea

"We don't have to stay too long. I'll make an excuse." Paris pats my shoulder as we walk toward the front door.

Earlier, she somehow found a spot to park for a moment so I could regain my wits. And I somehow found my calm without dragging her to a liquor store. To her credit, Paris didn't force me to talk. Nor did she try to contradict my words.

She silently let me have my tantrum. At the end of the day, what would she say? I'm a fraud.

"I'll be okay. Sorry you had to witness that." The amount of time I've spent lately staring at the floor or the ground will give me a stiff neck soon.

"For what it's worth, I agree with Vi. You don't have to exhibit ever again. You don't have to even sell your work, but I think quitting art to remain sober is stupid. Not creating will trigger you faster."

"I can't, Paris. I can't. It drives me crazy, and then I compensate with alcohol," I confess, reaching a new low. Just cut my balls off right now.

"You need a hobby, then. Maybe you can tackle some of my bucket list items with me."

I'd rather party myself to death while painting a masterpiece.

The door springs open. "What are you two standing here for? You're late." Mom yanks me to her. "Andrea, look at you." She hugs me and I fight the urge to recoil. I love her, but can't she fuss around my other seven siblings?

"Hey, Mom." I kiss her forehead. She cups my cheeks and stares at me for a moment, looking for something. The woman is clairvoyant, I swear.

"Have you been well?" She beckons us in. "Paris, you look great. Did you guys carpool?"

Shit. Maybe not clairvoyant, but definitely observant.

"My car is in the shop. What's for lunch?" I wrap my hand around her shoulder and pull my best game. "Is that a new hair color?"

"You're the only one who noticed, darling." We make our way to the main living room where everyone is already assembled. "Look who joined us." Mom pats my back.

Everyone greets us. Paris with joy. Me with an awkward hesitancy. Maybe I should just carry a breathalyzer to these visits to put everyone at ease, so they don't eye me like a caged monkey.

"You look good." Gio gives me a half hug. "What have you been up to?"

"I got a job." I shrug. I don't think I spoke loudly, but the room goes silent.

"A job?" Massi, my oldest brother, asks. He's fucking standing across my mom's sitting room that rivals a ballroom in size, and he still heard.

"Yes, everyone, I'm teaching at the Celestial Art Institute."

"That's wonderful." Mom claps. "Come help me in the kitchen." And here we go. I follow her, all eyes—most full of condolences—on me.

"Darling, promise me you'll get enough sleep." Mom surprises me with her random plea.

"Of course. It's a day job, Mom." I climb up on the stool at the island.

"Yeah, which means you'll forget yourself in your studio at night." She pins me with her gaze. It's full of concern, which I hate.

There is only a thin line between concern and pity. At least disappointing her has always been a familiar feeling. This current level of attention makes my skin crawl.

"I've just sold out my last exhibition, Mom. I'll take a break and focus on teaching for a while." I smile at her.

She jerks her head back. "Is that what you really want, darling?"

It feels like I'm the only one wanting it. "Yes, Mom, it's for the best." I slide down and kiss the crown of her head.

"Oh my God," London's voice slices through the air.

We both rush back to the sitting room. "What's going on?" Dominic, her boyfriend, dashes to her side on the sofa.

"I just got a generous donation. Someone sent us a quarter of a million. Anonymously." Her eyes dart between her screen and Dominic who kisses her.

I turn my gaze to my current favorite place, the floor, but I sense eyes on me. Paris shakes her head with a smile.

I shrug. I can still deny. London, Paris's twin sister, has been running a charity, and while I haven't spoken to her since my first ever exhibition, I've been sending money to support her cause every year. I might be hurt by her buying all my paintings back then and robbing me of true recognition, but I still respect her generous work.

As we make our way to the formal dining room where the dinner is served, Paris grabs my arm. "So, you don't speak to her, but you support her cause. A wild guess, given how brief your visit to the bank was, that this was not the first time?"

I put her in a headlock. "Wow, Sherlock, I'll have to kill you now," I whisper into her ear.

"Let go of me."

I do, and she almost collapses to the floor.

"Oh, kids, play nice." Massi's wife, Gina, snickers behind us.

"You need to grow up, Andrea." Paris shakes her head and leaves me behind.

Lunch is a loud affair, Mother commanding the conversation with machine gun-style questions. Luckily, she leaves me alone.

During dessert, I check my phone and find a message from an unknown number.

> I can have your jacket delivered. Send me your address.

Vivid.

All my reason screams not to answer. *Don't answer.* I type my reply. *Don't send it, asshole.* I hit send and save her number.

Is this a ruse to find out where I live?

Why do you want me to keep your
jacket?

How did you get my phone number?

Are you mad I did?

Why do you always ask, but never
answer?

I'm a curious vixen, what can I
tell you?

What's your name, Vivid?

Why do you call me Vivid?

Just answer one fucking question.

Ivory, and please don't make the
usual comment.

What comment?

That Ebony would fit me better
because my hair is so dark.

I chuckle and the room around me goes silent. Fuck. "Sorry, just a message."

"You're on your phone more than Gio used to be," Massi comments.

"Just return to your dessert, asshole. I'll be outside."

I kiss Mom's cheek on the way. "The lunch was delicious. I just need some fresh air for a moment."

On the patio, I drop onto one of the lounge beds and save her number.

> You're definitely not monochromatic to me, Vivid.

VIVID

> I'm starting to like Vivid.

That makes two of us.

> I'm not going to give you my address. I don't want to get fired.

VIVID

> I read somewhere your studio is at your house. I want to see it.

Fuck. She really is young. But unlike with any other obvious attempts to get to my house before her, in her case it entertains me. It's like her attention differs from anyone else's.

Genuine. Real. Innocent.

I have no right to engage in a conversation with her. It's against the rules.

The fountain chirps down the path and birds sing above my head. Amidst the peaceful sounds, I let my mind wander.

Let's sum up my recent situation. I fucked up an opening night, and sold out anyway.

I dragged a naked student from the model gig she was paid for and didn't get reported.

I pretty much accosted her in the schoolyard while everyone was watching, and then did it again in front of the bar. No consequences.

She is alluring, but I'm not a horny teenager. I can control myself. Okay, barely, but I can.

The biggest problem is the assault of inspiration she stirs in me. I swore off the work, but I couldn't help it and sketched her.

With each stroke of the pencil, a surge of anticipation coursed through me. Like foreplay. I was liberated at that moment of every trouble and doubt, just fueled by passion that couldn't be contained anymore.

I lost myself in the dance of lines, shapes and shades, chasing the beauty she doesn't even know she shares with the world. The pencil's graphite became the extension of my fascination, tracing the contours of the vision of her.

The satisfaction that comes with every stroke is something I've been chasing since I first discovered drawing. The agony of trying to capture the perfect form of what I see makes me alive.

And destroys me. But can I really go without that

intimate dance? My therapist might apply logic, but that is irrelevant when it comes to art.

Vivid truly is my muse.

I'm fucked.

Royally fucked.

My phone buzzes in my hand and I chuckle. She's calling. Fucking relentless little vixen. I shouldn't answer, but when have I ever followed the rules?

"This could be considered stalking." I smile like an idiot.

"Sorry. You didn't answer and, well... it was rude to invite myself to your studio, I know, but I've been staring at your sketch since last night. At the gallery you told me I was beautiful. I didn't believe you, but that sketch. The way you see me..."

"Stop babbling, Vivid." I chuckle. "Keep the sketch."

"That's not why I contacted you."

"You wanted to hear my voice and find out where I live. You're a stalker." My jaw is going to dislocate from the stupid grin.

"I want you to paint me."

Chapter 9

Ivory

I should have never shown that drawing to Julianna. I can't believe she talked me into this.

My car rolls down the vibrant streets. The entire block has such a Cassi vibe. Polished, but rough around the edges. A beautiful chaos of small cafes and eclectic little galleries. Everything pulses with art here.

It's no wonder my school resides in Chelsea, but I can also see that Cassi wouldn't fit anywhere else. This is his domain.

When Julianna forced me to write to him—okay, she was the one to send the first messages from my phone—I didn't plan on going any further with the innocent exchange. But that drawing, the way he sees me, made me feel bolder.

There are so many boundaries I'm blurring here

that it makes my heart skip beats. I love every minute. And regret it.

Or I probably will. Eventually. But if my father succeeds in his mission to marry me off for a profit, I might as well enjoy my freedom while I still can.

Andrea Cassinetti gave his phone number to all the students in his classes. I'm sure Julianna wasn't supposed to share that number, but as she said, "Let me live vicariously through your forbidden affair."

"I'm going to see him in action. Creating art, helping me feel better in my skin. That's all. There will be no affair," I told her, rolling my eyes and ignoring my thumping heart and fluttering stomach.

Under different circumstances I would be taking care of you, and you would love every minute of it.

Was he referring to his position at school? To our age difference? What circumstances hold him back?

I hate how needy I feel.

I hate that I'm lying to myself.

I told Julianna it's all about art and self-acceptance, but if he made a move... Jeez.

We turn onto a street lined with trees and meticulous green landscaping in front of every home. The townhouses look identical, with washed limestone facades giving the traditional design a modern feel. There is no doubt people here have money.

Oliver stops the car. "I doubt I can find a parking spot nearby. I'll have to circle."

"Maybe wait here as long as you can. I'll text you if I'm going to stay longer." I fidget with my compact, applying a bit of lip gloss.

"Who is this new friend again? I should probably have your father's security check him out." He observes me in the rearview mirror.

While Oliver is as benevolent as they come, being always on my side, he's still protective. He allows my freedom with Julianna and people he trusts, but this is beyond his comfort level. Well, his and mine—for different reasons.

Why did I even bring him?

Because I wanted to have an escape strategy.

Because I'm way over my head with this adventure.

Because I may be a little vixen, but I'm meeting a sorcerer with all the spells.

Because I want to be here, but I fear it at the same time.

Meeting Oliver's eyes in the mirror, I know I should have come by myself. Now I have his judgment and worry to add to my list of cons. Because yes, I made a list.

Not that it was useful in any way. The only pro on the list was that I'm attracted to the man. I'm touched by his art, and I want to spend time with him. It overwrites all other reasons in the opposite column.

"It's someone I met at school. Look where he lives —it's not like he'll kidnap me for a ransom." My chuckle sounds mad.

If Oliver wasn't suspecting anything before, now he is. I shouldn't be this nervous. It was easier to be bold via text and phone call.

Facing the man with my weird indecision about what it is I want from him is a whole different game.

I'm turning into my mother. Needy and desperate.

"Okay, I'll remain double-parked for as long as possible. I trust you, Ivy."

I open the door and rush out. I wish he hadn't said that, because I feel like I'm already betraying that trust.

I breathe and take the few steps leading to the front door. I glance back. Oliver is following me with eagle eyes. What will he think when he sees Andrea?

I care about his opinion, but not enough. The reckless thought propels me forward.

I ring the bell and practically bounce with anticipation. I wonder what he wears while at home on a Sunday. Shit, I should have brought his jacket. I completely forgot about that.

All my frantic thoughts come to a screeching halt when the door opens. I blink a few times and then smile, confused.

"I'm sorry. I must have got the wrong house," I tell a beautiful woman with gray hair. Who dyes their hair gray?

"Who are you looking for?" She leans against the door.

Before I answer, Cassi comes from around a corner. His eyes are bright with the mischief I like so much. His hair is mussed, falling into his eyes.

Now I know he wears jeans and a simple T-shirt on a Sunday. Oh, and he's barefoot. Looking like a model, he wears the casual outfit with a confidence and sexiness that are dangerous for my underwear.

He takes in my face with such an intent expression I swear he's trying to memorize my features. It's like he's not even seeing me, but different parts of me in a disjointed but somehow synchronized way. Right now, I could swear his hooded eyes landed on my lips.

None of it matters, because there is a woman in his house.

"Vivid," he rasps.

All the blood travels to my temples, pumping so loud everyone must hear it. I'm frozen to the spot.

"Oh, so you do have the right address," the woman chirps, beaming. She touches his shoulder in a familial way and pads away.

Why is she so pretty? *Wrong question, Ivy.* Why is she here? Is he married?

"Come on in," Andrea says.

I shake my head, turn before he can see the stupid tears pooling in my eyes and dash down the steps. Thank God Oliver is waiting.

I jump into the car. Before I close the door, I hear Andrea. "Oh, for fuck's sake, Vivid."

"Go. Drive away," I urge Oliver.

My driver doesn't need more encouragement and pulls onto the street. The loser in me turns. Cassi bounced down the stairs to the sidewalk. Without shoes. If I didn't just see his wife, I'd have thought he chased after me. I'm pathetic.

He shakes his head and puts a phone to his ear.

My phone rings in my pocket. The car takes a turn, but I continue staring backward, fighting tears.

I glance at the caller ID.

Him.

I decline the call.

I've acted like an idiot enough already, there is no need to expose myself to more situations to prove the point.

I start texting.

He's married.

JULIANNA

Who?

I roll my eyes. Not even my friend is helpful.

JULIANNA

Cassi isn't married. I've been
following him for years.

Then he has a girlfriend.

JULIANNA

Of course he does. Have you seen
the man?

Why did you encourage me to go
to him?

JULIANNA

I've never said there wouldn't be
competition. Again, have you seen
the man?

I groan and put my phone into my purse, averting my eyes to the traffic.

"Are we going home or to the Biachis'?"

Oliver's question startles me. Jesus, I forgot he just witnessed that. "Let's go home. Mother wasn't feeling well this morning. I better keep her company."

He nods and we drive in silence.

"It's none of my business, but the man didn't look like your classmate."

I close my eyes and sigh. This day has been too tiring already. "I never said he was a classmate."

"Be careful, Ivy. You know I'm on your side, but things will change once I'm gone." Oliver gives me a sad smile in the mirror.

"Gone? Where are you going?" I scoot to the edge and lean between the two front seats.

"You don't know?" Oliver fidgets. "Your father gave me notice. My employment with your family terminates by the end of the month."

I snort. "That's bullshit."

"No, Ivy, your father doesn't want my services anymore."

I fall back into the seat, absorbing the information. Without Oliver, I won't have an ally in the house. I won't have the elusive freedom he facilitated because my father trusts him. Trusted him.

The minute we stop in front of the house, I run out. Father has been and gone, but I still barge into the foyer calling him.

"Papa! Papa!"

I run to the dining room. Empty. I take the stairs two at a time into the dark hallway on the second floor. The office door is closed. "Papa!"

A soft groan from the other side turns me. "You woke me up, chérie. What's going on?" Mother, in her housecoat, blinks in the doorway of her room.

"Did you know Papa fired Oliver?" I march to her.

She gasps, covering her mouth. Of course she didn't know. She doesn't know much about any of my father's doing.

But then I realize she's not looking at me, and I pivot.

My father is standing on the other side of the hall, just in front of his office.

"I'm trying to work here," he bellows.

Fueled by the frustration of the day, I match his volume. "Why did you fire Oliver?"

"That's none of your business, young lady." His words fill the air with anger. Mother gasps again. "Look at her," he continues. "Look at your daughter. No manners... And what is she wearing?"

As usual, I'm thrown off by his bitter attack. I look at myself. Shit. I forgot I was wearing a revealing crop cut T-shirt and skimpy jean shorts, courtesy of my personal stylist, Julianna. I should have gone to the Biachis' first.

"Ivory, chérie, let your father work. It's his decision who he will or won't employ. It's not like you need a driver." Mother tugs at my arm. "Sorry, darling, we'll let you work now." She adjusts her hair, as if there was a chance my father would give her any attention.

"Don't you dare to talk to me like that again." He turns to his office, but doesn't go in. "Instead of questioning my decisions, you should make yourself useful and start acting like your status dictates. Otherwise I won't find you a husband. Stop acting like a brat. This family needs you."

* * *

I skip classes the following day. I don't want to chance seeing Cassi. Why did I run away? I mean, I went to him for a portrait—officially, anyway—and then I rushed out like he betrayed me somehow.

He's older and more experienced, and I'm acting like the little girl he believes I am.

Argh. I scream into my pillow.

But Andrea Cassinetti isn't the only man who drove me to staying in bed. Why has Oliver been dismissed? What did Father mean by this family needs you?

I've never asked him about his need to marry me off, because I hoped avoiding the topic would make it disappear. I didn't want to remind him.

But he hasn't given up on the topic. Does he so desperately need me to leave the house? If he thinks I'd marry someone I've never met, he's lost his mind.

I need to find a job and move out. But what about my mother? I would never forgive myself if she tried to end it again. If she succeeded this time.

And while she hasn't been here for me fully like Agatha has been for Julianna, she's the only mother I have. I can't leave her alone with him.

But if Papa goes through with his plan to marry me

off, I won't have a choice. I'll have to flee and leave her behind.

My stomach growls and I decide to go downstairs to eat something. I put on a sweater over my pajamas. When I quietly venture out from my room—I really can't cope with facing my parents—I'm met with the tantalizing aroma of fresh baking.

I check my watch. It's four in the afternoon. Weird.

Downstairs, Mother gasps when she sees me. "Ivory, are you sick? Why on earth would you come down wearing this?"

Have I been transported to a different dimension? My mother is dressed up and in excellent spirit. It should please me, but I know by experience how deep the lows are after her highs.

She's setting the dinner table. For four people. Whoever is joining us?

And then the aroma coming from the kitchen. This house, this scene, reeks of domestic bliss. But I've lived here long enough. I know we can't fake it.

"What are you doing?" I frown.

"Ernest Cornfield is coming for tea." She beams at me.

"Ernie?" My high school classmate? "Why would he be coming here? For tea?"

"Your father invited him." She fusses with the large flower arrangement in the middle of the table.

A laugh escapes me. "Oh, you mean Ernie's father?" I didn't know they shared a first name. "Does he do business with Papa?"

Ernie was a mean bully who I avoided for most of high school. We've never run in the same circles. It makes no sense he would come here for tea. It makes no sense anyone of my age would want to come for a formal tea.

"Not his father. Young Ernest. Mr. Cornfield and your Papa believe you two are a good match." Mother comes and kisses my forehead. "I was just going upstairs to help you get dressed."

The joy on her face is such a strange concept that it shuts me up. I don't retort. I don't fight. I don't protest. I haven't seen her this animated in months, and the little girl in me is overjoyed.

I abhor everything about this premise, but I'll go with it if it makes my mother happy for a few hours. I'll deal with the rest later. Maybe, just maybe, the happy hormones will win over the dark ones this time.

I make an effort and wear a classy black dress, and tame my hair into a simple bun at my nape. Ernie comes wearing a suit, and a bored expression that he maintains while he talks with my father about the markets and other things, mostly ignoring my presence.

Mother might dislocate her jaw if she maintains that wide smile. I recite the names of Greek gods in my mind, and then I move on to all the impressionists I know. All the while trying not to think about a certain professor.

I should probably apologize for running away yesterday. That's the only way to live down the shame and move on to coexist on campus. I'll text him later.

My father stands up, jerking me out of my inner world.

Ernie follows. "It was a pleasure, Mrs. Harrington." He bows. "Mr. Harrington, If you don't mind, I'd like Ivory to see me out."

"What an excellent idea." Mother rises to her feet. "Darling, we should leave them alone for a moment."

My father nods and shakes Ernie's hand. "Send my regards to your father, young man."

I walk Ernie to the door, formulating my text to Cassi in my head and moving on autopilot.

Ernie snaps me out of it when he yanks my arm, pulling me into a drawing room. I gasp and blink a few times, trying to step away.

"What the heck, Ernie?" I rub the arm where his hand clasped me.

"Oh, look, she speaks." Ernie rolls his eyes. He peeks around the door and then turns back to me. "Listen to me." His tone is a mean whisper. "I don't know what financial arrangements are going on between our fathers. Or why the fuck they believe those need to be sealed by our marriage like it's the medieval times, but I'm not marrying you, Harrington."

His words hit me straight in the solar plexus. It's not that I'm interested in him, but the blank refusal stings. "What a relief." I snort.

"Don't be impertinent. You'd be happy to land me." He runs his finger down my face and I recoil.

"Keep dreaming, Ernie." I step back.

"Whatever. Until I figure out how to get out of this without jeopardizing my inheritance, we'll play along."

"What do you mean?" I barely keep my voice in check.

"Keep up, Harrington. I need our fathers to believe we're gearing toward an engagement." He taps his foot.

"I'm not dating—"

"Keep your voice down, woman. I don't want to date you either, but I won't be openly dating anyone else, so we can keep up with the charade." He puts his hands in his pockets.

"What a sacrifice," I snap, but I have to admit his suggestion is the only proposal from him I'd ever entertain. It's a good plan to keep our fathers happy for the time being.

"Don't be smart with me. Can you do the same?"

I want to refuse him on principle because he's a bully, but his plan makes sense. And it's not like I've been dating anyone. Cassi's brooding eyes flash through my mind. It sets my heart racing for no good reason. Outside of my fantasies, I mean.

"We have a deal." I really hope I won't regret this.

"Okay, give me your number. I'll plan a few outings for us to keep them satisfied."

We exchange numbers and I see Ernie out.

"You think it went well? Jesus, your daughter didn't say a word. How can she attract a man if she sits there like a statue with no personality? As if that wasn't enough, she is all gawky, tall and so skinny, she can't behave," my father hisses.

I stop in my tracks.

"She was just surprised, darling. I think a quiet woman has its allure to a young man like Ernest."

"I don't know. You haven't taught her anything, Eden. If she doesn't step up, we'll be ruined."

"I'll make sure she knows how to charm young Cornfield." Mother's heels echo and I lean against the wall.

"Good, I'm going to my club."

"Cecil, you promised that if the tea went well you'd stay with me tonight."

"Well, until she's engaged, we can't judge the success."

My mother whimpers. I remain hidden while my father storms away. She pawned me in her attempt to gain my father's attention.

As I approach the stairs, I make the mistake of looking into the dining room and stop.

Mother sits straight in her chair, a ghost of herself, staring into space. Shattered. She's just used me in her own game, but I'm sure Father tricked her into it, and so before I can harbor my disappointment, I move to her.

"Come on, Mommy, let's start a bath for you." I stroke my hand over her slender shoulder. She doesn't look at me, withdrawn into her own world of sorrow and disappointment, but she stands up and lets me take care of her. Our roles once again reversed.

An hour later, I finally make it back to my bed. I'm emotionally exhausted, but sleep eludes me.

I grab my phone and write to Andrea. Then I erase it. I rewrite my message several times before I send a simple apology.

I'm sorry I ran away yesterday.

I turn off the screen, not believing he'll answer, but the screen lights up with a message.

CASSI

My sister can be pretty scary.

A smile blossoms on my face as my poor heart flutters. It was his sister. But even more, he's not throwing my idiocy into my face.

> So I guess I threw away a chance to have my portrait done by the amazing Andrea Cassinetti.

CASSI

> Flattery won't work here, vixen. Why do you want a portrait? Isn't your gen into selfies?

I'm not sure if he's reminding me, or himself, of our age gap, but I'm ridiculously pleased we're talking.

> Can it be flattery if your talent speaks for itself?

CASSI

> Here we go again, answering with another question. For the sake of keeping you on the topic, why do you want a portrait?

I sigh and flop back into my bed. I can't tell him I want to spend time with him, and I'm not yet sure if it's his artistic genius or his personal charm that drives my fascination. So I give him my other reason.

> I want to see myself through your eyes. It's pathetic, isn't it?

CASSI

> Stop with the questions, Vivid.

I giggle, wondering if I should keep the conversation going. I want to discover more about him, but what would be the point? I'd be falling for him in no time.

The dots dance on the screen.

CASSI

Good night, Vivid. Dream about me.

Chapter 10

Andrea

"Vi Mathison says that the best piece for my client's living room would be a Cassinetti." Leaning against the counter, Paris sniffs her steaming tea.

Today her hair is bright orange, and frankly I can't believe she steps outside with such a travesty on her head. And I've spent most of my adult life among eccentric people.

In the last two days, New York has unleashed wet weather on us. With the approaching fall and general gloominess, I better find a way to hibernate if I can't go to my studio. Not that my family is on board with that plan.

"Well, all Cassinetti pieces are sold out as she knows, so that's a shitty suggestion. And she seemed so business savvy." My irony doesn't deter Paris. Fuck.

"Perhaps a new piece can be commissioned?"

I open and close a few cabinets, not really finding anything to kill her with. Finally, I sigh and pin her with a glare. "Drop it, Paris. I'm not going to my studio. Period."

"Not even for me?" She cocks her head. "Come on, Andrea, it's an important client."

I narrow my eyes. "You should be supporting me, not driving me crazy. Why do you still live here, anyway?"

She flinches. "I'm avoiding my condo."

Frowning, I turn on the espresso machine. "Why?"

"I found myself in kind of a stalker situation." She sips from her tea.

I chuckle. "What the fuck, Paris? Go to the police?"

"I'm not in danger. I'm just trying to avoid someone's attention." She climbs on the stool by the island. "Back to you, bro. You really believe your art would drive you to drink?"

I'm tired of attempting to get people on board with my abstinence plan. "Why don't you commission Phillip Turner? Massi can get you a discount." I snort. My older brother's business partner is a talented artist.

"Phillip's style doesn't fit the space. Yours does. I'll stay here until you finish and—"

"Paris, I swear to God, this arrangement"—I point

my finger between us—"is temporary. As short as possible if you ask me. Oh, wait, nobody asked me."

She sniffles. For fuck's sake. Is she going to cry?

"Okay, I'll get a Turner. And I'll move out if I'm such a burden to you."

I bow my head. This is exactly why I don't need unwanted house guests. The chatty atmosphere each morning is giving me a headache. And now I have my sister's tears on my hands. Fuck.

"Look, stay if you need to, just fucking leave me alone." I down my coffee and leave, Paris's sobs echoing in my wake.

Goddammit. I return to the kitchen.

"I'm sorry. Being an asshole is what I'm good at. I need to go to school, but why don't we go out tonight? Nice dinner on me?"

"Okay." She sniffles again. "I'm sorry. I'm such a mess." She wipes a tear. "I'm worried about you, Andrea."

I kiss the crown of her head. "More than usual?" I wink, giving her a lopsided grin.

She shakes her head. "Actually, yes. This new you should be good news to all of us, but somehow it feels—"

"Careful, don't hurt my feelings." I touch the left side of my chest dramatically.

I might be jesting, but she's not wrong. This new

carefully crafted existence is... just that, an existence. I fucking wish my family would support me rather than challenge the premise.

"Like the quiet before the storm," Paris says into her cup.

"Let's hope it's a summer drizzle, not a hurricane."

* * *

"Sorry, I'm afraid you'll have to ask elsewhere." I step back, trying to extricate myself from this overzealous young woman who doesn't take no for an answer. She's been attacking me about private art lessons for days now.

"But, Professor Cassinetti, don't you think my work would benefit from your mentoring?" She bats her lashes and puts her hand on my arm.

"Yes, it certainly would, and that's why you're in my class. Keep at it." I lift her hand and drop it unceremoniously.

She giggles. "Maybe I can make it worth your while?"

"I have to go." I march away, leaving her in the shade of the courtyard corner.

While secluded, our exchange happened out in the open which might be a saving grace for me, and the only way to avoid rumors.

Though I'm not so sure after my eyes meet Wiggins's hawk-like glare. I grin, bow dramatically, and take a turn into the annex.

Fox was right—the only way to maintain some privacy is to hide in the studios here.

My first two weeks proved I'm not a good teacher. I mean, I'm a decent instructor, drawing on years of artistic experience. But I lack the key ingredient. A passion for teaching.

My time here is also proving everyone right. I'm bored out of my mind. My hand itches for a brush or a pencil.

I'm staying true to my commitment and leading this boring life. Whatever good may come of it. For some outlandish reason, I want to live. It doesn't align well with my former lifestyle. I just wish the alternative was more exciting.

Keeping up with my abstinence—substance and artistic—is even harder, because every corner of the Celestial Art Institute exudes an aura of creativity.

The kids here are brilliant, taking advantage of the space where imagination takes flight. I have to give it to Wiggins—she fosters an environment that nurtures and cultivates the artistic spirit of its students.

Me? I'm teased by the opportunities, disturbed by the level of interest students show in what I have to say, or my work in general. It grates on my nerves. If they only had the complete picture.

My boredom culminates in a new passion, and my mind has been manufacturing. Its vision has been growing in my head.

Irrationally.

Irresponsibly.

Irrevocably.

I haven't seen or spoken to Vivid since our last messages. Since that stupid good night message. Dream about me? If I wanted to serve Wiggins with evidence of my inappropriate conduct, I couldn't have done a better job. For all I know, the girl could report me.

I wish I wasn't attracted to her. I wish I knew why she wants me to paint her. Or why I ache to oblige her.

For some reason, her interest in my work feels genuine. Unlike some of her fellow students, who are more or less openly hitting on me through admiration of my talent and work—something that gave me a steady lay for years—Vivid feels different.

At least that's what my bored mind has constructed. I need to go out and fuck someone, because this infatuation isn't healthy. Or smart. Though the latter has rarely discouraged me.

The empty corridor with its floor-to-ceiling arched windows is a welcome solace. I open the first door quietly, not wanting to disturb anyone who might be inside.

The long neck and crazy curls stop me in the doorway. Vivid crouches down above a table, working with clay. I thought she was an art history major?

A decent human being would leave. Me? I clear my throat. A pathetic part of me wants her to spot me. The conversations with her, while providing no answers, are the most fun I've had since my last exhibition.

She remains focused on her work, completely oblivious to my presence. Drawn by her concentration, I step in and close the door silently. She still doesn't acknowledge me.

Hunched down, she gazes at the work in front of her. White pods in her ears explain why she hasn't heard me yet. With her stained fingers, she reaches into a bag of chips and pops a few into her mouth, crumbs falling into her clothes.

She's wearing a bright purple dress. It's more a sack really, and yet the slender, toned arms and her beautiful neck make the garment utterly sexy.

Stop it, asshole.

Under her fingers, the clay shapes into broken chains and what seems like shattered cages. The sculpture is not yet finished, but I'm drawn to it regardless.

The pieces are forming the beginnings of wings, I think.

Far from finished, the piece is already painful, full of longing and still beautiful, full of truth.

Why is a girl like Vivid, so vibrant and alive, sculpting chains and cages?

She struggles a bit to support the weight of the individual pieces and groans. It's a subtle sound of frustration, but coming from her it hits me directly in my chest, and my groin.

"You need to support it with something, it's too fragile to stand by itself."

She gasps, simultaneously pulling a pod from her ear and turning.

Shit. I forgot she didn't hear me come in.

A chain ring drops to the floor, and in her surprise Vivid steps on it. "What are you doing?"

"I'm sorry." I lean down to pick up the clay, but we both have the same idea.

"Ouch," Vivid squeals when our heads collide.

Crouched down, we both reach for what's left of the clay ring. Her fingers brush against mine and our gazes meet.

Time stops. It's like a fucking slow-mo sappy movie scene. My mind rebels against it, but my body awakens. Fuck me.

I jump up as if she tased me. "I'm really sorry. I didn't mean to startle you."

She stands up, molding the clay into a ball.

"Don't—" I extend my hand to stop her from destroying the fragile piece, and end up touching her again.

This time, she jerks away as if I burned her. We glare at each other, the air filled with pent-up tension. Fuck, she's beautiful.

Snap out of it, asshole.

"This"—I point to her work—"is powerful." I step to her working desk and trace my finger over the smooth surface of the chains. "There's so much emotion in it. What are you saying through this piece?"

A lopsided smile plumps one cheek. "What do you think?"

I chuckle. "Do you ever use a sentence without a question mark?"

We stare at each other for a few beats. I itch to reach out, but for once in my life I rein myself in.

"It seems to be a lapse only you inspire." She looks away.

"Finally, no question. Maybe I'm not such a bad influence."

Why did I say that? I'm the worst influence for her.

I don't know what it is with this girl, but I want to

bend her right over this desk, mold her into her sculpture and—

Fuck.

She steps closer. Close enough for her scent of jasmine and pure, innocent femininity to rob me of common sense.

She grabs another clay ring and squashes it, daring me with her eyes to stop her. Gripping her wrist, I turn her to me. She loses her balance and collapses against me.

And now I'll have to stay here hidden, or walk around with a boner. She lifts her gaze to me, her chest rising and falling rapidly. I stare into her eyes, but my mind is completely taken by the feel of her body against mine.

"Don't destroy it," I croak. "You have to finish it."

"Why?"

"You put yourself into this work. You started shaping a feeling, an idea into this piece. If it remains unfinished, it will haunt you."

I trace a finger down her velvet cheek. Her breath hitches. "Does your unfinished work haunt you?"

A humorless chuckle escapes me. "All my work haunts me, Vivid."

"Is that the reason you don't want to paint me?"

"Oh, I don't need to paint you for these eyes..." I trace her eyebrow. "These cheeks..." I brush her cheekbone. "These lips…" I dust the full contours of her mouth with my finger. "To haunt me."

She swallows.

I need to step back.

I should stop touching her.

But even the gentlest connection with her is intoxicating. Maybe I should paint her. Maybe my ridiculous infatuation will disappear once I capture her essence on the canvas.

"Maybe I won't haunt you once you paint me." Her words carry on a light breeze between us. And our minds have clearly synced up.

"Why do you want me to paint you, Vivid?" Instead of stepping away, I cup both her cheeks. She shudders and my cock stands in salute.

"I told you. I want to see myself through your eyes."

"Whatever for?" I don't know why I'm pushing her. What do I expect she'll tell me? "*Why* do you want me to paint you?"

"I-I… When I saw your paintings at the Mathison gallery…" She swallows again, as if the words are lodged too deep to extricate them. "Looking at your art, I can almost hear you thinking. And those thoughts are dark. They are like mine."

I crash my lips against hers. Without thinking, acting on the pure impulse her words triggered. The girl can see right into my soul, into the very depth of my being.

She exposes me, unravels my vulnerability, and it all sparks something in me. Exhilaration cruises through the dark crevices of my body.

She doesn't kiss me back. Not at first, but she melts into my arms. Like she's found a refuge.

I should stop. That's my last thought before I dive in fully, losing awareness of my surroundings.

Vivid grabs the lapels of my suit jacket, yanking me closer. Kissing her is like the first jolt of coffee in the morning, awakening dormant parts of me. Like dipping my tongue into the sweetness of the first summer peach.

She moans and I lose my mind. We stumble against her desk.

Another gasp reaches my deafened mind and Vivid jerks away. We both turn.

Fuck.

Julianna Biachi, from my class, stands frozen in the doorway.

"I'm sorry," she blurts and rushes away.

"Oh my God." Vivid takes off after her.

Double fuck.

I close my eyes, exhaling deeply. Not that it does me any good. I might as well walk into Wiggins's office and resign. It would definitely make her happy.

So much for finding solace here. What I found is temptation. I need to get laid. Vivid's luscious lips flash through my mind.

The fragments of the chains and cages goad me. The lower part of one unfinished wing is flattened, the small lines of Vivid's palms visibly imprinted in it. She must have leaned into it when I accosted her.

I carefully pick up the board with her work and place it on the shelves with all works in progress. She needs to finish it. I'll make sure of it.

I trudge out of the room and through the empty corridor. Wiggins's office is on the other side of the campus. I better go there now and face the consequences. It's not like I want to be here, anyway.

But without this job, I'm left exposed to my cravings and vices. Perhaps I should just take a trip to Europe. Or just fucking have a drink.

"Come on," a female voice reaches me as I almost turn to the inner courtyard.

"I'm not telling you anything." This voice I recognize. Vivid.

"I'm so jealous of you, but also happy." The voices get closer. I look around, but the smooth walls provide no hiding place.

"Don't get too excited. I don't even know what the kiss meant," Vivid whispers.

"Still hot. So hot." Julianna giggles and I want to

turn, but I'm too late. Both women step right in front of me.

Vivid's eyes widen when they meet mine, but Julianna doesn't register me and continues, "Imagine, he'd be your first."

Fuck.

Chapter 11

Ivory

"I see you're coloring today." I squat beside Emily who is sitting on the floor in the far corner of the room. This week's workshops are indoors, because outside the art supplies were flying in the wind.

The entire annex is filled with laughter and commotion that this space doesn't see on a daily basis. In every room, several of us are guiding the little ones through the process of creating. It's messy, it's loud, and it's way more fun than listening to the lectures.

The day would be perfect if it wasn't for this week's staff sponsor. Since we had to move the event indoors, two professors have been assigned to oversee the mayhem. One of them is Cassi.

The man who kissed me. Left me breathless with the sheer force of his masculinity. The man who overheard Julianna teasing me about my virginity. I wished for the ground to swallow me when our eyes met in the hallway a week ago.

I wasn't lucky enough for that to happen, so I turned and ran away. A mistake. At least according to Julianna, who believes I made things more awkward.

Cassi hasn't spoken to me since. If I lean into my paranoia and embarrassment a little more, I'm pretty sure he's been avoiding me on purpose.

What hasn't been avoiding me is the burning memory of that kiss. It's been etched into my soul. He kissed me like the artist he is, with all the emotions he possesses—passion, longing, pain, frustration.

Along with his natural dominance, it all mingled into the best kiss of my life. Not that I've had that many, but kissing a real man is nothing compared to the boys I encountered in high school. I haven't slept well for a week.

I wish I knew how to forget him. That's what I've been telling myself, but in reality I wish I knew how to make him kiss me more. God, if only I was more experienced.

"I'm drawing this one for you." Emily smiles.

"You are? Wow, I'm honored." I glance at her work. It's quite abstract for a little girl. "What is it, if you don't mind me asking?"

Emily cocks her head and beams at the colorful smudges on her paper. "Flowers, Ivory, of course."

"They are the most beautiful flowers I've ever seen." The voice behind us sends shivers down my spine.

Heat spills through my cheeks and my heart rate gallops freely, but I don't want to turn. His body heat engulfs me like a warm blanket, along with his scent. I should lean away.

"You like them?" Emily turns, her face lit up.

"I most certainly do. Ivory is fortunate to have you draw for her." He steps closer and now he stands beside me.

He shed his jacket somewhere and has his sleeves rolled up. His arm brushes mine gently. I don't look up. I want to be bold and above it all, but I'm not.

I want his interest.

I want his approval.

I want his eyes—and more—on me.

I don't want his rejection, so I stroke Emily's hair and don't react to his presence at all.

"I love it, Emily. Thank you for thinking of me." My heartbeat must be audible to all around me. Jesus.

"Can I talk to you for a moment?"

I don't see who he spoke to because I'm stubbornly staring anywhere but at him. A beat of silence sends shivers down my spine.

"For fuck's sake, Vivid," he hisses.

So, he was addressing me.

"I need to be helping around here. Maybe we can talk later?" I meet his gaze and shudder. There is a war brewing in his eyes.

"Follow me, Ms. Harrington," he growls and turns, expecting me to follow him. I wouldn't, if it wasn't for Emily and the others in the room. The last thing I want is a repeat of him dragging me outside.

I trudge behind him to the room next door. What the heck does he want? This is where he kissed me, and I would be thrilled if the room wasn't full of people this time.

He stops in front of the shelf with unfinished projects.

"You haven't worked on it. Why?"

What? He wants to discuss my art? "I haven't had time." I wring my hands in front of me.

He regards me, lowering his eyebrows while he cocks his head. "In seven days, you had no time?"

He's counted the days since our kiss? I fist my hands and look at the chains and broken cage.

The story of my life. I don't even know why I felt compelled to model it.

With everything that's happening at home, my father's outburst, his constant questions about my progress in locking down *the young Cornfield,* Mother's lows—because there have been no highs since that tea —I needed an outlet.

I wanted, at least figuratively, to break free from the chains that bind me, from the cages that hold me back. I wanted to take a stand, dare to be whoever I want to be, refuse to be controlled by anyone.

I look at the deformed, half-broken angel wings. To spread the wings, one has to know how to fly. I wish I knew.

"Maybe I had no interest," I spit. Partly because I'm pissed that this is what he wants to discuss, and partly because I don't want him to know I have no idea how to finish the sculpture.

"If you had no interest, you wouldn't have started," he says through his teeth. What is he so upset about? "You wouldn't have started expressing your struggle to find freedom, the pain, the fear, the longing. Because that's what this piece is, isn't it?"

His words are like physical punches and caresses at the same time. How does he see that in the mess of untamed clay? How dare he put my feelings into his words?

"This, Vivid, this right here is your fight to be who you truly are," he continues. "You can't give it up."

I continue wringing my hands and stare at the clay, almost feeling its ever-changing texture and form under my fingertips. I don't know if I'm anywhere close to depicting a fight for freedom, but I know what I felt when I lost myself in the moist material.

When I knead and lean into clay's subtle resistance and pliability, it's like a delicate dance between my intentions and the clay's nature.

And when it finally happens and the soft material becomes an extension of my own creative energy, the possibilities are limitless. It's the most exhilarating feeling.

I don't know how long we stand there. Me wanting to sink my fingers into clay and forget about him and the world.

Him glaring at me, waiting for my response, I suppose. The air between us fills with tension. And something else. I don't know what it is, but it's somewhat intimate.

While I'm aware of the life in the background, I also feel like it's only the two of us.

He makes me feel understood. He makes me feel seen. It's such a novel concept, I don't quite know what to do with that.

"What is it you study here, Vivid?" He finally breaks the silence between us.

"Haven't I told you already?" A wave of annoyance washes over me.

"Back to questions, I see." He smirks. "You told me you're an art history major. Did you lie?"

"What? How dare you?" Is he for real? "Why would I lie about that?"

"Stop with the dramatics, girl. I don't understand why you aren't pursuing your talent, that's all."

"One has to have one to pursue it." I fold my arms across my chest, barely keeping my voice in check. It's hard to yell at someone when you have to whisper to avoid attracting attention.

He opens his mouth, but I cut him off. "Is that what you wanted to talk about?"

I grab the shelf, wishing I could just rip it away from the wall.

"Yes, of course." He looks around, scanning the room. "What else?"

I gasp. "Maybe about what happened *after* you discovered I'm sculpting?"

"Vivid, that isn't a conversation for here and now—"

"Maybe not for here, but definitely overdue." I clasp my hands in front of me now, to stop myself from poking his chest with my finger.

He lets out a long breath and lowers his head. "I'm sorry about the other day. My behavior has been out of line on many levels."

He's apologizing? I wish I could yell right now. Scream out the frustration coiling inside me. "That's it? You regret it?"

He looks around. "Vivid, I think it's been established I'm not the man for you."

"*You* kissed *me*," I hiss.

He runs his hand down his face. "Don't act like you didn't want it. Just like all the others, flattering me about my art, trying to get my attention."

I flinch and step back. "Flattering you about your art? Your dark thoughts are not commendable, and they come across in your work with a boldness you clearly don't possess in real life."

I storm out. What an asshole. How dare he suggest I came on to him? Does he really believe I *flattered* him about his art? That my words were a means to an end? I wouldn't be talking to him if his art didn't move me.

He fell on me, *he* dragged me out of the class, *he* told me he'd take care of me, and there was no mistaking what he meant by that. And *he* kissed me.

I wipe a stupid tear and burst into the restroom. There, I can finally scream.

"What the hell, Ivy?" Julianna opens the door and stares at me in the mirror's reflection. "What happened?"

My exit wasn't as subtle as I hoped. I wipe my tears. "He said the kiss meant nothing, that he was out of line and he apologized."

"Oh, Ivy." Julianna wraps me in a tight embrace.

"I feel so stupid." I sob into her shoulder. I'm

stupid. Jesus. My teary reaction takes me by surprise. Have I developed a real crush on a professor?

"Don't you dare blame yourself. He kissed you and it was consensual." She grabs my shoulders and levels her eyes with mine. "It was consensual, wasn't it, Ivy?"

I roll my eyes and step away. "Jesus, Julianna, of course it was. But he made the move, and now I feel like... I disappointed him." I turn to the sink and lower my head, a sob escaping.

"Ivy, don't be ridiculous."

"I really feel stupid. I wish I didn't like him so much."

Julianna dashes to the stalls and pushes all the doors open. Gosh. I hadn't even considered witnesses.

"Have you thought about the pressure he's under? About the consequences of having an affair with a student? He might have pulled back because of that." She leans against one of the door frames, meeting my eyes in the mirror.

"Or learning that I'm a virgin scared him off." I wash my hands.

"If that's the case then screw him. You deserve better, Ivy. You might feel silly about falling for his charm, but you're not the only one on this campus, so stop this and let's have some fun tonight." She launches at me and wraps her arms around me from behind.

I sigh, a bit resentful of reality, but I will not join

his flock of admirers. "You're right. Let's finish with the kiddos and hit the town."

I don't do shots tonight. My dignity may have been dragged through the mud, but I won't bury it even deeper. I wish I was drinking though, because Andrea has been glaring at me like I stole his lunch. Or as if I was his lunch.

"You've been awfully quiet." Tim slides his hand around my shoulder. I move in my seat to face him, and his arm drops to hang over the backrest of my chair. He frowns, but as soon as I smile at him he relaxes.

Andrea's name for Tim, the Varsity boy, hasn't been too far from reality. He probably was a captain in high school. Nowadays he spends more time doing CrossFit than studying, and based on his bragging I think he's exactly the type to take pictures of his abs.

"Sorry, I have a lot on my mind." I fold my hands in my lap. Even not looking, I feel Andrea's burning gaze on me. What is his deal?

"I saw Cassinetti going after you earlier. What was that about?" He takes a curl of my hair and tucks it behind my ear.

The touch is doubly uncomfortable because I

know Andrea is glaring. It's not like he wanted the privilege.

I glance his way and see his receding back. I roll my eyes inwardly.

"It was just about a sculpture I messed up." Without thinking, I move, sliding back on my chair.

Tim doesn't pick up on my subtle body language and leans forward. "I didn't know you were sculpting. And what is it to him? He teaches drawing and painting."

And yet, he took an interest in my art. *This right here is your fight to be who you truly are.* I sigh. "It was just something I played with in my free time. I'm not talented."

"We can't all be, Ivory."

He winks at me as if that was a compliment. I study him like this is the first time I've met him. He's tall, bulked-up with gelled blond hair and blue eyes. He's attractive, I'll give him that, but equally as shallow. I hadn't noticed that—or cared—before.

"You're right, Tim. We can't all be. If you'll excuse me, I need to use the bathroom." I stand up and rush to the restroom, where I wash my face and decide to go home.

I make my way outside, my fingers flying across the screen of my phone as I type a message to Oliver. Shivering, I tuck my arms in closer.

Darkness has settled in, dusk slipping away with each passing moment. I turn to seek shelter under the bar's awning.

The scent of sandalwood and spice hits me in waves despite the wind. I groan. My gaze crashes into his dark brown-green eyes.

There is nowhere to hide but beside him, so I don't move. His stern face looks like he wants to rip me apart —like I wronged him somehow. Like I'm his biggest enemy.

"What is it with you lurking outside this bar?" I snarl.

He peers over at me with an enigmatic grin, then flicks his cigarette away. His silence weighs heavy in the air, but I've had enough humiliation around him, so I stare back steadily.

"And your questions never cease." He pauses for another beat, then adds as an afterthought, "I'm waiting for a car."

We glare at each other.

"Good. Me too."

"I didn't ask."

I let out a silent scream, raging within. "Why are you such an asshole?"

"You draw the best out of me, Vivid." He lowers his chin, glaring at me through hooded eyes. "Did you enjoy your little chat with the Varsity boy?"

"I did. Thank you for asking." My fake sweetness is nauseating. "He asked me out." The lie tastes bitter, but for some twisted reason I feel better throwing it in his face after his rejection. Petty. But I don't care.

"Good for you." He steps in my direction.

My heart races. My palms sweat. I can't let him any closer. I want to, but—

I step back.

My foot slips on the curb's edge and I lose my balance.

A car screeches. I yelp, flailing my arms in the air. Before I fall backward, Andrea yanks me away from the traffic.

My head hits his firm chest. My knees give in, but his strong arms hold me tight. The familiar scent has a calming effect on me, unlike its owner. My skin tingles at his nearness.

"What were you thinking?" he growls into my ear, holding me tighter.

I relish the comfort for a second before he steps back, glaring at me.

"You were going to pounce," I snap, regretting the words as soon as they come out. Can I get any more embarrassed when around him?

"I was getting to my cab." He beckons his head to the road.

"Ivy, are you okay?" Oliver's voice comes from the other side.

"I'm okay." I wave at him. "I'm coming." A sudden earthquake or alien abduction would suit me right now.

Opening his cab's door, Andrea's eyes bounce between me and Oliver.

"Why do you have a driver?" His question is so out of place at this moment that it sends a jolt of lava through my veins.

"Why do you live with your sister?" I hate my tone.

Andrea shakes his head and gets into the car, leaving me there stewing. I can't blame him, though.

If he was looking for a petulant child, he's just found one.

Chapter 12

Andrea

I roll over and stretch my aching limbs. What time is it? It's like I haven't slept at all. Thank God it's Saturday.

I used to sleep through the day, courtesy of nights in my studio or at a party. Well, apparently the lack of motivation to leave my bed is present even now, outside of my studio or clubbing.

I check the alarm clock beside my bed. It's nine in the morning. Who cares? I flip over and start drifting away again, my mind high on images of Vivid. Her brown-golden eyes shining with defiance, those luscious lips full of annoying questions, her slender fingers buried in the clay.

I'd prefer them buried in my hair while I eat her pussy. I want to fist that mane of hers and watch those narrow hips as I sink into her.

Creep. She's a virgin, and your student. Well, not mine technically, but I doubt Wiggins would make that distinction.

I roll to the other side, the images now replaced by thoughts. When have I ever considered playing by the rules? The exhilaration of doing whatever I fucking want is missing from my life.

Mostly because my therapist showed me how short-lived that thrill always was, forcing me to chase another hit.

But that fucker is far away and, as predicted by all my loved ones, I'm bored out of my mind. I haven't craved alcohol, weed, or any other substances. The same can't be said about painting or drawing.

Maybe it's safe to try. While Paris is here, I might just venture upstairs.

Jumping out of my bed, I don't bother with clothes or a toothbrush and pad barefoot up the stairs, wearing only my boxers.

The familiar smell of turpentine and linseed oil greets me. Four months since I've set foot in this space, and yet it feels like yesterday.

The reunion is bittersweet, like I'm seeing an old friend after a long time, and I'm not quite sure what to say.

The canvases are lined up where I left them, blank slates waiting to be filled. My brushes stick out of jars caked with paint that has no doubt dried into crusty clumps by now.

The thought of preparing them again fills me with a strange wariness. I know I'll get over it once I dive in, but that initial plunge seems like too much fucking effort.

A fine layer of dust coats everything, dancing in the sunlight streaming through the gaps in the blinds.

Clearly the cleaning fairy didn't visit while I was away. Not that I mind a little grime. It gives the place some character. Still, the dust is a reminder of time passing. Time I'm wasting, suspended in limbo.

I crack open the blinds, flooding the space with light. The blank canvases seem to call out in reproach, eager to be filled. I pry open a can of red acrylic paint.

I'm home, but it feels like I'm only visiting. Fuck.

Pulling one of the large canvases to the floor, I pour the paint on it, emptying the whole can. My breathing becomes labored, but that is the only labor here.

I stare at the paint seeping into the linen like blood. I chuck the can against the wall and groan. What am I even trying to prove?

I'd like to see myself through your eyes, Vivid said.

Well, girl, I'm fucking blind. I've been covering it well for years, but that's the fucking truth.

I rush out of the space and shut the door behind me.

Voices and laughter from downstairs alert me to visitors. Good, I need an outlet for this frustration.

"What the fuck is going on?" I growl when I enter the kitchen.

My stepsisters stand around the kitchen island. Sydney smiles at me like she's genuinely happy to see me.

"Did we wake you? Sorry," Paris chirps. Jesus, the orange hair is distracting.

"Yes. No. What are you doing here?" I've been accepting Paris crashing here, but this is a bit too much.

"Oh, what a warm welcome." Sydney shakes her head.

"Andrea." Paris's gasp startles me before I snarl at Syd. Or both of them. "What happened to you?" She clutches at her chest.

Red is smeared on my torso and my hands. "Chill, it's paint."

"Oh my God, oh my God, oh my God." She bounces like a fucking bunny. "You worked? Did we disturb your creative session? Oops"—she shrugs —"sorry."

"No, I just went to air out the room," I mumble. "It was an accident. To what do we owe the pleasure?" I smirk at Sydney.

She flinches. "If I knew I wasn't welcome here—"

"Don't be silly," Paris jumps in. "Of course you're

welcome here." She glares at me, beckoning me with her eyes to apologize.

Well, tough luck, sis, I don't feel the need. I'm an asshole today. Fully certified. At the top of my game.

"I came to talk to Paris, don't mind me." Sydney turns away from me.

"Oh, I don't mind any of you. I love you both, but mostly outside of my space." I make myself a double espresso and down it. "I'm going to shower. Nice seeing you, Syd. Say hi to Hunter." The sarcasm in my voice is unwarranted, but it's that kind of a day.

I leave them in the kitchen and go to shower and dress. When I don't hear voices anymore, I venture down to fix myself breakfast. They must have left.

"You're here?" Paris enters from the patio. I guess today is not my lucky day. "Syd is gone, and you owe her an apology."

"I don't do those." I take out a box of cereal from the cupboard.

"You apologized to Violet Mathison," she points out.

Very fucking helpful.

I get the milk and pour it into a bowl before I shake the cereal out of the box.

"You should pour milk over the cereal, not the other way around." She climbs on the stool. And there goes my silent breakfast.

"Any other opinions you'd like to share?" I groan.

"I'm leaving for a few days. A client would like me to design a vacation house on some island."

"And?" I won't make this easier on her. Mostly because I don't want to discuss it.

"Will you be okay alone here?" She sighs in exasperation.

"Of course." I play with the drowning cereal bits in my bowl.

"You don't seem all that okay this morning."

"What the fuck do you want me to say? I'm fucking going out of my mind here. Not sure why, and I don't want to investigate it further because it drives me mad." I realize I'm pacing the kitchen now.

"Does it have something to do with your visit to your studio this morning?" Her voice is level, low.

"Don't fucking patronize me, Paris."

"I'm going to postpone my trip."

I turn to the window. "Fuck. Fuck. Fuck."

"What happened in that studio?" Now she yells.

"Nothing." I whip around. "That's what happened. Nothing. Nothing has been happening in my life. Absolutely nothing." I sit back down and push the bowl away, the milk splashing on the counter.

Paris blows out a heavy breath. "Maybe don't start in your studio. Take a notepad, go outside, sketch."

"I kissed a student." This is what comes out of me?

My fucking brain is completely malfunctioning. I brace for her judgment.

"Maybe that's what you need." She shrugs. "To channel all that energy into a relationship."

"I'm not talking about a relationship. I sure would like to fuck her, though."

"Jesus Christ. This is more like something you should talk to Massi or Gio about. But if she's game, why not?"

"What if I relapse?" And there it is. I'm fucking confiding to my sister. Voicing my fears.

"Are you planning to?"

"It's not something you plan, for fuck's sake. You plan to eliminate the triggering situation."

"Do you think she can be a trigger for you? Or sex in general?"

I stare at her, my mind backfiring. I actually don't think of other women as triggers. It's only Vivid.

"She's talented, and drives me crazy, but there is something about her I crave. That I want to discover."

Paris shrugs again. "Give it a chance, then. You can't deprive yourself of all the joys in life. That is probably the surest trigger."

"I don't know. The dean is watching me like a hawk."

Paris laughs. "When did you start caring about anyone else's opinions?" She slides down and walks away, but turns in the doorway. "Have a clandestine affair."

* * *

I stare into my coffee, the dark liquid swirling like my useless mind. *Have a clandestine affair.* My sister is more free-spirited than I gave her credit for.

I wanted to spend my weekend sleeping. It worked for the rest of Saturday, but this morning Paris required proof of life, so I ventured to a coffee shop near the school.

For all I know, Vivid is dating the Varsity boy by now. And yet I came here because I want a glimpse of her. I'm done pretending that I don't care about her. She's been occupying way too much space in my head, my imagination, my fantasies.

Let her decide what's next. Dean Wiggins can shove the code of conduct down her throat.

My plan has several issues, one of them being it's Sunday and only a few over-achievers are at school. And the chance Vivid would show up here even if she's in school is slim to none. This is the result of having way too much time on my hands. I loiter.

The aroma of freshly brewed coffee is annoying after sitting here for two hours. Yes, I'm a stalker now.

A very unsuccessful one, but we all have to start somewhere.

I scroll through my phone contacts mindlessly, playing a memory game. Which woman belongs to which number? The sad part is, I don't remember most of them. Being sober, that lifestyle has no appeal.

A good lay, though, would help me out of this funk. Maybe I should blind dial one of the numbers?

What is the worst that could happen? Can I have a date without alcohol? Have I ever enjoyed female company alone? Obviously, yes, in the bedroom. But have I ever been on a date?

I've spent my life surrounding myself with people. The more noise I could orchestrate, the quieter the useless pity parties in my head became.

Now? It's too quiet. Aside from my sisters yapping in my house.

Maybe I should call one of my former lovers. To have a boring dinner. A boring walk through the streets of SoHo. Watch an uninspiring movie. I don't even know what steps progress to a nice, hopefully not boring, hook-up.

I should remember a few of these ladies. I recall fragrances, colors, glimmers, little details, but I can't really match them with the names.

None of them stayed around for repeats. I've avoided a relationship like the plague. I can't afford to have someone get too close. They would see me for who I am. A fraud.

Out of the corner of my eye, I notice a familiar shock of curls at the counter.

Vivid.

She gets her drink and glances around the shop. Her cheeks are flushed from the wind outside. Her hair is bundled on top of her head, but wild strands escape the tie, bouncing around her perfect face.

Her gaze stops at me for a beat before she passes right over, as if I were invisible. Feigning nonchalance, she saunters to the opposite corner.

She takes off her denim jacket and unwraps the bright yellow scarf from her neck. That neck will be the death of me. My fingers twitch with the urge to caress the tender flesh, to map the curves.

How could I stay away when every fiber of my being strains toward her? I have to speak with her, if only to slake this craving. If only to prove that she holds no power over me.

She sits down with her back to me, crossing one leg over the other. There is no way she didn't see me.

I grit my teeth, irritation flaring inside me. Two can play that game. I stalk over to her table and sit across from her.

She rolls her eyes but doesn't voice her protest. From her bag, she takes out a book. Even as she glowers, one look at her fills my senses, intoxicating like a liqueur I'm trying to avoid.

"Fancy meeting you here." I flash her a smile.

She raises one eyebrow, not lifting her gaze from the book. "Is it really? Or did you hope I might be here?"

"Don't flatter yourself, Vivid," I lie, though it's time to move past this passive aggressive approach to our relationship. "In any case, does it matter?"

She puts her book down. Picks up a bag of chips and rips it open. With her elegant fingers, she takes one round potato chip out and places it on her tongue. Fuck me.

She follows it with a deliberate sip from her drink. "Does anything really matter?"

I snort. "Too philosophical for me, little vixen."

"Is that so?" She leans forward, craning that beautiful neck I want to wrap my hands around. "Or are you afraid to ponder life's deeper questions?" She munches on more of her junk snack. I'm the last person to judge, but I've seen her with something unhealthy too many times. I want to see her taking better care of herself.

"With you?" My gaze drops to her mouth where traces of salt glisten. "I'd rather ponder more pleasurable pursuits."

She drops her gaze, but I catch the flash of longing. I'm not alone in this madness.

"I thought you weren't the man for me. I mean, you used those words, didn't you?" She licks the salt from her fingers. She does it casually, probably just cleaning them, but it sends shivers down my spine like it's the most sensual move.

I reach across the table and grab her wrist, leaning in. Our faces are close now. Too close. Too intimate.

She takes a sharp intake of breath, the magnetic pull between us buzzing like a current.

We stay frozen in that moment for a beat too long. "I'm trying to stay away for your own good."

She jerks her hand away. "Well, newsflash, Professor Cassinetti, I have enough people in my life deciding what's best for me. I don't need another one." She huffs and grabs her book again.

The chains and cages.

Her sculpture is an escape from her real life. That's the reason for its genius.

My eyes drop to her book, but I don't see the title. Her greasy fingers are smeared with dried clay.

"You worked on your sculpture."

She ignores me, pretending to read. I love it. Nobody has ever ignored me. My family has been fawning over me since I was young because I've always been trouble. Women dropped at my feet. Collectors tried to get a piece of me.

Their attention made me and broke me at the same time. All the while I've been trying to numb the noise, to escape it all.

And here is a girl who ignores me. I know I inspired her attitude, but still... She is so fucking real.

I annoy people, hoping to repel them, but they stick around for a multitude of reasons—not always noble. Here I successfully repelled someone I long to stay close to. *Great job, asshole.*

"You made—"

"You won't let me read, will you?" She sighs and closes the book.

I shrug. I'm also grinning, which is not uncommon. But it's genuine, and that is kind of scary. Honestly, I'd be perfectly happy just to watch her read. When she's in my orbit, the boredom and nothingness lose their power.

"Let's start over. I enjoyed that kiss very much. But I'm a staff member and you're a student, so it's my duty to correct the behavior. That doesn't mean we can't talk about art." I'm so full of bullshit.

She studies me long enough to fucking memorize the entire work of Shakespeare. Her expression is blank. It takes some practice to master a stony expression. Where did she practice that? Why does she need to hide?

"No smart question-come back?" I prompt her because I want her to come out of that shell. Art can't be such a hard topic for her—she studies it, for fuck's sake.

"We can talk about your art, because that sculpture remains unfinished," she says.

Okay, that's an olive branch. Not in a form I was expecting, but I'll take it.

"Why are you fighting your talent?" I lean back, bracing for another stare-down.

She snorts. "I can't fight what I don't have."

I blink. "Don't be stupid."

"What a gentleman. I think I'd like to read now." She picks up the book again and stuffs more chips into her mouth.

It's official. The woman drives me crazy. I want to reach out and squeeze my hands around her neck. Just the idea is satisfying and arousing. I fidget in my chair, making room because my cock has a mind of its own.

I sigh. "Fuck, Vivid, let's find a neutral topic, then."

"Like the weather?" She feigns excitement.

I roll my eyes. "Whatever. Go back to your book. Whoever told you that you're not talented was blind, mean, and stupid." I stand up.

"Wait." She grabs my arm.

Our eyes lock. This time, there is a war brewing behind those dark irises. Not sure what she's fighting, but I let her. Mostly because I'm enjoying her touch.

"You really think I'm talented?" She seems smaller. Her voice is just a whisper. Fuck, who did a number on her? The alive, feisty woman is gone, replaced by a little girl.

I take a seat next to her this time. "Your work is rough around the edges, lacking techniques and experience, but I know talent when I see it."

She cocks her head, frowning. She doesn't believe me. "But you liked Emily's flowers too."

"Who the fuck is Emily?"

"The little girl you praised at the kid's workshop on Friday."

I chuckle and look around, then say in a conspiratorial whisper, "Oh, those were dreadful."

She gasps and we both laugh, the tension melting a bit.

"You lied to her." Vivid challenges me.

"I'm not lying to you. Admittedly, your art needs more dedication or time to get better. But then you don't want to create." I wave my hand, as if dismissing the idea. "The difference between you and Emily? She is courageously expressing herself. Who am I to stomp all over that? Her efforts should be admired."

Vivid's eyes soften, a smile lingering on her face. "Only a few teachers recognize that."

"That is true. Was there a teacher who made you believe you're not talented?"

She lowers her eyes and wrings her hands in her lap, so I continue, "I'll go and beat him to death right now."

She chuckles, shaking her head. "It isn't a teacher. Though many of your colleagues can be less than encouraging."

"Don't I know that firsthand?" It isn't lost on me that he used the present tense. Someone is still scraping her self-confidence raw. But I don't delve into it right now, because she also masterfully turned the topic away from her.

"You? You seem like someone who was born with a paintbrush in your hand. I can't imagine someone critiquing your artistic attempts."

"Well, you've never met Mrs. Smiroyevski who taught art in my first grade."

She widens her eyes. "She must have been blind."

I let out a humorless chuckle. She probably was, but her dismissal had an avalanche of consequences that are still tumbling down, threatening to bury me. "Early experiences form who we are."

"True." She looks away and then smiles at me.

"The world is grateful you never believed Mrs. Smiroyevski."

"Oh, I did." I smirk. "I still do."

She laughs now, like a throwing-her-head-back full throaty laugh. It's beautiful. "I don't believe that, Andrea. You've achieved so much."

The way her tongue caresses my name sends a tingle down my spine. I need to hear it more.

For some outlandish reason, I'm comfortable with this woman. This girl. "One of these days someone will figure out I am a fraud."

She laughs again, not picking up on the truth of that statement. Thank God for that. Was there fucking truth serum in that coffee?

"Why do you want to see yourself through my eyes, Vivid?" I pin her with my gaze.

Her breath hitches.

She swallows.

The subtle movement in her throat beckons me to sink my teeth there. When did I develop a neck fetish?

"That drawing was beautiful." Her words float like a light breeze.

"Like you."

The air around us thickens. The murmur of the cafe falls into a blurry background.

She shakes her head slightly, as if my compliment invaded her senses.

"Who made you believe you're not beautiful? Or talented?" I urge.

She looks away. Her eyes darting around like spooked horses. Who hurt her? Who put chains on that gorgeous soul?

I fist my hands, wanting to punch whoever made her feel this way. Standing up, I startle her. "Come on. Let's go."

"What? Where? I—"

"Move, Vivid."

Chapter 13

Ivory

His command is impossible to ignore, and I grab my bag and scramble behind him. Completely drawn by his sheer masculinity. I even leave my book behind, but I don't dare turn to get it.

When I noticed him earlier, I almost ran away. I'm glad I didn't. This conversation is similar to his kiss.

Caressing my soul.

Challenging my needs.

Discovering my wants.

I needed it after the weekend I had. My father has been in the worst mood, harping on at me anytime he saw me. Nothing is to his liking. My looks. My lack of progress with Ernie. My attention on my mother.

My mother. Oh God, she's been so devastated after his last betrayal, she refuses to leave her room. Or eat. I finally forced her to drink some clear broth this morning and eat a piece of toast. Exhausted, I left the house to seek a moment of solitude.

The Biachis have a family function, and while I'm always invited I craved peace today. Somehow I ended up at the school's studio. Not that I progressed with my sculpture, but molding gave me a jolt of purpose, so I dove into it.

I lost myself in work all morning. I called my mother to make sure she's reasonably functioning and listened to her whining about her friend getting divorced. How did she even find out? She's been stuck in her room for days.

I love her, but parenting one's own parent is exhausting. She was fussing enough for me to allow myself more time away from the house, and I decided to read in the cafe. Well, read I did not.

Andrea grabs my hand and drags me behind him. I'm surprised he passes the front entrance and leads us to the far end of the establishment. He pushes the door open. Wait? What?

"Why are we going into the bathroom?"

He pulls me in and locks the door behind us. It's a small room for one person only. Just a toilet and a sink to the side.

"What are you doing?"

Instead of an answer, he pivots me, so my back is to

his chest. "Making you look at yourself through my eyes."

I meet his gaze in the mirror in front of me. My heart hammers. I should be annoyed by this, but I'm not. I'm thrilled. I think. And a bit scared.

His solid body against mine creates a sense of protection. I exhale, leaning in, not breaking eye contact.

He lowers his mouth to my ear, his breath dusting the sensitive skin, sending shivers down my spine. "Look at yourself, Ivory."

This is the first time he's used my name. Hearing it on his lips jolts me with nervous energy. When he calls me Vivid, we're in our own world. He sees Vivid.

Being Ivory exposes me. Reminds me of reality. Makes me... me.

"Look at yourself," he growls. This time he cups my jaw and I force my eyes on my reflection.

We stay still for what feels like an eternity. This room is too small to sustain us with enough oxygen. I already feel its lack, panting to fill my lungs.

"What color are your eyes?" He holds my chin, his touch firm yet delicate. His voice fills me with a sense of calm, but my mind rebels against it.

"Brown," I grunt.

"They're sprinkled with golden sparkles. When you

laugh, they glimmer. When you're upset, they dim. You have the night sky in your eyes. The tiny lines here..." He traces his fingertip along the outer edge of my eye. Jesus.

"They get deeper when you're concentrating. Or when you smile. And when you look down, blushing..." He dusts my thick lashes, though I'm not sure if he really touched them. "These lashes fan around like butterfly wings. So delicate, yet so alluring."

I close my eyes, his words and touch leaving a trail of fire on my skin. I can't believe how much he notices, how much he sees. It's almost like he's been studying me, learning every inch of me.

"Open your eyes," he demands, and I snap them open so fast I get dizzy. It's a good thing I have his support.

He's still staring at me, his gaze intense.

Like he's peering into my soul.

"You're beautiful," he murmurs, his hand still on my jaw. "So damn beautiful."

I swallow hard, my heart rate reaching a dangerous cadence. Jeez, it must be audible. My mind rebels. I don't want to believe him, but at the same time the raw honesty of his words crawls into all the insecure crevices of my heart.

His words are riveting. Exhilarating. Scary.

He traces my cheek with the back of his hand.

"These cheekbones speak of your femininity. Like they were sculpted by Bernini."

I gasp. His breath on my skin, hot and heavy. I'm burning, assaulted by a myriad of sensations.

A part of me wants to leave, to hide, to retreat into safety. That part is muted by all the other parts that are coming alive.

"And these bee-stung lips of yours. God, if you knew what they've been doing to me. Just one look at the caramel of them and I lose my mind."

He lets go of my chin and now both hands move down to the base of my neck, and he traces the curve of my spine.

My skin is on fire as his hard-on presses against my back. But I don't move. I can't. I'm frozen in place, hypnotized by his touch and the way he talks about me.

"Now, your neck," he rasps, his lips brushing my sensitive skin. "It's my favorite part of you. Long and slender, like a swan's. I could spend hours kissing it, biting it, squeezing it, and marking it as mine."

I whimper at his words, feeling the wetness between my thighs. This is wrong, I tell myself, but my body betrays me. It wants him, needs him, and I'm powerless to resist.

He wraps his huge palm around my throat, squeezing. Not too tight, but not lightly either. I part my lips, seeking oxygen, but also more of him.

"Mine," he whispers, staring at where his palm connects with my tender flesh. My throat bobs against his rough skin.

I watch in the mirror, not recognizing what I see. In the fog of my arousal, I catch glimpses of the girl he sees. Jesus. She is beautiful.

She is so beautiful that tears prickle my eyes. I want to blink them away, but his next move steals all my attention.

He unbuttons the top button of my blouse and ever so gently brushes the swell of my breasts. My knees give in, but he thrusts forward and pins me between the sink and his hips.

"I can't wait to discover these. They are a tantalizing promise, teasing me every time you push them together when you're cold. Or when you hide them under your baggy top. Teasing me. Driving me crazy."

He takes my hand, dragging it up to the side of my face. "These fingers, Vivid, long and slender... When I saw you sinking them into the clay, I was jealous, longing to be touched by such a gentle strength."

There's so much sexual tension in the air it's suffocating. But I don't want it to end. I want more of him, more of his touch, his smell, his taste. I want to give in to the pull, to the heat that's consuming us both.

But he steps back, leaving me cold and empty. My skin. My blood. My bones mourn the loss of him.

"Tell me you're beautiful," he growls.

I grab the sink, afraid I might collapse. His eyes narrow on me in the mirror.

"Say it," he commands.

"I'm beautiful," I whisper, my mouth dry and the lump in my throat ballooning.

"I didn't hear you." His words are a cold shower and a jolt of current.

"I'm beautiful," I parrot.

"Louder."

His dominance washes over me with its intended effect. My nostrils flare. What does he want?

"I'm beautiful," I yell.

A smile spreads across his handsome face as I glare at him. "Now we're on the same page, little vixen."

Someone bangs at the door.

"Just a minute," Andrea hollers.

For some outlandish reason I laugh. This man is a lunatic, but I haven't felt this empowered... ever.

We stare at each other, grinning, until another bang snaps us out of the stupor.

"I'm beautiful," I whisper.

He cups my face and lowers his forehead to mine. "You're beautiful, Vivid." He kisses me lightly.

I part my lips, but he steps aside. I'm deflated, but I understand. This moment, however intimate, wasn't about us. It was about me.

He clasps the back of my neck to keep me in place and lowers his lips to my ear. "In another life, I would continue admiring you in a full-length mirror." I shudder and utter a sound that hasn't been captured in a dictionary, somewhere between a whimper and a gasp.

He looks down at the tent in his pants. "You certainly affect me, Vivid." His chuckle is dark. "Off you go, or I'll have to stay here forever."

He unlocks the door and pushes me out. "Give me a minute, dude. She's been sick," Andrea lies nonchalantly, and the guy who's been waiting swears.

I stumble out and lean against the wall. What the heck was that?

"Are you okay?" the toilet-seeking dude asks.

I pry my eyes open, annoyed by his intrusion of my euphoria. "I'm good," I croak.

"Fuck it," he says and storms away.

I take a minute or a year to locate my brain, normalize my breathing and remember how to walk.

Each time our paths cross, I yearn for his attention, craving his touch and desiring to be seen in a way no one else has ever seen me before. And little did I know what an explosive way it was.

As I recover my basic functions, I stumble to get my book. Like a newborn fawn, I totter into the main room.

In an instant, the bliss disappears. Tim smiles at me. I forgot I messaged him earlier.

"Hey, gorgeous. I thought I got the wrong place. Is your phone off?" He drops his into his pocket and saunters up to me.

My eyes widen as he lowers his face to mine, his arm snaking around my waist. I turn my face and his lips land on my cheek.

"Hi," I croak.

With his arms still around me, I push against his shoulder and whip us around to see the bathroom door. Andrea is nowhere in sight. A sense of panic grips me. What am I going to do? Why did I invite Tim?

Because I didn't want to be alone. Because when I texted him, Andrea was still in the unattainable asshole category. None of these reasons bode well for my current reality.

"I'm sorry, Tim, I started feeling sick." I'm not even lying much as my stomach tightens with anxiety. My eyes dart between the bathroom and Tim. "I think I need to go home."

"Oh, well, let me get my coffee and I'll walk you to the subway."

No! I want to scream, but instead I attempt a smile. I don't think it fully forms and I'm the master at feigning. "I need fresh air. I'll wait outside?" My voice is high-pitched.

He steps to the counter and blocks my view. Oh my God. It's not like I'm doing anything wrong, but I don't think Andrea would see it that way. Besides, he's already made it quite clear what he thinks about the Varsity boy.

I need to get rid of Tim. Why did I call him? Why?

"I already ordered. Just give me a moment. Have you eaten something?" He tucks a strand of hair behind my ear and I flinch.

Tim is oblivious to my reaction, because he is mostly oblivious to anyone or anything that isn't him.

"Actually, I haven't eaten since this morning." Why I decide to tell the truth now is beyond me.

My hands shake, sweat drips down my spine. All the self-confidence Andrea instilled evaporates with my current conundrum. If I leave with Tim, how would I explain my disappearance to Andrea?

I can text him and lie. I groan inwardly.

If he steps out now and sees us, I think he'll act cool, but the chances of him listening to my explanation are slim.

I'm riddled with indecision, spiraling into panic. Tim can't see I'm here with Andrea. Am I here with Andrea? I can't risk anyone in school finding out.

"Well then, let's go—" His name is called by the barista. I nod like my life depends on it. Yes, yes, let's go. Tim turns to pick up his drink and finishes the sentence. "For late lunch. What do you say? It's a date."

I freeze. Behind Tim, Andrea glares at me, a storm brewing in his expression. My mouth goes dry and I lose all my words. Not that there is much to say. I can't explain without giving Tim ammunition to run to the dean's office.

He would report us in the blink of an eye.

"Professor Cassinetti, what are you doing here?" Tim takes a sip of his drink and to my utter horror wraps his arm around my shoulder.

Andrea's eyes narrow on the spot of my shoulder where his hand was just moments earlier, and where Tim now rests his.

He lifts his gaze up and smiles at Tim, baring his teeth in an ugly snarl. "Having a coffee, obviously." He glances at me. "I was going to get dessert, but I've lost my appetite."

"Oh, the bakery next door has a better selection." Tim whispers, leaning in like he was sharing a secret. "Not as cozy as here, but truly homemade. I'm telling you, an honest craft."

"Thank you, Tim, I can use a bite of honesty." His words strip me of any hope that I can salvage this. "Well," he continues. "Have fun on your date, kids."

Chapter 14

Andrea

"Okay, everyone, let's wrap it up," I announce ten minutes before the end of my class. A class I spent staring at the wall while pencils scratched across the paper everywhere around me.

Simple daily functioning has been a bitch lately. My body hurts, my mind floats in a fog, my soul is buried in darkness. Yesterday I almost went to a bar, but Sydney showed up.

Fuck. Paris is gone, but it seems like my overbearing family is taking turns dropping by or checking on me, calling.

That's how much faith they have in my recovery. I can't blame them. It's probably more than I have right now.

"Professor Cassinetti, could you have a look?" A

girl with a nose ring—what's her name?—shoves her sketchbook into my face. "Did I get the perspective right?"

I look at the black lines in front of me. Shit. She is good. "Yeah. Good job." I stand up, pushing the notebook back into her hands.

"So there is nothing I can improve?" Her deflated expression bothers me, but not enough to act like a human. Like a dedicated teacher. Can I give her a few pointers to improve? Yes. Do I want to? Kind of. Is it too much of an effort? Definitely.

"Practice makes perfect." I trudge out of the room.

Fuck, this headache is blinding.

My eyelids lower under the searing pain. I bump into someone.

"Are you okay, Andrea?" Fox grabs my shoulder.

"Yeah, sorry, Virginia. I have a headache."

"Jesus. You look horrible. I have painkillers in my drawer." She keeps holding my shoulder. Does she believe I'll faint? I must look worse than I feel.

I wince. "Thanks for the compliment, but I'm good."

"Are you sure?"

I nod. She might be aware of my party boy past from the media, but I won't confirm to her I'm trying to stay clean.

Though a good dose of painkillers might color my life in more vibrant colors. More vivid. Fuck.

Vivid.

I mumble something to Fox and stumble down the hallway.

Vivid is like an unfinished painting. She drives me crazy. Unhinged. Infiltrating my dreams, turning them into nightmares. Nightmares that feed my soul with poison. With an exhilarating drug.

When I paint I'm alive, but I also feel like I'm going to die. Like the connection to my work is a lifeline. And just before I need to finalize my vision, I start hating the work, chasing perfection. Drowning in the mediocrity of the result.

Vivid, on the other hand, is perfection. But she is not mine. She can't be mine. Her raw beauty and wounded soul pull me in like the crashing waves of the ocean. Powerful, but dangerous.

And yet I can't let go. I need to get another fix of her, only to discover it's not enough.

Like an unfinished painting. Or a drug.

Intoxicating.

Not good for me.

That doesn't get her out of my head. In fact, this impasse we've been fluctuating in creates a sense of pure need and want. Anticipation.

Without knowing it, she is teasing me.

Like an unfinished painting.

What do I do to finish a painting?

I suffer. Drink. Party. Indulge.

All of that is off the table.

Over the last few days, I've picked up my phone to call one of my faceless contacts. I felt nothing. I couldn't imagine hooking up with any of them.

There are artists who work on several projects at the same time. I have to finish a painting before I move on.

Vivid, who is dating the Varsity boy, is my unfinished painting.

I walk through the school aimlessly, and somehow I find myself in the annex. Staring at the door where her unfinished sculpture waits. Fuck.

I squint in the dim hallway, trying to cope with the pain. I should call my therapist to see if painkillers are such a big transgression. Staying clean might have different interpretations.

Stumbling into the meditation room, I'm relieved that it's empty. I plop down into one of the bean bags and close my eyes.

Fuck this pain.

Fuck this life.

Fuck the unfinished painting.

I shiver, goosebumps covering my body while it's covered in sweat. My back is stiff like I slept on the floor of my studio. Did I?

My mind catches up and I crack my eyes open. Rolling on to my back, I hoist myself to sit up in the wobbly sack.

I fell asleep in the meditation room. Great. Teacher of the year. At least the fucking headache is gone. Is it?

I blink a few times and stretch my neck. I'm good as new. No migraine. Only stiff muscles, cold shivers, a fucked-up mind and a still-dark soul. Yay, my life.

Briefly, I consider sleeping here tonight. The idea of rolling out of here in the morning is slightly less appealing than the prospect of going home.

I push myself up and take off my wrinkled jacket, the chill causing me to shudder, but also waking me up properly.

As I step outside, I groan.

Vivid's eyes meet mine. She's leaning against the wall opposite me. Wearing a black dress that looks like a long button-down shirt and golden boots, she looks like a model. A goddess.

She perks up, shoves an uneaten bag of chips into her backpack and removes her buds from her ears, but then she takes me in and frowns. "Are you okay?"

"You shouldn't eat that shit all the time. It's late.

What are you doing here?" I toss my jacket over my shoulder, hooked on my finger.

"Waiting. Are you okay?" she repeats.

I sigh. "I had a headache. I'm good. Why are you still here? Isn't your driver waiting?"

"No, he isn't," she says simply, studying me, wringing her hands in front of her. Is she nervous?

"You never told me about your driver. What's up with that? Are you a trust fund baby?" I step closer. I can't help it. The scent of jasmine hits me like no substance before. I want to bury my nose in the crook of her neck.

"Like you?" She lifts her chin, but her voice hitches.

God, I enjoy this tug-of-words with her too much. "You read my bio." I smirk.

A curl falls from her bun, bouncing in front of her face. She blows it away, but it springs back. I reach out, tucking it into the beautiful mess on her head and sinking my fingers into her mane, stepping even closer. "Who are you waiting for, Vivid?"

"You," she breathes.

"Why?"

She looks down, licks her lips and takes a fortifying breath. "Can you help me with my sculpture?"

Her words are light, floating between us tentatively. It cost her to ask.

"So you're going to finish it?"

She nods, still not looking at me.

She should finish it herself. She should fight her own doubts and discover the truth of her demons through the work. She needs to set herself free while she creates.

I have no place disturbing that tender bond between the artist and their work. As a teacher, I should encourage her to push past her limitations.

As a man, and not a very honorable one, I want to spend time with her.

"Okay, let's see if I can help you." I start toward the studio.

When we enter the large room filled with tables and art supplies, I'm relieved no one else is using the space.

Her work is on one of the large tables. She's progressed a bit since I saw it the last time.

She drops her backpack and stands by the table. "I want the pieces to form wings, but no matter what I try the weight is too much to support the structure." Her eyes dart around. Is she ashamed of her work? Is she uncomfortable after our last meeting?

I put the thought of the Varsity boy aside and refocus on the clay in front of me.

"Wings? What a brilliant concept. Broken chains

morphing into the wings of freedom." I smile at her, and she beams back. A sudden jolt of flow hits me.

I haven't got back to my studio since last weekend, but now I feel I could conquer the world if I picked up a brush or a pencil.

Rummaging on the shelf, I do just that. I tear off a page from the sketchbook and, leaning above the table, I start drafting the wings.

"You need to be a bit more technical here. I like that you create from your imagination, but at this point you need to measure. Decide how big the wings should be, and then choose the material to marry with the clay." My hand runs across the paper as I sketch what I think is her idea for the sculpture.

She cranes her neck over my shoulder. "Andrea," she breathes, and touches my arm. The electricity zaps through me and when my eyes meet hers, her sudden shiver gives me an unwarranted sense of satisfaction.

"Yes?"

"This is exactly what I had in mind. How could you have known?"

I feel it, vixen. "I guess you described it well enough."

We stare at each other, the heat rising up my spine. Her eyes. Her freckles. Her uneven breath. All snapshots I'd like to capture. Along with her lips.

"Large enough," she whispers.

I frown. "What?"

"I want the wings to be large." She looks away and turns to examine her work. My eyes linger on her body, admiring her shape as she moves.

"Okay, that's not very precise, but let's turn it around." I step closer. Standing behind her, I feel her shudder again. The jasmine fogs my mind momentarily.

I should step away. Not only because I'm the professor here. Not only because someone might come in at any moment. Not because she's dating the Varsity boy. Okay, that thought does it, and I step aside.

"Turning it around?" she croaks, as affected as me.

We both reach for the same piece of the chain. Unlike my calloused fingers, her skin is pure silk. I stare at the connection between us, feeling her gaze on me. I can't look at her.

Because fuck my position here. Fuck her boyfriend. Fuck the school. Fuck common sense. I want her, and if I see a similar longing in her eyes again, all bets are off.

"Yeah." My mind scrambles while I keep my fingers on hers. "What material are you comfortable with? Plexiglass might create a solid base. You can consider wood—"

"Or metal rods." Her voice is equally excited and breathy as she removes her hand and turns to me. This time it's she who ignores the reasonable distance between us.

I face her, our bodies flush. "Metal rods and wires are an excellent idea. It's broken chains, after all."

"Flying free from the cage." Her breath fans my skin. "How would I go about it?"

I snake my hand behind her, pressing my fingers between her shoulder blades. Her breath hitches, and now I see the longing in her eyes. It matches my ache.

Her breasts burn into my torso. Her hips are too alive pressed against me.

"Imagine it being your wings. If they start here..." I press into the spot where my hand lays and it pins her closer to me. She fits. She fits perfectly. "The wires would go up." I trace up her back to her shoulders. "These are your wings." I surprise her by lifting her arms above her head.

God, she would be a vision, lying like that under me. I slowly trace my fingers up her arms, admiring every inch of her, marveling at the small quivers. Her breath is on my neck, having a direct line to my pants.

She must feel my length against her, but she doesn't move or say anything.

"If these are your wings, the wires would support the clay, but it would be a very meticulous process to make sure the clay is layered enough not to break. Or you can decide to expose the wire."

I hold her wrists above our heads and my mouth is too close to hers. I'm practically breathing my words into her mouth. I'm not even sure what I'm saying.

"Expose..." She relaxes her hands into mine, slightly shivering against me.

Lowering my head, I brush against her lips, when a sound in the hallway jerks us apart.

"Right," she says loudly. "Right, I'll find the wire and rods now. I think I saw some over there." She waves her hand in no particular direction.

"You do that." Watching her rush to the shelves across the room, I rearrange my cock, painfully straining against the zipper of my pants.

She comes back with a spool of soft wire and some rods and pliers. She puts on an apron and with shaky hands she gets to work, testing the new material and the idea.

I watch her, helping when she needs it.

Our hands keep meeting in tantalizing touches. Our eyes keep engaging in short duels. Our bodies keep finding each other as we try to stay focused on her work.

In some twisted turn of events, I'm helping an art piece come to fruition, and it's almost as exhilarating as my own work. Just watching this beautiful woman so enthralled in the grasp of creativity makes me want to go back to my studio.

She is like my fountain of life. Awakening the beast in me, but also uncovering my soul under layers of sod. Making me feel alive. Real.

And let's not forget that my cock remains at half-mast.

"This is working. Andrea, you helped me progress." She beams at me, her genuine joy contagious.

I walk to the other side of the table, admiring the piece. Fuck, I'm proud of her. "It's easy to create when the theme is familiar."

Leaning on my hands, I hover above the sculpture that is coming alive under her fingertips.

She looks at me and bites her lip, but then looks away and starts tidying up the surface, swiping the clay crumbs and wire clippings into her hand.

I grab her wrist. "What is the theme? Who are you, Vivid?"

She lets the mess fall from her hand and sighs. Without letting go, holding her hand above the sculpture, I round the table to join her.

"I... The idea just came when I touched the clay. The first parts of the design just came out. But yeah, I want to be free. Free from the expectations, the judgments, the rules."

Tracing my finger gently down her cheekbone

while still holding her wrist, I smile. Her heartbeat pulses against my grip. "Whose?"

"I've spent my life trying to be who my parents want me to be. My mother needs me. And I guess my father too. It's a lot of responsibility."

"Family is about love and support."

She snorts. "Yeah, I guess love in the Harrington house is shown in a very twisted way." She looks away for a moment and then meets my gaze. "This..." She nods toward the sculpture. "Makes me feel like I'm getting closer to the real me. Like I'm tapping into something raw and true. Finding courage."

"I can relate to that."

"Yeah, but you express yourself without shame. I'm not sure if I'm strong enough to do that."

Oh, how I wish I could show her what a wonderful human being she is. How I ache to punish her parents for sprouting so much self-doubt.

"You are." I cup her face and kiss her gently. "You're stronger than you realize. I believe in you. In your talent, your passion, your spirit. I want to see you fly." I brush my lips against hers again, and her breath hitches. "I see your pain, but I see your courage and strength. It's all beautiful."

Tears glisten at the corner of her eyes as she glances at the sculpture and at me again. "Thank you," she whispers, her voice barely audible. "Thank you for seeing me."

"I'm glad you let me. I'm glad you waited for me today."

There is a sense of beauty between us. Not just the sexual tension. Not the aftermath of creative work. Something pure. Intimate. It scares the shit out of me.

I move away from her, reaching into the reservoirs of my sabotage tactics. I can't have her getting too close. Not like this. Bodies, yes. But beyond that. Fuck no.

"How did you know I was in there?" I grab my jacket and shove my arms into the sleeves.

Vivid wipes her hands on the apron and walks to the corner, untying it. She jerks it off with frustration, getting her hair stuck as she pulls it over her head.

I groan inwardly and go to help her, the closeness welcome and hated in equal measures. I untangle the fabric, trying not to think about fisting that mane.

"I saw you going into the meditation room. Though I didn't expect you to be meditating for that long."

"You waited for almost an hour?" I hang up the apron.

She shrugs. "I came to work on the sculpture and hit a dead end. I had nothing else to do."

"The Varsity boy wasn't available tonight?" I don't even care that the jealousy is obvious in my question.

She looks at me wide-eyed, but before she has a chance to respond, I step in. Her back hits the wall.

"I don't share, Vivid," I growl into her ear. Pinching her chin between my thumb and finger, I lower my face to hers. I can count all those beautiful freckles on her nose.

"At least he knows what he wants," she snarls.

Her nipples graze my chest through the fabric of our clothes. They are perked up, begging for my attention. Oh, they have it. Mine and my cock's.

I thrust my hips against her, pinning her to the wall. What am I doing? The thought briefly floats through my mind, but the sheer need to own this woman drowns it.

"He wants to pop your cherry, vixen, and then move on." Not that my intentions are more honorable, but I still warn her.

"How do you know he hasn't already?"

I groan, pressing myself against her harder. The friction of her body against mine stirs a beast in me I can barely contain. "He doesn't deserve the honor."

"Too late," she spits. "It's not like you wanted it."

My arousal mingles with a wave of anger. "You have no idea what I want."

She pants, glaring at me. "Yeah, you hide that pretty well. Hot and cold. Wanting me and then pulling back. Denying yourself. The whole troubled artist shit."

"Watch your mouth." I squeeze her chin harder, tilting her to me. My lips can almost taste her.

"Why should I?" Her frustration mirrors mine. She's taunting me. And winning, little vixen.

"Do you know what I want? Ever since you landed under me with that fucking yellow dress, you've been the only color in my life. I'm drawn by your beauty, fascinated by your talent, exasperated by your defiance. You're intoxicating. You're mine, Vivid. But I can't have you. You're too young, and I'm broken."

I let go of her chin and punch the wall beside her head. She flinches but takes my face in her hands. "Maybe I need a villain in my story."

Our lips crash together in an explosion of pent-up passion. Her hands burn on my skin, drawing me closer. I lean into her, crushing her with my weight, but I need to feel her. To fuse with her.

We devour each other, our tongues dueling in a fierce battle. But it doesn't matter how much I take, I can't satisfy my craving. Blinded, deafened, only remotely aware of my surroundings, I taste her, trying to satiate my senses.

She's like a first taste of water after a long trek through the desert. Like touching the brush to white canvas for the first time. Like everything that has been missing from my soul. She feeds my passion addictively.

Addictive.

Fuck.

I pull away. Step away. She gasps and grabs the wall to regain her posture.

"We shouldn't—" I lie, because there is no fiber in me that doesn't want to continue. Fuck should or shouldn't. It's all must and want now.

But reality crashes down on me like a ton of bricks. We're in the middle of the school, for fuck's sake.

We both pant like runners after a sprint.

"We shouldn't fight it, you mean?" She recovers.

I smirk. "You'll be the death of me, Vivid." I lean my back against the wall beside her, the coolness sending shivers down my spine.

She takes her turn now, pinning me against the wall, and I groan into her mouth. Our tongues move in a wild dance.

"We shouldn't..." I repeat when we come up for air.

"I agree with that." Wiggins's voice slices through the air like a sharp blade.

Chapter 15

Andrea

"What I saw seemed consensual, but..." Wiggins's nostrils flare as she keeps rearranging stacks of papers on her desk. A few papers fly around.

I'm standing by the door. I don't think I should sit while she's having her nervous fit. Or bout of anger. Whatever it is, I'm pretty sure my nonchalance is further feeding it.

I don't give a shit, though. None. She can fire me, but nothing can keep me away from Vivid anymore.

"You should be grateful it was me who walked in on you."

She lifts the three-hole punch, and for a moment I fear it's destined to land on my head. To my relief she uses it to abuse some papers on her desk.

Punching holes, she continues her tidying up

without looking at me, like catching up on her filing is equally as important as firing my ass. Making more mess by the looks of it, but who am I to judge?

"You're lucky there are people on the board who stand behind you. But your talent isn't an excuse for such behavior." She forces a stack of papers into a binder and snaps the rings closed.

I'm not versed in office management, but that sounded a bit too close to losing skin on her fingers. She pushes the binder between two others on the shelf behind her.

With her back to me, she lowers her head, exhales and remains frozen. Fuck. The silence stretches through the air like a virus, threatening to pry an apology from me. I don't want to lie. I'm not sorry, so I remain silent.

She turns around, and while her cheeks are flushed, her little tête-à-tête with the binders helped her to recover her composure. She fixes her perfectly styled silver bob and sits down, her breathing slightly faster than normal.

"You're lucky..." For the first time she looks me in the eye.

I fight the need to tell her she's mentioned that particular fact a few times, though I fail to see what's fortunate about any of this.

"...I don't want or need a scandal at this moment. If

you, however, continue to disregard this institution and the rules, I'll make it my personal mission to have your ass dragged through the courts if I have to."

I nod. Not necessarily to acknowledge that I understand the gravity of my circumstances, but to hopefully finish this conversation. Monologue, I mean.

I want to go and find Vivid and reassure her she isn't in trouble. I want to hug her, kiss her, bend her over the desk and fuck the Varsity boy out of her system. The idiot stole what was mine.

I also need to stop thinking these thoughts right now, right here, for fuck's sake.

"You're suspended for two weeks, and you're not to speak about this," Wiggins snaps at me.

I frown. "How do you plan to explain my suspension?"

She purses her lips, probably annoyed by the lack of sense her punishment makes. Or maybe by her decision not to go for the jugular. At least not this time.

"Right. You'll take two weeks' unpaid leave," she orders.

"If that makes you happy, dean." I turn to leave.

"Andrea..."

I exhale, holding the door handle, but I don't face her.

"If you don't care about your reputation, show

some regard for that girl. She doesn't need to start her life, her career, tainted by a scandal like this."

I wish I was a bastard who could shake this off and go find Vivid and do things to her I've ached to do for weeks now.

For a moment I consider that any connection to me might be a boost for her career. A good thing.

But even I know she deserves a better path. A path not stained by my selfishness. A path that leads her to freedom. Without being dragged through the mud.

It's official. I've known all the feels. I'm a man tortured by drowning whirlpools of all the emotions, but something is happening inside me I don't recognize. And the result is that I care for Vivid enough to stay away.

I can forget her.

I can avoid her.

I can survive this.

A week passes by, and surviving is just about what I've managed. The first two days I tortured myself, reading her worried messages. I finally sent her a message.

And a fucked-up part of me was hoping my attempt to hurt her would land, because I don't want to be the only one with this pain.

She hasn't reached out since, so I guess my bile

landed where it should. I probably sent her into the Varsity boy's arms.

That was three days ago.

Since then, I've just been moving between my bed and my sofa, like right now, and staring. At my phone, hoping she will write again. Why would she? Or just staring into space. What else is there to do?

These are certainly not the best circumstances for a recovering addict. It's not lost on me that I replaced all my vices with one. A tall, elegant one, with golden-brown eyes and caramel lips and a scent of jasmine.

I lie down on the sofa, swinging my legs over the armrest. My eyes land on the stairs. I could go up and dust things in my studio. I felt invigorated watching Vivid molding the wire and clay into something so breathtakingly beautiful.

It was as close to my own creative flow as I remember from the last time I finished a painting. When was that? Four months ago? Five?

The loud screeching of my phone brings me back to my bleak reality. I want it to be one person in partic-ular, but I'm not that lucky.

"Hey, Gio, what's up?"

"What's up with you, bro? Mother has been calling around to confirm you're well. Is Paris back?"

"No, Paris got stuck on some island due to weather, and Mom can fucking call me herself."

"But she doesn't, so be a good boy and call her. Or even better, visit her. Surprise her with your cheerful presence. It's a thing children do."

"You say that as if you drink tea with her daily."

"Mila checks on her," he answers a bit too quickly, the bastard.

I chuckle. "Well then can Mila cover for me as well?"

"Don't you fucking take Mila's name into your filthy mouth. Find yourself your own girl to do your errands."

"Oh, so it's an errand to check on our mother, not a privilege. Not that thing children do."

"Touché. Look, for years it was mostly Massi who visited her often, but he has his own family now. She's worried about you, and with Paris God knows where, she doesn't get enough info to satisfy her concern. Though to be honest, why she spares you a thought is beyond me."

"Hey." I clench my fist. Gio should be glad I'm across town from him. Or across the planet— who knows where he is? "Okay, I'll call her. Happy?"

"Indifferent, as long as she doesn't pester me about you." A keyboard clicks through the line. Clearly my brother is done with this conversation. "But consider my advice."

"What advice?" I stand up, because this conversation is driving me to the kitchen.

"To find yourself a girl."

I stop in my tracks, halfway to opening the fridge. "How will that help keep Mother off my back, or yours?"

"I'm new to this whole relationship thing, but I can attest that it gives you a new sense of purpose. And you've been trying to settle into some sort of routine with your prestigious teaching job," he mocks.

"Fuck you." I open the fridge. A normal person would find a bottle of chilled wine. I find diet soda.

"Don't be so testy, I'm just messing with you. But a girl could give you the sense of calm you need."

It's not lost on me that instead of a woman he's referring to a girl. Like he's too lazy to finish the word and call it a girlfriend. Or the universe has a twisted sense of humor, because a particular girl has already stolen all my depraved attention.

"Well, I've never imagined a day when Gio Cassinetti would promote relationships. Mila must be special."

"That she is, bro, that she is. Okay, I gotta go. Will you call Mother, please?"

"And now he says please." I fake shock. "Whatever Ms. Ward did to you seems too drastic."

"Go to hell, you idiot. But call Mom before you do."

He hangs up. I lower my forehead to the fridge. Maybe I can call on my mother. It would be a regular thing to do, an opportunity to get out of the house, potentially get a warm meal out of it.

I open the fridge again and look at the foil-wrapped meals my housekeeper left for me. I shut the door promptly. My eyes land on the sofa, and the idea of spending one more minute there without alcohol, drugs or Vivid—not that she's ever been on that sofa— propels me to action.

I call an Uber and do something I haven't done since I moved out of our Riverdale house. A spontaneous visit.

Chapter 16

Ivory

"Mommy, I'm exhausted." I try to leave, but she drags me into another corner of the department store.

We've been at it for hours. My feet hurt. My stomach growls. My head spins. I follow her into the gallows of more clothes and accessories, the multitude of shopping bags in my hands bouncing off the racks, hitting my legs.

"Come on, chérie. We haven't shopped in such a long time. I want to surprise your father with some new outfits. And you need to update your wardrobe as well. Ernest is well-bred—he has expectations." Mother winks at me.

I groan and roll my eyes when she turns. She grabs a dress and props it against me.

"What do you say, chérie?"

I look down, the bags cutting into my palms. "It's perfect if I was a thirty-year-old housewife."

Mother huffs and turns to peruse the display. Why did I agree to this shopping spree? Well, I was too excited about her interest in getting out of the house. I was anxious to leave our mansion, where every corner cowered before my father's threatening mood.

Most of all, I needed a distraction from my thoughts. Andrea hasn't come to school for a week now. He simply disappeared. If I wasn't a coward, I would have gone to the dean's office and asked her about him.

Julianna said they were told he's sick. I don't buy that. But then if he was suspended, we would have heard.

I want to go to his house, but he sent me a nasty message, making sure I stay away.

I haven't slept well since that evening in the studio. Just my luck, when we finally embraced our mutual attraction, we got caught.

When I asked him to help me with my sculpture, I didn't have an ulterior motive. Okay, perhaps a little. But never did I expect our creative session to shake my foundations like that.

He awakens a dormant passion within me, igniting a fire that blazes. The depth of his understanding stirs something profound within my soul. It's as if he sees the hidden layers of my being, and with each interaction he peels away the walls I've carefully built, exposing my true self.

The way he sees my work. Never laughing at my lack of talent, experience, or ability to express myself artistically. I've never felt so understood, so seen, so valued.

It sounds and feels crazy, but it's like my entire life led up to that moment in the school studio with him. This connection with him, this realization of my own power and worth.

"Ivory!"

"Yes, Mommy." Just thinking about him makes me breathless.

"Oh, I know that look." Mother abandons the dress she was holding, throwing it carelessly over the rack.

"What look?" I frown. "Let's go. My feet are killing me and these"—I lift the bags—"are heavy."

"Okay, okay, let's pick up some lattes and go home. But that look... you're in love." She shrugs in glee.

I'm about to protest, but she keeps going, "Ernest and you will be such a great couple. And your Papa will finally be able to relax a bit."

Oh God, my mother can't read people at all. She lives in her own world. And it's not even a pleasant fantasy.

"I don't think Papa's mood could be aided by my happiness," I mumble.

"Oh, chérie, he needs a powerful connection, and you'll secure it for him, and everything will change."

I sigh but perk up quickly when my phone beeps. I drop half of the bags and pull my phone out.

"Oh my, is it him?" Mother is so cheerful she even takes the bags without complaining.

My heart hammers, also hoping it's him. Not Ernie, but the him who has been invading all my dreams and waking hours. But the universe has a weird sense of humor. The message is indeed from Ernie.

And a few unread ones from Tim. I haven't opened those because I don't want to encourage him, not even with a simple read check mark.

He behaved like an asshole when I told him I wasn't interested after Andrea stormed out of the coffee shop.

He doesn't deserve a chance to apologize. All these messages in my inbox, and none from the man I wish to hear from. I open Ernie's text.

ERNIE

Tell your parents we're going to the Caribbean for Thanksgiving. I'm taking my girlfriend there. EC.

And where exactly would I be getting tanned?

I'm grateful he's not into this stupid arrangement, but he could put some effort into planning things better.

ERNIE

You're not coming with us, but I'll pay for your hotel here.

I sigh.

"What's going on?" Mother sounds alarmed.

"He wants us to spend the Thanksgiving weekend together." I throw her a bone and she attacks it like a starving stray, salivating over the news.

"At their place? Is he inviting us over to their house in Florida? Or the one in France?" she chirps.

"Not us, just me. And it's somewhere in the Caribbean." I can't sound less enthusiastic even if I tried.

Mother gasps and several people turn their heads. "He's going to propose. Probably somewhere on the beach." She drops the bags and launches at me. "Oh, my chérie, Papa will be so happy."

The irony of my mother hugging me for the first time in I don't know how long isn't lost on me, but the little girl in me rejoices at the attention. I let her cling to me, basking in the rare display of affection.

Then reality hits me. "You can't tell him. We don't know if he's proposing. It's your wishful thinking."

"You're right. Let's not keep his hopes up. Oh, my lovely girl"—she cups my cheeks—"I'm so happy for you."

For a moment, I pretend this is all real. I'm getting engaged, and my mother is happy for me. Not grasping at the opportunity to appease my father. Actually happy for me, because she knows me and wants me to be happy.

For a moment, I imagine she loves me unconditionally like I do her. That she isn't a woman broken by my father, but a proud wife and mother. That the gentle, caring woman I still remember—though the memories are fading—is the one hugging me right now.

For a moment, I wish this was all real. That I'm the daughter who can make her parents proud by marrying the chosen man and feel that that's enough for her.

But it's not enough. It would never be enough, because I want—I need—my own choices. And a pair of adults in my life who will respect those choices regardless, and then comfort me when those backfire.

Then I accept reality once more and let my mother hug me for a bit longer, because while the reasons behind it are all sorts of wrong, she needs the hug as much as I do.

When we return, we've barely put the bags on the floor in our large foyer when my father's voice startles me.

"I said I'll take care of it. You agreed to wait one more month." His voice, coming from the dining room, shakes the china in the cabinets.

Mother covers her mouth with her gloved hand and frowns at Martha, who is standing in the entrance to the kitchen. Martha shrugs and scurries away.

The tension stretches as we both stand there, unable to move and worried to breathe.

"You owe me a few more weeks of patience. I'll take care of everything." The words bounce around the ground floor like bullets.

Followed by the shattering of glass—he probably smashed a vase—are his footsteps. It's too late to disappear.

He looks at us bewildered like he's just realized where he was. His hair is all messed up, like he's been raking his hands through it. But while that is very unusual, the real shock comes from his loosened tie. My father has always been impeccably dressed.

He notices the bags and I step back involuntarily.

"What is this? Eden, have you lost your mind? I told you no more unnecessary shopping sprees." Father marches over to us and kicks one of the bags.

Mother jumps, but then quickly re-arranges her face into a smile. "This was necessary. Ernest invited Ivory for the Thanksgiving weekend."

Father was already turning to walk away, but this

grabs his attention. "Did he? Shouldn't he ask for our permission first?" He puts his hands into his pockets, relaxing despite his words.

"Oh, Cecil, nowadays they don't ask for permission. He's taking her somewhere in the Caribbean. Isn't that just fabulous?"

"I guess it's a step in the right direction. You should gain some weight. No man wants to see your boyish figure in a swimsuit."

Heat rises into my cheeks and stupid tears prickle behind my eyes. "Maybe I won't go then." I don't know why I decide to piss my father off, but I guess even I have my limits.

His eyes widen, but he recovers quickly. "You don't have a choice in the matter."

"She doesn't need to gain weight. I'm sure Ernest likes her the way she is, otherwise he wouldn't invite her. Cecil, the boy *wants* to spend a long weekend with her."

I don't remember the last time my mother stood up for me. This is in her own slightly twisted way, but it counts. Warmth spreads across my chest and the little girl awakens again, craving Mommy's attention.

"Good. You better come back with a diamond on your finger. I'm going to the club." He storms to the back of the house where the door leads to the garage.

"Cecil." Mother dashes behind him. I don't stay for her cooing and begging, but run upstairs to my room.

I close the doors, slide down the wooden frame and pull out my phone.

> My parents are hoping for a proposal during our weekend away.

The three dots dance around.

ERNIE

> Fuck.

I close my eyes. I hear Mother and crack the door. I'm not in the mood to resuscitate her, but I can't help it and check what state she's in after his refusal. To my utter shock, both my parents are entering Mother's bedroom.

Wow, I guess my almost engagement has lifted some of the troubles in their paradise.

* * *

"Ivy, come on in. Julianna went to meet with some guy from school, but you can wait for her." Agatha greets me like she's genuinely happy to see me.

I hesitate. A guy from school? Why wouldn't Julianna tell me?

"Don't stand there. I cooked your favorite pasta."

Even though I'm exhausted, I couldn't stay at home. But I'm in no mood to spoil the joyful atmosphere at the Biachis'.

"No, thank you, I'll just call her later."

Agatha frowns. "Are you sure?"

I force a smile. "Yes, thank you."

I wander around the neighborhood aimlessly for I don't know how long, and then my legs take me to the subway station. I don't even make a conscious decision about my destination.

But after almost an hour, deep in my turbulent thoughts, I find myself in front of the gallery in SoHo.

It's been four months since I came here, but in some ways it feels like yesterday. In others, I feel like I've aged years.

A bell chimes as I enter. Unlike the last time, the gallery breathes freely now, practically empty aside from the art giving life and purpose to the space.

A woman I vaguely remember comes from the adjacent room.

"Hello, I'm Violet Mathison, the owner. May I help you?" She extends her hand.

I shake it, but I don't tell her who I am. It's not like I can afford anything here. "I was here a few months ago."

"Oh." She smiles. "I love it when people return.

Did you come for anything in particular, or would you just like some alone time to enjoy the work?"

There is something about the woman that puts me at ease. "Do you have any pieces by Andrea Cassinetti?"

Just saying his name, my heart hammers in my temples. What am I doing? I can't afford any of his paintings.

"I'm afraid Andrea sold out immediately. There are still two pieces in the last room waiting to be delivered to their new owners. I'm afraid that's all I can offer right now."

"Thank you. Do you mind if I have a look?" Why do I feel like I'm doing something illegal?

"By all means, go ahead. Cassinetti can touch one's soul in the most profound ways."

Don't I know it?

I make my way to the back room, ignoring the other art on display, though just in my peripheral vision I can see the owner has an excellent selection.

The colorful explosion taking up the farthest wall assaults my senses. I don't have to read the plaque to know it's Andrea's.

The vibrant strokes of color captivate me, pulling me closer. I stand before the painting, my fingertips tingling with anticipation.

It's a breathtaking masterpiece—an abstract representation of emotions and desires. The canvas comes alive with a whirlwind of hues, blending and dancing together in perfect harmony.

The fiery reds intermingle with gentle blues. Just like the artist, hot with passion but cold in his denial. Splashes of yellow and orange burst forth, exuding warmth and vitality.

But then I notice what's hidden behind the ostensive colors. It can't be?

I step away and tilt my head, blinking a few times before I refocus on the piece in front of me. It's there. Contours of shackles, so well hidden, I doubt anyone has noticed them before.

His shackles to my chains. Jesus.

It almost explains the inexplicable connection, a profound intimacy. It's as if Andrea has taken a glimpse into the depths of my soul and translated it onto this very canvas.

But he didn't know me when he was painting it. He still doesn't know about my hidden emotions, the desires I've longed to express. Yet my pain mingles with his, laid bare before me.

The vulnerability in his brushstrokes, the raw honesty resonates within me. I trace the contours of the painting with my eyes, absorbing every intricate detail.

In this moment, I understand that our connection goes beyond the superficial. It's a meeting of minds, hearts, and souls—a profound intimacy that ignites a spark within me.

And as I stand before his masterpiece, I know I can't simply pretend nothing is happening between us.

I don't care how old he is. Who he is. I forget about Papa, Mother, Ernie. About the school rules, and the lie that I told him about being with Tim.

There is no doubt in my mind: the only man I want to be with is Andrea Cassinetti.

If only I could make him feel the same. And accept it.

"Oh, this one has been captivating everyone." Violet's voice startles me.

I don't look away from the shackles. I want to cut them free. "I wonder why."

"There is something special about it. I can't quite grasp what it is, but somehow Andrea captured pain within a chaos of joyfulness. It's like... like the artist. Have you met him?"

I swallow. "Yes. Yes, I have."

"Are you an artist?"

I want to say no, but it seems like a lie. *My chains.* "I'm studying."

Violet chuckles. "If you're studying the craft, you're an artist already. Maybe one day you'll show me your work."

I finally look away from Andrea's work. "I don't think—"

"You never know. It's not a simple path, but when the soul needs an outlet, it finds one whether we want it or not. Take my card."

I take the simple white business card and thank her. I leave the gallery and my steps have a renewed purpose. I know where I need to be.

Chapter 17

Andrea

"Andrea!" Mother smothers me in a tight embrace, which by itself is an achievement since she barely reaches my chest. The woman is strong. Inside and out. "What is wrong, darling?"

I unclasp her arms from around me and kiss the crown of her head. "Nothing is wrong. Why?"

She takes my hand and drags me to the kitchen. "Sit," she orders and gets a jug of lemonade from the fridge.

Some things will never change. I smile inwardly and climb on the stool. Picking up an apple, just to have something to do with my hands, I take a bite. She places a full glass in front of me.

"To begin with, you came, on your own, so I'm assuming there is a reason for that. And forgive me for not assuming it's good news to share." She cups my cheek and looks at me like I was fragile and even a gaze could break me.

It doesn't break me, it pisses me off, but I swallow her pity and smile. "There is no news, good or bad. Gio told me you're worried and we can't have that." I wink at her and take another bite of the apple.

"Let me warm up some pasta. The cook is off already, but I can still use the oven." She perks up and starts fussing around the kitchen.

"Thank you. I haven't had a good Italian meal since I was here the last time."

"You can come for a good, homemade, made with love meal anytime," she says, as if she was the one cooking around here. "You don't look very good, darling. Have you been sleeping? Working?"

"I took leave from work, but I'm fine."

She swats her hand like the idea is bothersome. "I'm not talking about your little play at teacher—"

"What the hell, Mom?" What is it with everyone discounting my livelihood?

"Oh, please, what do you want me to say? You're a talented artist. If you were teaching because it's your calling, that would be one thing. But you're doing it to avoid your studio. It makes no sense."

I drop the apple. "It makes perfect sense, Mom. I can't work in my studio. I'm not strong enough."

She observes me for a long moment. I swear her eyes have an X-ray vision quality and she can see the darkest, deepest areas of my soul. It's unnerving. I grab the apple again, taking a generous bite while playing the silent duel of stares with her.

"You believe your art is your trigger?" And bingo, her sixth sense is at its best.

"It's not a belief, it's a fact."

"You've been living your life as far away from your family as possible, so I might not have the full picture, but I think it's the acceptance of your work that's your trigger. It's the fear people won't receive it the way you intended. That it fails."

And now I definitely remember why I've been avoiding coming here. It's a therapy session. The only difference is that I'm not paying for it, and she nails the situation better than a stranger who takes an hour just to tap the surface.

"Mom, don't—"

"Sorry, Andrea, but I have to, because you're old enough and successful enough to have learned that you are enough. That is something you have to accept in here"—she touches the left side of her chest—"and no amount of perfection, of sold-out exhibits, of awards or accolades for your work will ever give it to you. Only you. You're enough."

I lower my head, my stomach swirling with nausea.

Her words pound against my temple, blinding me. I push away from the bar and rush to the back door to get outside.

The crisp air fills my lungs, and after a few deep breaths I swear and return inside.

She takes a dish out of the oven, the silence loud in the kitchen. The steam dances from my plate as she transfers a portion of lasagna onto it.

"Enough of the drama. You know I'm right, and you're smart enough to stop fighting it. Eat now." She pushes the meal in front of me.

My stomach is too knotted to eat, until the tantalizing smell hits me with such comfort that I sigh and dig in.

"Go back to your studio and create for yourself. Paint the demons out of you and never show them to anyone. And find yourself a new outlet to cope with the unwarranted self-doubt," she scolds.

She acts like I just failed a test in school, not like she's talking about the foundation of my existence.

"Unwarranted? Do you remember who bought out my first ever exhibition? Who established me in the art world without giving me a chance to prove myself?" I shove another spoonful into my mouth to shut myself up. To shut away all the feelings that are bubbling up.

"Is that your reason for all your troubles over the years? Because your sister wanted to make you happy and bought all your art? It was a gesture of love and admiration on her part. And it did indeed catapult you to a new level in your career, so holding that against her and against yourself is a bit too dramatic even for you."

"Oh, is it? We will never know if my work was any good because I didn't get a chance to show it to anyone. Puff." I snap my fingers. "Those dreadful drawings sold out, and suddenly the attention was on me. Not because of those pieces I sweated blood over, but because the market accepted them. What a fucking lie."

"Enough." Mother's voice carries across the kitchen. "Even if the opportunity wasn't the one you wanted, it was an opportunity. None of us ever dared to buy any of your paintings, and you keep selling out, so I'm pretty sure those collectors want to own them. You can't change the beginning you got, but you can surely stop destroying your present and your future."

I push the plate away. If she only knew half of it. "I'm full."

She throws her arms up in exasperation. "Suit yourself. You haven't spoken to London in years. Isn't apologizing part of the recovery process?"

My eyes widen.

"Oh, Andrea, you really think I believed you were in Europe? I'm glad you're sober. I'm thrilled you're trying so hard to stay that way, but don't stay away from your studio. It's a gift, and you have to nurture it."

* * *

To say that the visit helped me in my state of self-loathing would be an understatement of cosmic proportions.

I return home fed but also fed up. How dare she speak the truth? How dare she force me into the naked reality I don't know how to resolve?

Though she might have uncovered one important piece I've been ignoring. I may find myself painting, and if I don't intend to show the piece to anyone, I might survive.

I rush up to my studio. I almost trip over the canvas with the red paint splatters from before. I stop and close my eyes, breathing in the energy of the space, finding the flow I've been missing.

My imagination fails me miserably, because the only thing I see in my mind's eye is the golden speckles in Vivid's eyes, the sprinkles of her freckles, the small lines around her eyes when she smiles.

I'm fucking obsessed with her. My muse. So Vivid.

I grab a pencil and start sketching her. From my memory, but it's almost like she was sitting here with me. Perhaps if I capture her on the paper, she'll leave my fantasies.

I don't know how long I'm at it, but the process is as tedious as ever. It's like the weeks without the pencil or brush between my fingers left me stiff. I go through several attempts, but I can't find her.

Frustrated, I throw the sketchpad on the table and go downstairs. My fridge is just as disappointing as it was earlier.

Fuck it. I grab my phone and order three cases of premium wine.

The clock ticks slowly in the living room as I sit there waiting for the DoorDash. My palms sweat, my wrist hurts from the sketching attempt, my mind is numb with everything that's happened in the last few months. In the last few years. In my fucking life.

Finally the bell rings, and I trudge to the door, considering giving the wine to the delivery man as a present. I don't know what I want anymore. Or rather, what I want isn't available.

I open the door and almost shut it again. "What are you doing here?"

Vivid jerks her head back but recovers quickly. "I missed your glower. Were you expecting someone else?"

I snort. "Again with the questions." God, it's so good to see her. It's like she got even more beautiful in the last week. "This is not a good idea, Vivid. You should go. I don't want you here." The words hurt like hell, but not as much as the look on her face.

"You mentioned that in your message. I didn't know you were into ass kissing." Her words are confident, but she's wringing her hands in front of her.

"Ass kissing?" I lean against the door. I can't invite her in. For her own good. Fuck.

"Isn't that the line that Wiggins wants you to use? To protect the school's reputation?" She clenches her fists now.

"To protect *your* reputation, silly girl."

"Oh, I see, you've joined the ranks of people deciding what's good for me. How I should look, how much talent I have, how I should behave, what my worth is?"

"That's not..." Fuck. Fuck. Fuck. "I can't give you what you deserve."

"Why?"

"I can't be chained." But the only person I want to be chained with right now is you. I can't tell her that.

"Well, I need someone to teach me how to break free."

This girl. "Vivid—" It hurts to say her name.

"I don't believe in love, Andrea, you're safe with me."

We stare at each other. Who hurt her this much?

So young. She should still believe in love and happily ever after.

Fuck.

We're two lost souls, drawn to each other to burn for eternity.

I groan, and with the last remains of decency in me, I make the final attempt to send her away.

I even deliver it with detached coolness. "Is the Varsity boy busy tonight?"

Chapter 18

Ivory

I roll my eyes and sigh. I'm exhausted to the bone from this denial, the chase, the unresolved feelings.

"You can't decide what I deserve. I deserve to explore what this is between us. For once in my life, I deserve to make my own decision and not care about the rest of the world. I might be young and inexperienced, but I'm not stupid. So stop pushing me away. I'm not with Tim. I'm yours."

He utters a sound like a wounded animal, filled with frustration and a hint of capitulation. The latter might be my wishful thinking.

"I'm trying to protect you." The words come out strangled, and my heart swells.

"Can you protect me inside your house?"

He groans, grabs my hand and pulls me in. Kicking

his door closed, he captures my lips. My back hits the wall. He devours me like a man possessed. It's not our first kiss, but... Jesus.

Every fiber in my body reacts to his lips owning me. He fists my hair and angles me to his liking.

I can't breathe.

I can't think.

I can't move.

I'm at his mercy, and I love every minute of it.

His length hardens against my lower stomach. His body is solid against mine. But he's not touching me anywhere.

The man is purely dedicated to kissing me so thoroughly I might never find his equal.

He's taking everything with that kiss. My inhibition. My doubts. Me. And I give willingly. Eagerly.

When he finally comes up for air, he lowers his forehead to mine, cupping my face. "I don't give a shit about me. I want you, and the rest of the world can be damned. But you need to think about your reputation. You're young. I'm your professor. People will—"

"Judge? Condemn? Assume that anything I achieve is thanks to you?" I pant.

He closes his eyes briefly, nodding.

"I'm here because I don't want to be anywhere else. I've been judged, condemned, and everything except recognized for who I am my whole life. We can keep it a secret if it makes you feel better, but I'm yours. Maybe it's just for this moment in our lives, but we need each other."

Our lips fuse again, and I try to keep up with him, be an equal in this connection, but it's quite clear I'm not, so I let him lead. Dominate. Own me.

Andrea hoists me up, wrapping my legs around his waist. Walking down the short hallway, he nuzzles my neck.

"Did you eat a good, nutritious meal?" He sets me down and studies me like I'm his dinner.

"What?" I'm sitting on his kitchen island, but is he really going to feed me?

"I've been waiting for this for too long. You'll need your energy, vixen." He smirks and rolls my jacket off my shoulders.

What the heck is he planning to do with me? I chuckle, or I hope that's what it sounds like. "I had two bags of chips."

He unzips my boots. "Don't be smart with me, Vivid, because I'll feed that pretty mouth of yours. With my cock."

He throws it out there casually and my cheeks heat up.

He snorts. "Not yet. Close your mouth." He takes off one boot then the other. I'm perched on a cold marble surface, but I don't get a chance to take in the surroundings before he cups my neck and yanks me close for another kiss.

Tracing his lips down my neck to my clavicle, he awakens all the cells in my body. My desire pools in my core, soaking my panties.

The man explores my body like it's his life's mission. I'm wearing a light sweater with a boat neckline. It fits me tightly, but he tests the elasticity of the fabric and pulls it down, exposing my black lacy bra.

"Look at you, my little vixen, dressed like a good girl, but underneath it all you're my little slut." He takes my nipple into his mouth through the skimpy material and I gasp.

Falling onto my elbows, my head falls back as I close my eyes, trying to deal with the sensation and with his words. He's a dirty talker. My first one.

My first one.

I should tell him—

"And to think you gave this beautiful body to the fucking Varsity boy. I'll fuck him out of your system." He grabs my jaw. "I'll fuck all thoughts of any other men from you, Vivid."

Before I can speak he seizes my lips again, squeezing the back of my neck and my breast.

I need to tell him, but I'm so aroused and full of anticipation I don't want him to stop. He pushes my bra out of the way and sucks my nipple like it's a popsicle.

"You taste so good, Vivid. So good." He hums against my skin and I shudder, my body acting of its own accord. Or rather of Andrea's accord, because I'm slowly losing all my faculties.

I'm succumbing to his skillful ministrations, and he hasn't even moved below my waist yet. I moan.

"Oh, those sounds, you're perfect. Just perfect."

His words alone may send me over the edge. It might be just dirty talk, but he says it like he means it. Like there are no other women on Earth.

Just me. The goddess.

He bites my nipple and I arch my back, gasping. The guttural sound of a predator echoes throughout the room. My ovaries scream with anticipation.

"Oh, Vivid, just for those pretty little sounds, I'm going to make you come on my tongue, on my fingers, and on my cock. And you will take it like a good girl. My beautiful vixen."

He gazes at me with hooded eyes and I whimper, because his praise, his filth, his hands and the reverence in his eyes are spreading in my chest, setting my core ablaze.

My whimper is the sound that strips him of patience, and before I know it, he rips off my tights. He pushes my knees apart, flattening them against the counter.

My skirt rolls up at my waist, the remains of my tights hanging from my left leg. I'm widespread for him and speechless. If I thought his gaze before was reverent, I don't know what this is.

I'm utterly exposed as he takes in the drenched spot between my legs with a look of a conqueror, a worshiper.

"Look how wet you are for me already." He grins. "God, I can't wait to taste you."

I open my mouth to speak, but all the words leave my brain along with my destroyed underwear when he rips it off and dives in with his tongue.

The neighbors must hear my moans. He nibbles and sucks and laps until my clit is on fire. His whiskers burn my skin, his hands dig into my thighs, holding me still as I thrash.

It's all too much. Too good. Too intense.

Falling flat on the counter, I fist his hair, not sure if I want to push him away or pull him closer.

"Andrea," I cry out. I want him to stop, and I want him to continue and never stop. Ever.

"You like my tongue there." He looks up and drags himself up my body.

I was so close, but I'm grateful for the reprieve. I try to collect my thoughts, but it's a lost battle. He kisses me, and now his taste is mixed with mine. It's the sexiest thing.

I wrap my legs around him, pulling him as close as possible, crazed by the taste of us.

"You're a mixture of the best flavors in the world. Taste yourself, vixen."

I moan against his lips, holding him tightly, fearing the loss of contact might tear me apart.

He lifts on to his elbows. "You're so beautiful, all flushed. Do you want to come?"

I blink a few times. Scrambling for words, I end up nodding. Jesus. I'm as articulate as a sedated sloth.

"Finally, no questions." He chuckles again, kisses me, and his head disappears, diving into my pussy again.

I close my eyes, trying to deal with the overload of feelings. Lost in the tantalizing sensations he's inflicting on me, I let my body take over and ride the wave.

The orgasm hits me with such intensity I must bruise my vocal cords screaming. My body tenses, my core clenches, and I drench the counter and his face, coming and coming while he murmurs praises.

"And she's a screamer," he rasps, and reaches for my sensitive nipples. "I can't wait anymore, vixen."

I'm still dazed when he flips me over and yanks me to the edge of the counter roughly. Oh God, I need to—

The burn spreads and I whimper. Jesus, that's uncomfortable. Painful.

Not as painful as my embarrassment, because Andrea halts. For the longest second of my life, everything goes still. Tears prickle my eyes.

His hands on my hips tense. I squeeze my eyes shut. I didn't tell him soon enough, so there is no point telling him now. Clearly, he knows.

God, I wish it didn't burn this badly.

After what feels like an eternity, he growls. "Vivid."

Leaning over me, his breath warms my neck. Still sheathed inside me, he shifts, and I swallow another whimper.

Andrea cups my chin, turning my face and forcing me to look at him.

"Open your eyes, Vivid," he orders.

I know it's childish, but I shake my head. Humiliation mingles with pain, and my until now void brain offers useless thoughts. Like how am I going to go home without my underwear?

"Stupid girl," he grumbles and withdraws, leaving me empty.

Filled with pain, I fight my tears.

Discarded.

I won't cry. I won't cry.

Andrea paces, I think. "You didn't sleep with the

Varsity boy. Why did you lie?" A hint of annoyance and regret colors his voice. But it's not anger, at least.

I don't know what to say. What's the point anyway? I didn't speak when I should have.

With shaky legs, I push off the counter.

"Fuuuuck," Andrea shouts.

He snakes his arm under my knees and hoists me up, bridal style.

I can't look at him. My heart hammers against my chest. For one horrible moment, I fear he's going to dump me in the street, but he turns toward the stairs.

"Stupid girl. I want to punish you right now so badly." Despite his words, he kisses my forehead gently.

His heart thumps against me. My confusion, embarrassment, stupidity and vulnerability have collided, knotting my stomach and sending my heart into overdrive.

The worst part is, I'm filled with regret. We've danced between attraction and denial for so long and... I spoiled it all.

"Where are we going?" I croak into his neck. Not sure why I ask, because right this moment I'm just relieved he's holding me.

He stops and glowers at me, shaking his head. "You, Ivory, have no regard for your own body. It fucking pisses me off."

Ivory. Ouch. I guess I deserve it. I don't even know why I suggested I slept with Tim. It seems a lifetime ago now. But I should have told him.

He examines me with sadness in his eyes. "Why didn't you tell me? You deserve so much more. Fuck."

"Well, I don't have any reference, but I'm not even sure you took my virginity." I try to lighten the mood. I'd say anything right now to negate the heaviness of disappointment. His. Mine?

"Don't be fucking smart with me, Vivid. It's more like Livid right now," he scolds, growling, and restarts our ascent.

He's upset on my behalf. I don't know what to do with that sentiment. I don't know how to accept it.

We enter a room at the back of the house. It's large and luxurious, but also very masculine with its navy and light brown colors. He marches to a massive bed and lays me down like precious cargo.

"You don't have to—"

"Shut up. I'm going to finish what I started, and you're going to enjoy it. You'll scream my name until you lose your voice. You'll leave this room when you're thoroughly fucked, but before then, I need to show you how to treat your body. And you will let me. Do you understand?"

Oh, the confidence, the dominance, the testosterone oozing from him... it renders me speechless. If he asked me to jump from a bridge right now, I would.

He put me first. No one ever, not even me—especially not me—has ever put me first.

"Do you understand?" He locks me with an intense gaze, assessing me with hungry eyes.

I have no idea what he's asking, but I nod. Andrea traces his fingers down my calves and rolls down what's left of my tights.

"Are you very sore?" he asks with a husky voice.

"A bit." My physical discomfort is inconsequential right now.

He shakes his head like he doesn't believe me. He snakes his arms under my legs, meeting his hands at my behind. With care, he drags me to the edge of the bed and drops to his knees. He kisses the inner side of my thighs and I shiver with pleasure.

Trailing feather-like, reverent kisses up one leg and then the other, he finally reaches my mound and stretches my folds with his fingers. He blows slowly and my hips buck of their own volition.

He places a caressing hand on my hipbone and blows again before he kisses me there and then licks the last remains of the burn away.

I'm losing myself again in his care, overwhelmed by it all. By his consideration. By his reaction to my lie. By his tongue gentle and urgent between my legs.

This time, he just kisses and licks me tenderly. But it's so much worse because it's a tease, I'm shivering with desire, my mind completely fogged. His tongue seems to have discovered all the right spots.

His hands are too strong, holding me pinned against the silky sheets of his bed. I reach my second orgasm, crying out, but it doesn't stop him. He goes on relentlessly, like he never wants to stop.

"Andrea," I cry out.

"Yes, vixen?" he rasps.

"Please," I whimper, but I'm not even sure what I'm begging for.

He chuckles and bites my thigh softly before he moves back. He offers me his hand and pulls me to standing. I'm not even sure how I stand because my legs wobble.

Andrea rakes his eyes over me with a wolfish grin. I'm sure my hair looks like a lion's mane, my boobs still hang from my sweater and my skirt is rucked up around my hips. I'm a mess, and I immediately hunch my shoulders.

"No, no, no, you will not hide." He steps closer and lifts my arms, then pulls the sweater over my head.

Goosebumps cover my skin as he kisses my shoulder while he undoes my bra. For some outlandish reason, I want to cover myself. As if he hasn't seen or tasted my breasts.

He grabs my wrists, tutting. "You'll let me admire you." He wraps his arms around me and unzips my skirt. It floats to the ground and pools at my ankles.

Andrea buries his nose in my hair, his body solid against me. "So beautiful. So fucking beautiful."

His breath on my ear weakens me and I grab his shoulders, quivering with desire and anticipation.

The energy is so different from downstairs. There he dominated with need and arousal. Here he still dominates, but with a sense of worship. I'm not sure which is better. This slower pace leaves too many beats for my brain to riot. I need to stop thinking.

He kisses my forehead, my temple, the corner of my eye. "I want to kiss every inch of you. Mark your skin. Brand my name inside you, so there is no doubt this beauty belongs to me."

Jesus. I'm so wet for him again, completely stripped of my will. I'm just pure desire while he steps back and starts unbuttoning his shirt. I want to help, but I can't move, locked in his gaze and drowning in the thick sensual atmosphere.

He shakes the black shirt off his shoulders and then lowers his briefs. He must have lost his slacks in the kitchen. When he straightens I gasp, and my eyes widen.

His erection stands between us. Huge and hard.

Okay, it hurt a lot before, and there is no way he even got it all in.

He takes my hand and brings it to his shaft. It feels like velvet under my fingertips, but I'm too stunned and frankly shy to explore it.

He nudges my chin up and our eyes meet. "Don't worry, vixen, we know it fits. This cock is yours, but first let's finish your lesson."

"Lesson?" The word dies on my lips. Mostly because what little brain function I have left is dedicated to useless thoughts. How can he like my body? He's just saying that. Will it hurt again this time? Should I be doing something? I'm so out of my depth here.

He takes my hand and leads me around the bed. In the room's corner is a large mirror on a stand. He grips both my wrists behind me with one of his hands and wraps the other around my neck.

"Look how your beautiful neck looks with my hand around it. I sense your heartbeat, wild with anticipation."

He slides his hand slowly down my shoulder, my arm to my hip. His touch ignites my skin, blazes and goosebumps mingling.

"Look at these hips. The way you sway them when you walk hardens my cock every single time. That's the effect you have on me, Vivid. You think I'm in charge here, but all the power is in your hands. Your beauty is a source of light for me."

I close my eyes, the air not really filling my lungs anymore. "Andrea," I breathe.

"Look at yourself," he whispers darkly. He squats behind me, not letting go of my wrists. His hand caresses my leg. "Look at these gorgeous, sexy legs."

With my gaze, I follow his hand, trying to calm my racing heart.

My mouth is dry, mind blank. I'm nothing but feelings, exploring my body through his eyes.

Andrea moves to my side, grips my ankle and yanks my feet apart. I lose balance, but he lets go of my wrists and I find purchase holding his shoulders.

"And the jewel, the prettiest pussy in the world. Yours." He cups me between my legs and my knees buckle.

He's so handsome looking at me from down there.

I believe him. I believe his reverent words. I trust his admiring eyes. I feel beautiful. Not because he told me, but because he showed me.

I snap my eyes back to the mirror and look at myself—really look. And for the first time in my life, I don't see the imperfections. I see me, and a smile stretches across my face.

The road to self-acceptance is long, but tonight,

right here and now, with the hands and eyes of this dark man on me, I accept my body.

I find his eyes in the mirror, grinning at me. "Don't ever hide, Vivid. You're a goddess." He stands up and kisses my shoulder.

My heart flutters and I turn to kiss him, taking the initiative. We both moan into the kiss. Andrea walks us backward until my legs hit the bed.

"Let's get that beautiful pussy ready for me. Nice and slow," he rasps and pushes me.

My back hits the soft sheets and Andrea lowers himself over me, capturing my lips.

We continue discovering our bodies. Somehow he makes me come two more times, on his tongue and with his hand.

I don't know how he has so much self-control, because that erection must be painful by now. When he said nice and slow, I didn't expect this level of commitment. I'm wild with desire. Crazed. Completely out of my mind as he continues getting me ready.

No wonder he is so successful if he creates beauty with half the dedication he's using to destroy me.

My clit is raw, my nipples sensitive, my need for him exploding. "Please," I whimper.

Chapter 19

Andrea

Our bodies glisten with perspiration. The room is filled with the beautiful sounds she makes, and the dirty words I can't stop reciting as I explore her.

Time has stopped. The world outside doesn't exist.

I don't remember when I last had sex sober. Fuck, it's intense. It's exhilarating. It's delicious.

She's delicious. A beast awakened when I hurt her earlier while taking her on the counter. She was a fucking virgin. Why did she lie about it?

Thank God she hasn't slept with the Varsity boy. Tonight, she is truly mine. I get what no other has ever gotten before. And if that doesn't make me want to pound my chest and roar, nothing does.

"Andrea," she breathes. Fuck, my name on her lips gets me even harder, if that's possible.

"What is it, Vivid?" I lean back on my haunches.

"Please," she groans in frustration.

I chuckle. Her plea is music to my ears.

"Look at you all greedy now, my little vixen." I reach into my drawer for a condom. Fuck. I got so wound up downstairs I went in bare.

I fist my cock and give myself three rough jerks. Okay, self-control might be an issue here. I'm so hard for her, I might just come in my hand.

Her eyes go wide as she looks at my cock again.

I grin. "Shh, little one. I'll go slow."

I roll on the condom and cover her as I position myself between her legs. On my elbows, I frame her flushed face between my hands and kiss her. She wraps her arms around me, but I can sense hesitation.

"It's going to be okay," I murmur against her lips. She smiles and nods.

Gazing at her, I absorb her features and hopefully give her encouragement. With one hand, I guide myself to her entrance. I push in just an inch, gritting my teeth at how snug she feels.

"Breathe for me, Vivid. Relax."

She takes a deep breath, and I slide in more. She winces and I pause. "I know, vixen." I kiss her forehead. "Your pussy feels amazing." She relaxes a bit. "I'll make you feel so good. Do you trust me?"

She nods, breathing heavily, and I stop.

"Don't you dare to stop again." Her husky voice almost fucking makes me come.

I rock gently, going deeper with each thrust as her body yields to me. The friction is exquisite, almost too much. I have to clench my jaw to keep from losing control.

"Christ," I growl when I'm fully sheathed inside her. "You feel like sin, hot and wet and tight. My good girl."

A moan escapes her lips as she arches against me, and I take it as my cue to move. My thrusts drive deeper, and her body responds to me with wanton abandon. I can barely contain myself as a wave of sensation ripples through me—an electric heat that threatens to send me over the edge.

With firm, deliberate moves I pound into her core, pleasure and pain consuming us both.

"Andrea!" she cries out in ecstasy, her nails scraping across my back as I push her closer still to another rapture.

I kiss her savagely, our tongues tangling as I pick up the pace. The bed creaks under us, our harsh breaths and the sound of skin slapping the only noises in the room. Well, that and Vivid's beautiful symphony of pleasure.

"Come for me again," I demand gruffly, the rhythm of my hips becoming faster with each passing second.

I feel her inner walls flutter just before my own release takes hold. As I spill into the condom, she clenches tightly around me, sending aftershocks of pleasure ripping through every nerve ending in my body.

I collapse on to my back beside her. We lie breathless for a moment, and I pull her close, savoring the feel of her body.

It's almost too much. "I'll be right back."

I peel off the condom and tie it off then pad to the bathroom where I toss it in the trash. I wash my hands and stare at myself in the mirror.

What the fuck? I feel empty and full at the same time. This woman has ruined sex for me. How will I ever find someone who makes me feel this alive? No longer an unfinished painting, Vivid is a muse and artwork of her own.

I wasn't planning to want her after I had her.

"Andrea?" Her voice sounds small. Our eyes meet in the mirror, and... Fuck, I left her there alone after this.

She's a vision, that stunning face flushed, her raven, curly hair sticking in all different directions, and those swollen lips...

"Are you okay?" We both say at the same time.

Christ. What am I hiding from? I grab her hand

and pull her into a hug. She buries her face in my chest and I hold her like she was about to disappear.

"I think you're my trigger," I whisper.

She lifts her head, frowning. I tug her closer, now really feeling like she may disappear, leave.

"I'm a recovering addict," I croak.

She wraps her arms around my waist and lowers her cheek to my chest. "I'd rather be your addiction. You can fuck me again instead of using." She traces her tongue around my nipple.

I chuckle, grateful for her lightness. I nudge her chin up. "Are you okay?"

She sighs. "Still... processing." A shy smile curves her mouth. "It was—"

"Careful there," I warn, grinning.

She rolls her eyes and chuckles. "I don't know..."

"Clearly I fucked the vocabulary out of your brain. Amazing? Earth shattering? Life changing?" I can't keep the smugness from my tone.

She laughs, smacking my chest. "Don't get too cocky."

"But that's my most endearing quality, woman." I kiss her. Deeply.

"It was all of the above."

She squeals when I hoist her up and sit her on the vanity. "Let me clean you up." I grab a washcloth and soak it in hot water.

"No. I can do it myself." She hunches her shoulders again, averting her gaze.

"Nonsense." I force her legs apart, while she looks at me like I was about to drown a litter of kittens. I gently clean her, leaning in for tender kisses. Fuck, I hope I didn't hurt her.

When I look up, tears are rolling down her cheeks. "What's wrong? Are you that sore?"

She shakes her head, wiping her face.

"You're scaring me, Vivid. Talk to me."

Her breath hitches a few times—longest fucking second in my life—before she speaks. "No one has ever taken care of me."

I dump the rag in the sink and pick her up, kissing her forehead. "I was planning to fuck you again, but let's talk."

She chuckles against my chest. I get us both under the covers, tucking her under my arm.

"You're too young not to remember your parents taking care of you."

She lifts her head, propping her chin on my chest. "There is nothing to remember." She sighs. "I don't want to talk about it."

"Too late, vixen, I suspect they are responsible for your lack of self-confidence and your appalling diet. I just gave you the best sex of your life, so the least you can do is explain the tears in the bathroom."

She huffs. "You gave me the first sex in my life."

"And I'll give you your last one as well, and all the sex in between."

"Possessive." She chuckles. "Is that a threat?"

"Yes." I nod, and her eyes widen. "Now stop changing the topic and talk."

She releases a long breath and rolls on to her back, covering her eyes with her forearm. I don't like that she's distancing herself, but I sense she might need it for this conversation.

"I had nannies when I was little, because my parents never had time for me. My mother was sick often and my father traveled. I acted out a lot, and the nannies only stayed for short periods of time. And then, when I was eight, Mother tried to kill herself."

Finding her hand beside me, I squeeze it.

"She didn't succeed, but I... I can't imagine going through that fear again. So I've been taking care of her. She needs me. After her attempt, Father started traveling even more, and generally had time only to berate me for being too thin, too tall, too clunky, too useless as an heir—"

I can't stand it and I roll over her, pulling her arm away. "I'm sorry, vixen." I brush my lips against hers. "Though I want to kill your father right now. None of his vile words are true." I kiss her.

"He's under a lot of stress, and so disappointed at

not having a male heir, and I guess I was just an easy target. I don't think he really means—"

"Stop it right now. There is no good reason to talk to you the way he's apparently been doing for years. You're making excuses for him because he's your father. He's your father, and that's the reason he shouldn't be using you as his coping mechanism... a punching bag to deal with his stress."

"It's not that easy—"

"Vivid, you say you don't think he really means it, but you believe him." I swipe the hair from her forehead.

She opens her mouth and then closes it, deflated. "I do, don't I?" Her voice is so soft, so dejected, I almost get out of bed and leave her here to wage war on her fucking father.

"What about your mother?" I sit, too agitated to remain still.

Vivid joins me, settling beside me, leaning her head on my shoulder. "She keeps the peace with Father. She needs him."

I kiss the crown of her head. "You're beautiful and talented. Repeat."

"You're beautiful and talented."

Tackling her down, I hover above her. "Thank you for telling me." I smirk.

"I'm cheaper than therapy. Very good for your ego as well." She grins.

"What did I tell you about being smart with me?"

"What would be my punishment?"

"That sounds like a dare. I'll spank your pussy so hard it will throb to be fucked."

Her eyes widen and I laugh.

"Don't worry, not yet. First get used to my cock, and then we'll upgrade." I capture her lips, said cock already begging for attention, hard and heavy between us. "Are you very sore, vixen?"

She bites her lips, but doesn't answer. Instead, her stomach growls.

I chuckle. "Okay, I can feed you my cock." I wiggle my eyebrows.

Her face is a mixture of horror and curiosity. "Okay?"

"And we're back to the questions." I laugh. "Let me make you something to eat first."

"You don't have—"

"Shush, woman. I know it's hard to accept, but unlike your shitty parents, I want to take care of you. Besides, I don't want you to bite off my precious possession out of hunger." I point to my crotch, where my length is definitely not on board with the kitchen detour.

Vivid giggles, but gets out of bed, looking for her

clothes. "Oh no, vixen, this is naked chef edition." I swat her ass and lead her downstairs.

After I shove chicken kung pao in the oven and set the temperature and timer, she gives me a surprised expression.

"What?"

"I didn't expect you to know your way around the kitchen." She shrugs.

I lean against the island and guide her between my legs, her back to my torso. "Yeah, Vivid, it's an accomplishment. I know how to reheat a meal."

"What is it? Who cooked it?" She shivers when I nibble on her shoulder.

Having her here, in my kitchen, naked, feels so good. It feels like home. The thought crawls up my neck like a tarantula, fuzzy but scary.

"It's kung pao, and my housekeeper prepared it."

She hums, and my cock twitches against her back. "It sounds delicious. Where is your housekeeper now?" She tenses, and the urgency in her voice makes me laugh.

"Don't worry, she doesn't live here."

She relaxes into my arms, and I spend the rest of the meal preparation nibbling on her soft skin.

When the timer sounds, I take out a bowl and ladle the dish into it. After getting a spoon, I lead us over to the living room. I sprawl on the couch and pat my thigh. "Sit."

Vivid's laughter dies when she sees my expression. "You can't be serious?"

"Deadly." I pat my leg again and she sits on my lap with a frown. "Open." I hold the spoon to her mouth.

"You're going to feed me?" She raises her eyebrows.

"Obviously." I shrug, and she opens her mouth reluctantly.

Her lips wrap around the spoon, and I almost drop the bowl, ready to pound into her again.

She hums. "This is good."

"I can't wait to see those lips wrapped around my cock, vixen."

She swallows. "I'm not saying I don't want to do it, but I'm eating right now. Can you tone it down?"

I laugh and feed her another spoonful. "I can't. You bring out the beast."

"I really wish you would let me eat by myself." She sighs but takes another bite.

I kiss her shoulder. "It's not happening, beautiful."

She looks at me with a soft gaze, her shy smile lingering. "You do make me feel beautiful."

I feed her in silence for a moment, digesting the air heavy with feelings I don't want to name.

"Why didn't you want to paint me?" she asks when she finishes her meal, stroking my hair.

I sigh. "It's not you. I haven't gone to my studio for a while."

She plays with my hair, and it brings an odd sense of peace, so I continue. She trusted me with her demons, after all. I put the bowl on a console table behind me and meet her gaze.

"When I told you earlier that I worry you're my trigger... Well, art *is* my trigger."

She frowns. "But how?"

"When I try to finish a painting, I'm torn by so much restless energy and... well, doubt... that I need to numb the thoughts. So I do. I haven't finished a painting while sober in the longest time. And then when it's out there, I need to deal with all the noise and attention—"

"Like the night we met." Instead of being disappointed or repulsed, she kisses me. I groan into the kiss. I don't deserve her absolution.

I jerk my head away, but she straddles me and cups my face. "Maybe I'm not your trigger. Maybe I can be your outlet. I can be there for you to fight the monsters while you make me scream your name."

Her words hit me right in the chest, spreading warmth through me. This girl. Fuck.

She holds my cock between us with a shaky,

unsure grip. Lifting her hips, she positions the tip at her entrance and looks at me for guidance.

I give her a quick kiss and reach behind me into the console table drawer. Thank God there are condoms there.

She sheathes my length and then looks at me again, her eyes full of wonder that's going to kill me for sure.

I grab her neck and bring her in for another kiss, before I dig my fingers into her hips and guide her down. The entire time she watches where our bodies unite with such reverence that I can barely control myself.

She's fucking perfect. "Your tight pussy is driving me crazy."

She wraps her legs around me and I take my time unraveling her.

"You make me feel beautiful," she whispers, and I lose all my control.

* * *

The third time I take her in my bed, and we experiment with other positions. Vivid is an eager learner, and soon she will take everything I'm craving to give her. Having her opening up for me feels like a privilege, and a responsibility.

The first I don't deserve, and the second I don't want. And yet... here we are.

Her breathing evens out as she drifts off, while I draw mindless circles over her silky skin.

I haven't slept much lately, but sleep eludes me. My mind is racing, swirling with thoughts of her and this thing growing between us. It's too much. I know I should put distance between us, for her sake and my sobriety, but the idea makes me want to drink.

I don't know how long I lie there, wondering how this young girl with enough parental baggage for a worldwide tour is somehow stronger than me. Her dreams and self-awareness have been drained dry by the two people who should support her the most.

She has every right to feel unworthy and untalented, because someone kept telling her that. Unlike me, supported by my family, adoring fans, collectors, teachers, everyone, and I believe in myself less than she does. Or just as little.

I'm hiding it better, but... Fuck. I buzz with energy and need to find an outlet. Looking at the woman beside me, I lean in and kiss her forehead. She sighs and smiles in her sleep.

Carefully extracting myself from her embrace, I pad upstairs to my studio. The familiar scents of paint and canvas calm my frazzled nerves.

Before I know what I'm doing, my fingers trace the

brushes and I select one, weighing it in my hand like a precious instrument. I set up a clean canvas on an easel.

Squirting some paint on the palette, I dip the brush into it and I lose myself in the work, in capturing the beauty of life I've just discovered.

Back to work, back to life. When I paint time stops, and I enter this new place... the fourth dimension.

Often it's not enough, and I can't capture the essence of the feeling I want to imprison on the canvas. But today, my strokes are bold. The flow is unbreakable.

By the time my stiff neck calls for attention, the day is bright outside. Shit. I wipe my hands with an old cloth and look at my work. The woman sleeping downstairs is definitely a muse.

In the light of a new day, the guilt settles in. I stayed away to protect her reputation, but now? Are we supposed to sneak around in secret? Am I even capable of tending the fire between us, or will it consume me?

Keeping her is foolish. Reckless. She's so young, and I'm still clawing my way back to solid ground. But when I'm with her, when I look at her, everything feels brighter and more alive. I can't give that up. I won't.

High on creativity and possessive desire, I stride downstairs, eager to gather her in my arms again. Maybe even show her what she inspired.

I enter the bedroom silently, careful not to wake her. The sheets are rumpled where she lay earlier, still holding the scent of sex and her, but she is gone.

"Vivid." I check the bathroom.

Her skirt and sweater are gone.

I jog down and scan the kitchen and living room. I even open the patio door, calling her name.

Icy dread washes over me, followed swiftly by anger. My hands curl into fists, nails biting into my palms. The familiar urge to drink until I can't feel anything threatens to overwhelm me.

How dare she? After everything we shared, everything I gave her, she ran.

She left.

Chapter 20

Ivory

"**O**kay, slow down, this is all too much. You slept with Cassi." Julianna bounces off her bed and hops around the room in some sort of celebratory dance. Focused on the wrong part of my story.

I giggle, the images of last night flicking through my tired and confused mind. "Can we talk about this morning?"

Sitting cross-legged on her bed, I clench my pelvic muscles. I'm wonderfully blissed out and still sore.

And hurt by his disappearing act.

And exhausted.

I left Andrea's at five in the morning after I searched the entire house for him and tried to call him, only to get his voice mail. I messaged Ernie to get a cover story for the night, but he hasn't answered yet.

I don't know what my parents will do when they realize I didn't spend the night at home. Chances are they won't even realize. But I don't want to risk it, so I'm crashing at Julianna's until Ernie responds.

It's a stupid plan because it would have been easier to sneak in at six in the morning, but here I am. I couldn't have imagined being alone in the caverns of my house.

"No, we can't. Not until you share some details," she huffs.

"Stop it, Julianna." I throw a pillow at her.

She makes puppy eyes at me. She's in her pajamas with messy hair, but she's here for me even though I woke her up. "Come on. You wouldn't even know about him if I hadn't told you and took you to your first meeting."

I roll my eyes. "You know he's a professor at our school."

She jumps up to sit next to me. "And that's another thing. What now? You broke like a gazillion rules."

I sigh. "I'm pretty sure we broke only one. I hope." Gosh, I was brave last night, not caring about the consequences, but things look different in the light of a new day.

Especially since I'm not even sure where we stand. "I don't know what's next. It's not like I had a chance to talk to him after."

Though we talked so much last night. I shared more than I'd ever admitted to anyone. And then I pushed him to share, which apparently made him run. I groan and lean my head on Julianna's shoulder.

"I scared him enough to run away from his own house." I blink away tears. What if I really am his trigger and he's drunk or high somewhere? I can't even share that suspicion with my friend.

"What if he went to get breakfast and coffee to bring to bed?"

"At five in the morning? He just vanished. I tried to call him, but it went right to his voice mail. Besides, why hasn't he call me back yet? He doesn't want to see me." I groan again. "Jesus, Julianna, how am I going to avoid him now?"

"I'm sure there is an explanation. Maybe he needed to go out of town? Catching an early flight, and he's in the air with no reception?" My friend is looking for any explanation, despite logic and all the odds.

"And he couldn't leave me a note?" I deadpan.

"Maybe he did and you didn't find it." She wraps her arm around my shoulder, patting me.

I wish she was right, but it makes no sense. "He would have ordered me a cab and not lulled me into sleeping there."

"He lulled you into sleeping there?" She tuts. "There is good news here." She perks up, but her enthusiasm can't reach my aching heart. "If a man wants you to stay overnight after your first time together, that's a great sign."

"And if he stayed there with you that would be even better," I counter. "I guess he just had a delayed reaction and didn't want to face the awkward send-off."

"Nice of him to let you sleep though," she offers unhelpfully.

I drop into her pink throw pillows and whimper.

"Come on, Ivy, at least tell me how it was." She flops next to me.

I turn my face to her, a shy grin on my face.

Her eyes widen. "That good?"

I bite my lip, nodding. "Amazing."

"Bitch, you're the only woman I know who had amazing sex their first time. Lucky you."

"I don't feel all that lucky right now."

"Girls, breakfast is ready," Agatha yells from somewhere in the house.

"Coming," Julianna shouts back, almost piercing my eardrum. "Listen"—she sits up and turns to me —"what about your parents?"

I follow her out of the room. "I called Ernie to cover for me, but I haven't heard from him."

"Normal people are still sleeping," Julianna groans.

"I made a frittata. Sit, sit," Agatha announces when

we get to the kitchen. She's fussing around, tidying the counter covered with takeout boxes.

I'm starving, but seeing the boxes from Chinese food steals my appetite. Stupid kung pao.

"Ivy, what's wrong? You look pale." Agatha grabs my shoulders and studies me, frowning.

Maybe it's just my general state of exhaustion. Or the conversation about my parents from last night. Or the overall state of dejection I've been nursing since I woke up, but the contrast between my mother and Agatha feels sharper today and I burst into tears.

She wraps me in a motherly embrace, which only makes things worse, and I sob into her blouse. She lets me have my moment, patting my hair.

"Get out," Julianna snarls. I'm assuming she is protecting the dining room from her brothers, who are now denied their breakfast because of my breakdown.

"I'm sorry," I sniffle.

"Hush, no need to apologize. Is there anything I can do to help?" Agatha's hand on my back threatens to throw me into another meltdown, so I step back, wiping the snot and tears from my face.

"She met someone," Julianna offers.

"Darling, but that should make you smile with joy. Is he mistreating you?"

I look at Julianna in a panic. Jesus, this took a turn. "No, no, I-I think we might want different things."

"Love can overcome any obstacles. When I met—"

"Mom, she doesn't need to hear your sappy story right now." Julianna sits and serves herself a generous portion of the steaming dish in the middle of the table.

"Can we eat?" one of the Biachi boys complains from the doorway.

As we all sit down to eat, my phone rings.

* * *

I push the front door open, deep in my thoughts. After Ernie called me—his voice less than awake—to say that the ruse would actually work for him as well, I decided to go home and sleep.

Voices stop me in my tracks. Martha is at the base of the staircase, her hand over her mouth.

"Maybe I should have divorced you a long time ago." Mother's words carry from upstairs.

"And what would you do? Slink back to your daddy with your tail between your legs?" Father speaks in a composed manner, not even raising his voice, but his calculating words slice like a scalpel. "He's no longer here to help you out, and if you think I'd give you a penny, you're mistaken."

"If it wasn't for my father, you wouldn't have doubled your assets. The least you can do is treat me with some respect."

I click the door shut carefully and tiptoe to where Martha is standing. One glimpse up and my hand flies to my mouth as well. Father is leaning over my mother, holding her by the throat over the banister.

They glare at each other, oblivious to our presence. My heart hammers against my chest. I've seen them arguing before, but with my mother's torso hanging in the air, I pat my pockets to get my phone, ready to call 911.

And then I wish I didn't bother coming home. My father whips Mother around and lifts her skirt. Martha rolls her eyes and scurries away. I rush to the kitchen behind her. Jesus.

Martha clatters around, producing as much sound as possible, but the groans and moans echo around the house. I sit down, covering my ears, now even more upset with Andrea for leaving me so vulnerable this morning.

"I'll make tea for her. She will need you, Ivory." Martha sighs.

"I'm not going on another shopping spree."

"Oh, it won't be a high she'll chase. Usually after these encounters she's depressed, because he never stays. He's not available, but somehow she holds on to her hope."

I tap my head against the counter. "Why?"

"Love."

When the silence stretches for long enough, I decide to venture outside. A glance up confirms my parents are not in the hallway anymore, but as I turn to take the first step, my father's voice roars from the dining room.

"Where were you all night?"

Without a convenient invisibility spell, the next best thing is the magic of Ernie. "I was with Ernie."

My mother descends the stairs with a spring in her step, freshly showered and changed.

Martha comes out with a breakfast tray, and I use the opportunity to sneak upstairs, but I'm stopped by my father's steely voice.

"Did you hear? Your daughter is a whore."

Mother stops in the doorway between him and me and looks at me wide-eyed. "Cecil," she breathes.

"Don't you Cecil me. She was with Ernie all night. Do you think he wants a wife who is too easy? You haven't taught her anything."

"Cecil," Mother repeats, looking disoriented.

"Stop repeating my name. If you fucked up the engagement with your loose behavior, I swear to God—"

He stands up, sending the chair tumbling to the floor. My phone rings, blasting through the air. Startled, I look at the screen in my hand.

Jesus. Now he calls?

"Where the fuck are you?" Andrea snarls the minute I put the phone to my ear.

"Can you believe her?" my father shouts at my mother.

"I would ask the same," I snap into the phone. "But I can't talk right now."

More words are exchanged between my parents, but I tune them out. My relief at hearing Andrea's voice is overwhelming. And inopportune, given the circumstances. But God, it's good to hear him.

"What's going on there?" he asks.

My father looms over my mother, who seems to plead.

"I can't talk right now." Why did I even answer?

Because I was desperate to find out what happened, to seal the hole in my heart his vanishing caused. Because in the middle of a family crisis—a common occurrence—I knew he'd make me feel stronger.

"Don't you dare hang up on me, Vivid," he commands. Thrill, panic, dismay, and annoyance are just a few of the emotions hurling through me like a tornado.

Mother sits down, wiping her tears.

"Where are you?" Andrea demands.

"Home," I whisper, watching my father march to the door.

"I'm coming."

"You—" *Don't know where I live,* I finish into the air, because he hung up.

My eyes meet Mother's, who cries silently, gracefully, at the table set with a breakfast that will probably go uneaten. She takes a long, fortifying breath and smiles at me.

"Papa went to work. Will you join me for breakfast?" The nonchalance in her countenance worsens the tornado inside me.

But the good girl in me wins and I smile. "I'm not hungry. Thank you."

I desperately need a shower and a change of clothes. Or at least a pair of underwear, but I can't imagine staying here. Running to my room, I shove some clothes into my backpack and dash back down.

Mother is drinking her tea, composed. "Where are you going, chérie?"

"I'll spend the weekend at Julianna's. We have exams next week."

Mother nods. "He doesn't mean it, chérie. He's been under a lot of stress." She stands up and walks to me.

She wraps me in an embrace. It's like a prickly blanket, giving me warmth, but also hives. We stand there while I let her draw strength from me, because I know this hug is more to console her than me.

She squeezes my shoulders and looks at me with a weak smile. "He doesn't mean it," she repeats. "Things have been difficult for him at work."

The hope in her eyes hits me hard. She isn't just making excuses for him—she truly believes that's the reality. That the problems of her marriage stem from outside, work-related issues, and that one day those will pass.

For years she's been living denied by him, and in denial of the truth. Now she believes the excuses she formed in her mind. To save her heart.

I kiss her forehead, exhausted from the roller coaster of emotions. In a span of twenty-four hours I lost my virginity, connected with a man who somehow sees beyond all my masks, then worried I had lost him.

I witnessed a new low in my parents' marriage, and became the target of yet another of Father's tantrums.

And I'm watching my mother's desperation from the front-row seat right now, and frankly, it's all too much.

"Is this going to be a problem?" She breaks the silence, lifting her chin. It's like she sensed my pity and now needs to prove me wrong.

"What?" I swallow.

"You and Ernie." She returns to her seat. "Ivory, I can't emphasize how important this engagement is. You need to come through for your family."

Her words hit me right in the solar plexus. The little girl who wants to see her Mommy happy and the girl who became a woman last night fight within me. Why is this shit happening when I'm so tired?

My phone rings again, startling me. *Andrea.* My heart soars.

"I have to go now." I rush out the door before she can guilt me into staying with her, caring for her, filling the void in between the fleeting moments when she belongs to my father.

"I don't know where you live," he growls. His frustration curls the corners of my lips up.

"I'm coming over."

"Thank fucking God. I swear, Vivid, I'm going to spank your ass red."

Chapter 21

Ivory

"Finally." He steps outside and drags me into his arms. His bewildered look and disheveled hair are the sexiest thing ever. "Why did it take you so long?"

"There was a delay with the trains." He's holding me so tight I can't breathe, but I don't need to. Not here, with him.

"Where is your fucking driver?" He moves us inside and kicks the door closed. Kissing, he walks us to the kitchen.

It's so similar to last night, and yet so different. Holding my hands, he stares at me, inspecting me like he can't believe I'm really here.

"Where did you go?" My hazy brain snaps me back to the issue at hand, and I fold my arms across my chest.

He drags his hand down his face. "Me? I was fucking here. You—"

"No, I woke up and looked everywhere and you were not here. You didn't leave a note or pick up your phone." I wipe a stupid tear.

"Clearly, you didn't look everywhere." He tugs me to him and I want to resist, but he's stronger and... Okay, I guess my resistance isn't that important.

He seizes my lips with such fervor that I collapse against him, barely able to catch my breath.

One thing is clear, Andrea Cassinetti kisses like the devil possessed, consuming me. And I surrender with abandon. Never have I felt more alive. It's scary. And wonderful.

"I guess it's my fault for not giving you a tour last night." He takes my lower lip between his teeth and nibbles. His eyes are hungry, and I'm pretty sure I'm on the menu. "Let me correct that."

I snort. "To show me where you were hiding?"

"Don't be smart, there is a lot of spanking in your immediate future." He drags me to the staircase. "Kitchen and sitting room." He flails his hand, half-assing the tour, leading me up the stairs.

"Two guest rooms, guest bathroom." He points to the closed doors on the second floor. There are black and white photographs on the walls of abstract objects, nothing personal anywhere.

The decor is luxurious but understated. He doesn't care about flaunting his money in people's faces like my father.

He stops abruptly by the entrance to his bedroom and points to the door to my right. "This is a linen closet. I didn't hide there," he says, his eyes glistening with mirth.

"Stop it. I was really..." Jesus, I'm not going to tell him I was hurt.

"Worried, pissed?" he offers, glowering. "Welcome to the club."

Okay, that sounds less needy than what I've almost blurted.

He kisses me again, but I back away. "I feel filthy. I didn't get a chance to shower."

He nuzzles my neck and inhales deeply. "You smell of me and sex, just like I want you." Humming, he squeezes my breast.

A moan breaks free from my chest. This man owns my body already. I have no control of my reactions the minute he's in my vicinity. I marvel at that discovery for a moment, expecting anxiety to follow, but there is none.

I'm perfectly comfortable belonging to him. For now, anyway.

Andrea picks me up with ease and carries me to the en suite bathroom. He undresses me and then sheds his clothes.

"Let's get you clean, you filthy girl." He smirks and slaps my behind. I gasp. "Oh, you're going to like it." He winks, and my heart launches into an Olympic race. My face must show it because he laughs. The bastard.

His shower is a large marble space with one glass wall and a small stone bench in the corner. Andrea fidgets with the black handle on the wall, testing the temperature with his hand, and then pulls me under the waterfall.

"The madness brewing inside me dies when you're around," he whispers, "I'm just not sure if it's a permanent peace or the calm before the storm."

He kisses me and it's a good thing, because his words unravel me. I close my eyes, letting the warm water melt the tension of the past few hours.

I'm slowly relaxing—as much as possible when showering with a sex god—when he begins to massage my shoulders. I moan with pleasure and lean into him, my back against his solid body.

He squirts shampoo into his hands and rubs it into my hair and then gently washes it out. I'm speechless, the emotions lodging in my throat.

"What's wrong?" He pours shower gel down my chest and then washes me.

"You taking care of me again." The words hitch out

of me and die on a moan when Andrea massages my breasts.

"My sweet girl, you better get used to it." It sounds like a dark promise and I'm glad I'm wet, because the evidence of his words is dripping between my thighs.

He washes my breasts, my torso, my back, my ass, my legs with such reverence I'm losing my mind, completely aroused and shocked by his care.

His touch on my skin seems ten times amplified, burning me and driving me out of my mind.

"Hands on the bench," he orders.

Wait? What? He chuckles at my expression, but that doesn't ease my confusion.

He pivots me around and whispers into my ear, his erection hard against the small of my back, "Don't make me repeat myself."

I swallow hard, dazed by arousal, my head spinning, and drop my hands on the bench. The approving hum deep in his chest gives me confidence.

My ass is up in the air, and I almost jump when Andrea strokes it gently.

"Beautiful vixen, are you ready for your punishment?" he croons, and dusts the softest of kisses on my ass cheeks while dragging his fingers through my folds.

"Andrea," I moan, pushing my ass back, needing more.

He chuckles but doesn't relent. He kneads my ass

with one hand while rubbing my clit with the other. "Answer me," he commands.

Jesus. He's just touched me and I'm a complete mess already. I don't even know what he's asking, but I need him.

"Please," I whimper, and cry out when his hand connects with my behind, the sting spreading through me.

Now I know what he was asking. Before I can protest, he slaps me several more times in rapid succession.

The heat travels all the way to my core and leaves me moaning in pleasure.

"Andrea," I plead and push my ass back into him, but he holds me steady. "Please," I beg, not even sure if I want him to stop or not. It doesn't matter, because he keeps on spanking me.

I'm ready to beg him to fuck me when he finally stops and washes the sting away with a soft caress.

"Andrea," I gasp.

"Such a good girl, taking your punishment. You liked it, didn't you?" His voice is deep and hoarse. Instead of answering, because I can't yet admit it to myself, I jut my ass higher, inviting him.

"Admit it." He spanks me again hard, and I moan at the pleasure and pain mixing.

"I liked it." I pant, and get rewarded with two of his fingers inside me.

"My good girl. This pussy is so hot for me. So responsive, learning fast." He's panting too, his erection twitching between my thighs as he works me with his fingers.

I moan and push back against him. He spanks me, and it leaves me swollen and aching. He withdraws his fingers.

The first thrust is hard and deep. I'm surprised how well he fits. It might be the water streaming on us, the steam, my arousal from the spanking, but there is no resistance or pain this time. We fit perfectly.

He keeps working me, thrusting again and again, his hand stroking down my back, over my burning behind and then around my hip to my clit.

My knees give out and I almost collapse, but he snakes one hand around my waist, supporting me. How is he so strong?

Never slowing the pace, he lowers us. The tiles scratch my knees, but the momentary discomfort is negated by the growing pleasure in my core.

Fisting my hair, he pulls me to him. I'm like a rag doll in his hands, completely at his mercy. And grateful for it. He wraps his hand around my throat, holding me in place. Just the way he wants me.

I whimper loudly. The pain, the pleasure, his hand

on my throat—I can't take any more, but he doesn't stop, murmuring dirty praise in my ear.

"Come for me, now," he growls, fucking me harder, relentless in his assault.

"Andrea," I cry out as my orgasm rolls through me, so intense it makes me shake uncontrollably.

He withdraws, grunting and spilling himself onto my back. Jesus. We didn't use a condom. The thought is just a fleeting concern in the overload of sensations as he gathers me into his arms. We sit under the running water, trying to come back to reality.

I don't know how long we stay here. Not moving. Not talking. Hugging out the worries. Or trying to reconcile the intimacy that is growing against our will. Against my will for sure. The closeness is over-whelming.

His care is overwhelming. And so welcome at the same time.

Andrea peppers small kisses down my face and neck, but he seems lost in thoughts as well. Is he as affected as I am?

My stomach growls and we both chuckle. He stands up and lifts me with him. After shutting off the water, he leads me out of the shower. He dries me, combs my hair, and then pulls one of his T-shirts over my head.

I don't even protest at his care anymore. The man

loves it, and frankly, I do too. And it's not like he'd listen and let me do it myself.

We don't speak as he leads me to the kitchen, but when I sit and observe him working the coffee maker, I can't help myself. "I feel like we unloaded heavy stuff and never got a chance to discuss the small, normal facts about each other."

He looks at me, his eyes hooded. "I don't think it's the facts that help forge a connection. Those you learn over time."

I tease, "So you don't need to know my favorite food, color or—"

"I already know your favorite food is an atrocious sodium-packed snack, and it has changed nothing. Though it should." He smirks.

"Hey. My father cut my allowance." I glower.

He pushes a cup of coffee and a piece of toast in front of me. "Eat, vixen."

I stare at the plate, hungry but annoyed by his judgment.

"Okay, tell me what your favorite meal is." He nudges my chin up with his finger. Reluctantly, I lift my gaze. And while his tone earlier felt patronizing, there is not a trace of it in his eyes.

"Pasta." I pout, and he kisses me.

"My mother will love you." He kisses me again. "What are your favorite flowers?"

Maybe he was right, and the facts are unimportant. They don't add to the intimacy, or the connection I felt when I saw his paintings before I even met him.

"Cactus." I take a bite of the toast.

He snorts. "Being smart again? You know what that means?"

My ass is still smarting from earlier, but Andrea's look and words ignite my entire body. Jesus. I didn't get a chance to process what happened in the shower, but as much as I don't understand it, I want a repeat.

We eat in silence, electricity zipping between us. When I finish my coffee, Andrea leans in and kisses me.

"Let me show you where I was this morning."

Chapter 22

Andrea

Vivid stares at the canvas for what feels like two lifetimes while I die and resurrect myself, practically ready to jump out of my skin or hurl myself down the stairs.

She looks at me—her just-fucked face beautiful in the light spilling through the roof windows—and then back at the canvas.

In the mixture of colorful strokes, her face hides. Full lips, the slope of her nose, the warmth in her dark eyes. It's an abstract painting, but where I used to hide my pain, this time I hid my joy.

She wrings her hands in front of her, looking utterly gorgeous in my T-shirt. When I spilled my cum on her skin earlier, I worried I went too hard on her. Fuck.

I lost my self-control, not even thinking about the

condom. Thank God I realized that when her walls collapsed around me.

She loved it, though. She loved it as much as I did, my little vixen. And her attempt to move us into a lighter inconsequential territory while we were in the kitchen was adorable.

And smart, but we might be a bit late for that. There is a bond between us we can't deny or fight, as much as we both may wish to.

"Are you going to say something?" I tap my fingers on my thighs.

Vivid looks around, her gaze touching the shelves with paints, the table with the chaos of brushes and other tools, the unfinished canvases in the corner.

"So this is your studio?" she speaks finally.

What the fuck? I snap my eyes to her and catch the smile she's trying to hide. "Yes, Vivid, I see you may have enjoyed being punished too much." Her eyes light up as she bites her lips. "This is my studio. Your observations skills are uncanny."

She shrugs and walks around, touching things, purposely avoiding the easel in the middle of the room. Goddammit.

I lean against the door frame and watch her, savoring her in my space but hating that she's taunting me.

"I like it here. Thank you for showing me." She comes to me and brushes her lips against mine.

I cup the back of her neck roughly, forcing her to look into my eyes. "Don't tease me, Vivid. Do you like the painting?"

She looks at the ceiling, pursing her lips, pretending to think hard. "It's not like your previous work."

I frown. "Meaning?" Why is my heart looking for escape routes?

"It's more alive, joyous. It's..." She exhales into my face, kissing me lightly. "It's vivid."

I capture her lips, whipping us around. Pinning her against the door, I raise her hands above her head, devouring her. Pressing my body against her hard, I won't let an inch of air between us.

She's mine. She's a part of me already.

"I thought you didn't want to paint me," she murmurs against my lips.

"You see it?" Something inside me explodes. "Do you like it?" Suddenly her approval is the most important thing in the world.

"I love it." Her breath on my skin ignites something in my chest. I don't want to name it. I'm not an asshole who falls for a girl because she praised my work.

"I could relate to the shackles as well," she continues.

Fuck. Yes, I'm that asshole. This woman is etched on my soul already. And if I had a heart... Fuck.

Not even my most loyal collectors notice some of the imagery hidden in my work. Like secret messages, they form the whole painting, evoking feelings without being seen.

"My beautiful girl." I kiss her again.

She smiles and looks at me with hooded eyes. She opens her mouth and then she closes it again.

"I thought work was your trigger." She looks down, voicing her concern, but not ready to face it head on.

I step back, and her arms fall to her side. She lifts her gaze, full of worry.

I take her hand and walk to the center of the room. There I stop, pulling her in front of me, wrapping my hands around her waist. Much like last night in front of the mirror.

"And I thought you were my trigger, as well. But look what you triggered. What you inspired."

Sighing, she leans against me and strokes my forearm as we stare at the painting. I want to show it to the world. Not because it's my poor attempt at capturing my feelings and her essence. Because I know deep down it's superb. Without hesitation. It's like she injected confidence in me.

Or maybe my mother was right. If I paint just for myself, the pressure dissipates.

"I don't want to drink when you're here, Vivid," I whisper into her ear, a slight shiver raking through her. "Maybe having you by my side is enough. Stay."

She turns. "What do you mean, stay?"

Fuck. I don't know what I meant. A selfish prick, I want her by my side, so she can rub my ego. She keeps me sane in this fucked-up world. She's my salvation, whether or not she knows it.

"I need you here to work. I want you here to fuck. I enjoy your presence. Even the fucking questions."

Her lips curl up. "I'll stay this weekend and we'll see."

"What do you mean we'll see? You're giving me a trial period?" I snap. What does she want? For me to beg?

"I'm twenty-one. I don't have an income or an education or anything to live on my own. I can't leave my parents' house."

"They're shitty parents."

"They're the only ones I have. I can't move from them to you. They will never take me back. What's going to happen when you..."

She looks away and steps to the side, wrapping her arms around her middle.

"When what?" I growl at her. Doesn't she understand how much I need her? How I'll take care of her?

She throws her arms up in exasperation. "When

you tire of me," she huffs. She shakes her head and bolts for the door.

I catch her before she reaches the door handle.

"Let go of me." She stomps on my foot.

I turn her around and grip her jaw in my hand, forcing her to look at me. Her defiant gaze is fucking sexy.

"Listen to me carefully, Vivid. I'll never tire of you. You may get discouraged by my madness, but I will always take care of you."

"Your madness is driving me crazy already. This is all too fast for me. We can't even go outside without getting in trouble at school."

Fuck. I forgot about school. "Okay, you're right. Go home." I drop my hand and turn to the window.

I hate this. It's too soon, too much and too fast. I don't even know what I'm asking of her. Or if I can deliver. Well, I can't.

But when the door clicks, my voice of reason dies a quick death. I abandon my fucking pride and rush after her.

Her quick steps echo throughout the hallway. Fuck, she's fast, but I catch her on the landing before she takes the second flight of stairs.

As she tries to yank away, we lose our balance. My ass hits the floor, sending searing pain through my back.

Vivid yelps and propels me farther. I topple onto my back with a thud, and she lands on top of me.

Her knee digs into my leg and her elbow bruises my side. We both grunt.

"Are you okay?" I fidget slightly to make sure she's comfortable.

She winces, but then smiles. "At least I'm on top this time."

"And I bruised you again." I chuckle.

"I'll take my punishment from you anytime," she says darkly.

My little vixen.

"Stay."

She closes her eyes and lets out a heavy breath.

"This weekend," I add, and she crushes her lips against mine.

"I don't want to go home." Vivid drops her torso on the kitchen island, resting her head on her forearm.

"I'm sure you like being fed normal food and the general attention I pay you." I put our plates into the dishwasher.

"Oh, such a hardship for you." She stands and walks to the window. "I wish it was warmer and we could sit on the patio."

"Hardship it is, but I make sure you pay me for everything with your sweet little pussy." I cup her between her legs from behind and she yelps but melts into me.

"You're insatiable."

"Are you complaining, Vivid?"

"I wouldn't dare. My ass is still stinging." She turns and wraps her arms around my waist.

"Fuck. I'll buy some ointment."

She throws her head back and laughs. Her laughter has echoed through this house in the last two days. Her presence has filled the air with lightness and brightness.

We spent the weekend together, fucking, sleeping, eating. And we spent a lot of time in my studio, where Vivid sat in the corner while I painted.

The process is unfamiliar. My energy is undiscovered. The flow is unstoppable.

I'm enchanted by her presence, but I don't push her to stay because... well, because as much as I want to, I can't reassure her I want her to stay forever.

"What are you thinking?" She strokes my cheek. God, she's so beautiful and young.

"We'll sit there all summer." I kiss her forehead.

"What?"

"Jesus, your memory is concerning. On our patio." I wink and leave her there standing, staring at me.

Our patio? Yes, Vivid, if you think rational arguments work with me, you're mistaken.

I open the dishwasher and almost dive into it when she jumps on my back, wrapping her long arms and legs around me.

"Crazy woman, do you want to break my back?" I straighten and dash to the living room, where I drop her on the sofa and immediately pounce on her.

"I can't wait to sit there with you this summer. On our patio."

We grin at each other, the mood light but also heavy with all the feelings soaring in my chest. I can't taint her with any declarations.

"I'll talk to Wiggins when I'm back in a week."

She frowns. "Oh, I forgot you can't come back yet."

"Play hooky this week." Wow, I'm an excellent influence on her. "Though as a teacher, I advise against it."

She laughs. "I have an exam tomorrow, but I can go sick for the rest of the week."

I kiss her. "You should call your driver, before I make you my sex slave and never let you leave."

"I don't have him anymore. My father let him go."

"What the fuck? Why? I don't want you to hop around the subway." I stand up. "When is he getting you a new one?" Jesus, I hope it's a woman. I'm irrationally jealous of her non-existent driver.

Ignoring my voice of reason around Vivid has become a theme. That fucker has been just a whisper for years, anyway.

"I'm not getting a new one, but your concern is duly noted." She sits up.

"Why not?"

"I think my father is having financial issues."

"So you'll just get robbed or something worse on the subway?" Over my dead body. I'm chaining her to my bed. Fuck.

"You are crazy." She snorts. "Plenty of people use public transportation. Have you ever?"

"Don't fucking change the topic. I'm calling you a town car, and then I'll get a car and driver sorted out for you tomorrow."

"Are you out of your mind?" She stands and throws her arms up.

"Vivid, I swear to God, stop fighting me on everything. You want to sit on that fucking patio this summer, you're getting a driver. I'm taking care of you now."

She widens her eyes and then narrows them. I brace for her comeback, but of course she floors me with her response.

"Okay."

"Just like that?" I frown.

"What? Were you testing me? Did you want to see

how fluidly I float from my father's controlling claws to yours?" She puts her hands on her hips. A goddess of war. Captivating.

I yank her to me and kiss her roughly. "Don't you fucking compare me to your father." I kiss her again, diving deeper this time. She moans into my mouth, and I rein myself back from the notion of bending her over the sofa's backrest. "I want you safe. I'm getting you a car and a driver. Nod nicely."

She glowers but nods.

I kiss her forehead. "That's my girl."

I arrange a car and we make out by the door like teenagers. "Good luck on your test tomorrow."

"Well, I didn't study much, and I'm pretty sure you fucked my brains out, so..."

I snort. "Hmm. You fail, and I'd have another reason to punish you and keep you in detention."

She beams. "I can't wait."

The bell sounds. "Your car." I yank the door open and freeze, all the bliss of the weekend evaporating.

Chapter 23

Andrea

"Oh, Paris, hello," Vivid chirps.

"That's the evil twin," I growl. "Ivory, this is London. London, what are you doing here?"

My stepsister glowers with her arms folded across her chest, utterly unimpressed. Then she moves her gaze over and smiles. "Nice to meet you, Ivory."

"I guess my car is here." Vivid kisses my cheek.

I pull her to me. "Call me when you get home." I kiss her deeply. She tenses, unsure of our audience, so I swat her ass and send her off.

As soon as the car leaves I pin London with a glare, not inviting her in. We haven't spoken for over a decade.

"What are you doing here?"

"Right now, regretting that I came." She steps forward.

"Then leave." I block the door.

London smirks. "Really? Are we ten again?"

Grunting, I step inside, not inviting her but not shutting the door in her face. I turn and glare.

"Ivory looks nice. Young…" She throws it out there, her judgment lingering.

"Your presence here makes me want to drink." I'm not above guilting her into leaving.

"Sorry." She shakes her head, as if she needed to shake off the feeling of this entire exchange.

Or she is shocked that she apologized, which is not a readily available weapon in her arsenal.

"For what?" I lean in the doorway to the sitting room.

"I came to talk to you about…" She purses her lips. "Not about your girlfriend. Any chance we can sit?"

Asshole that I am, I plop on the stair and rest my elbows on my knees. "Sorry, there is no room to sit here. And I'm not inviting you any further because you might just poison the air."

She rolls her eyes. "Fuck you, bro. Anyway, I'm here, so I'm going to say what I came to say. It's been ten years. Have you finally figured out why I bought all your drawings back then?"

I snort. Who the hell does she think she is? Why

would she come here after all this time, tainting a perfect weekend? "Because you didn't want to embarrass me when no one else would."

She rolls her eyes. Again. "Yeah, you idiot. I bought them because you worked so hard and you were so nervous. I'd never seen you losing your shit like that. It was the first time I saw you drinking and getting high. I was worried about you, and I was sure those pieces were decent and would only increase in value. Boy, was I wrong."

Is she for real? The memories of my first exhibition crawl out from the hidden crevices of my soul, grating on my nerves, sprouting sweat beads on my nape. "Sorry, I'm not getting you a refund after all this time." Fuck, I need a drink.

"You're such a jerk. I was wrong because I didn't save you from yourself. Instead of riding the wave of success, you've been riding against it every chance you get. You drank more, and you... Simply, me trying to protect you from yourself didn't work. And you hated me because you believed you didn't deserve the break the sold-out exhibition got you. Years later, you still can't accept that your work is valuable."

She shifts from one foot to the other and then steps closer. She shoves my shoulder and somehow squeezes in to sit beside me.

"I can't fix that," she continues. "But I learned this

year that sometimes we do the wrong things with good intentions. My intentions were good, and I'm not asking you for forgiveness, but I miss my brother."

I stare into the void in front of me, my world crumbling. The hatred, the resentment, the denial, all losing their foundation, scaring the shit out of me. "Thank you."

"Don't thank me, Andrea. I should have come a long time ago. Or you should have come to me. I don't know, but if you need anything, I'm here. I won't try to save you without you asking for my help, because nothing good ever comes from assuming, but I'm here and I'm proud of you."

I stand up, sighing. "Why now?"

"Okay, not only to get Bianca off my back." Of course, Mother wouldn't let go. "Dominic and I are moving, and he hates those drawings, but I promised myself I'd keep them until you forgave me," she adds.

I snort. "Dom hates them."

"I kind of do as well." She looks at me, biting her lip. "More what they represent than how they look. They have been a part of my apartment, but they don't really fit into our new place."

I shake my head. "You had them on your wall all this time?"

"Yes." She pushes off the stair, standing up, and shrugs.

"Why?"

"To remind me that my good intentions are not always for the good of others."

We stare at each other for a long time. I'm searching for signs of cravings, the need to drink, to do something crazy, but the strange peace that Vivid inspired only settles deeper.

"Do you want coffee?" I say finally.

London scrunches her lips to the side, but then nods. "Sure." She follows me to the kitchen. "It's a nice place you have here."

"Thanks. I don't clutter it with my art."

She widens her eyes, but then catches my grin. "Asshole." London climbs on the stool by the island. "So, was that your girlfriend?"

"Yep." I start the coffee maker. Admitting my relationship status feels strangely right.

"Is it serious?"

"If it was up to me, it would be."

It's odd confiding in London. Not only because she's the most cynical of my siblings, but because we haven't spoken in so long. But I'm feeling quite comfortable doing it. I guess I fucked my brain out this weekend.

"She seems quite smitten by you."

"We've been together for two days. She doesn't

know what she's gotten herself into yet." I put an espresso in front of her and lean against the counter.

"Two days and she's met Paris already?"

"As observant as ever. We've known each other for longer."

"Oh, I like her even more if she resisted the famous Cassinetti charm." London grins.

I utter a humorless chuckle. "I was the one doing the resisting. She's a student at the Institute."

"So, a clandestine affair? Is she old enough to drink?" London doesn't hold back.

I snort. "She is, but she keeps me sober and level. Peaceful."

"Then I hope she stays around." She downs the coffee.

"I'm bound to fuck it up, so don't keep your hopes up."

"When you meet your person, they tend to put up with a lot. Look at me and Dominic. Neither of us was ready to go exclusive, let alone fall in love, but somehow nothing else made sense once we accepted what we felt."

"The intimacy scares me. I don't want her to know who I really am." I don't know why I'm admitting this to my stepsister.

"It only means you care. And if she feels the same,

she'll see all of you, no matter how much you try to hide it."

"Oh, I'm sure she will uncover the worst of me. The question is, will she stay around?"

"I really hope she does. For as long as you both need and want."

I laugh. "You avoided the word forever."

"Well, that word scares the shit out of me."

We talk for a moment longer before she leaves. It's like no time has passed. The closeness we used to share seeps through effortlessly.

I clean up the kitchen a little once she's gone. Not tidying up, more moving shit around, restless. The house feels strangely empty and silent without Vivid here.

I make my way upstairs, take a shower, and wander around like a lost puppy. My phone lights up with a message.

I drop on the bed and unlock the screen.

> VIVID
>
> I'm home.

> You should be here.

> VIVID
>
> I wish I was.

> Then come back.

No response. Sitting up, I wait for a moment longer and then dial her.

"Answer me," I growl.

"I just did." I can almost see her grinning on the other side.

"Vivid," I warn.

She laughs. "I couldn't find my charger. You're awfully bossy."

"I miss you." I'm not yet sure if I miss her or the company to keep me from getting bored and thinking of sources of entertainment. Okay, who am I kidding, it's both. The former screaming louder and louder in my head.

"I'll be there tomorrow after school. Good night."

"Good night, vixen."

I stare at the ceiling, but there is no way I'm going to sleep. I toss and turn for a moment and then turn on the lamp again. It casts a cone of light across the bed, and there, on the pillow, is a single long, wiry dark hair.

Such a small thing, but it steadies me. I pick it up and rub it between my thumb and index finger, taking comfort in this tiny piece of her.

She's mine.

I jump off the bed and head to my studio. I need to chase my muse.

Chapter 24

Ivory

"What a beautiful venue, chérie!" Mother exclaims in a high-pitched trill. "Don't forget to smile." Her perfume, a heady mixture of flowers, envelopes me when she adjusts my gown for the umpteenth time.

My black dress is embroidered with a delicate golden pattern. It's open in the back, plunging down to my behind where it flares into a maxi skirt. I'm wearing it with a dose of anxiety.

I told Andrea we'd be here, but I have no idea how I should survive the evening pretending we don't know each other.

My eyes roam the venue. We're at some unfinished building by the river, but its transformation is evident in the exquisite details that have turned a ruin into a swanky hall.

I wish I could enjoy it more. Where is Andrea?

The soft murmur of conversations blends with the faint strains of a string quartet. It's too much noise for my frazzled nerves.

My mother's voice registers, but I have no idea what she's going on about. I keep nodding absent-mindedly.

"Ivory!" Mother glares at and then turns her fake smile to a man whose eyes on me are anything but innocent. "She's mesmerized by the venue. How are you?" I didn't even realize when this dude joined us, but I wish he left.

"You look ravishing." He kisses my hand.

His palm is clammy and holds my hand a bit too long. I'm acutely aware of a strand of hair that's escaped my updo. It tickles my nape, along with a sheen of sweat trickling down my spine. So much for an open-back dress.

"Chérie, don't just stand here." Mother's voice gets through to me again. "Forgive her, George."

He kisses Mother's hand and shakes hands with my father. "It's nice seeing you both tonight."

Father clears his throat, his eyes roaming. "George, let's have a drink. I have something to discuss with you." He leaves, and luckily his friend with the wandering eyes leaves with him.

Mother's chest heaves as she watches her husband,

who abandoned her without so much as a glimpse back.

She tries to smile. "Perhaps I'll go and see if the Cornfields are here."

I hope they're not. Ernie would have mentioned something. I hope.

"Ivory, so nice to see you. Andrea didn't tell me you were coming."

I whip around, almost toppling my mother. "Paris? London? Hello."

Andrea's stepsister's throaty laughter fills the space between us. "It's London." She extends her hand to my mother. "London Lowe. Thank you very much for supporting the cause."

"Oh, thank you. It's an important cause and it's our pleasure to be here." I'm pretty sure Mother does not know what cause we are supporting. She's here to support her social status, gossip, and appease my father. "I'm Ivory's mother, Eden Harrington."

They shake hands.

"How do you know each other?" Mother asks.

My eyes widen and London smiles coyly. "We met..." She seems to scan her memory while looking at me. "At my brother's art exhibit. If you'll excuse me, I need to greet other guests. I hope you have a fabulous night."

London's little lie helps me breathe, but if

someone else speaks to me before I find and talk to Andrea, I'm going to run away. Cinderella style. I shouldn't be this nervous, but I can't help it. The idea of him and my parents in one room overwhelms me. It's like I want to hide my family's dynamic from him.

He gives me courage and encourages my freedom, but I never feel that around my parents. So having my two worlds mixing like this makes my body tingle with all sorts of conflicting feelings.

"Well done, my dear, making connections in our world. Maybe that art school of yours is a good thing after all." Mother beams, her eyes roaming. When she seems to find whoever she needs to mingle with, she perks up. "Okay, let's move around."

"I need to get water, Mommy." I look around, hoping I will spot him.

There is a part of me that got all dolled-up just for him. Hoping he'll see me like this and... I don't know. It's not like he doesn't make me feel beautiful all the time, but today I've dressed the part.

"Okay, get your water. Careful not to stain your dress." Mother talks to me, but her eyes and mind are already on someone else. "Come and find me then."

I'm shaking with nerves, and I don't even know why.

I have never seen Andrea outside of our art world

or our little bubble, and for whatever reason I'm not sure how to handle it.

I'm all giddy and restless. And very aware of our age difference. It hasn't bothered me before, but tonight... I'm here with my parents, not even being able to speak to him without explaining myself.

I need to compose myself first. I walk down the hall toward the bathrooms. Stopping by the large industrial window, I watch the shimmering river. I'm making this a bigger deal than it is. I'm sure the minute I see him, all will be good and clear.

"Are you hiding?"

The hoarse voice sends shivers down my spine. I whip around and my gaze meets the brown-green eyes.

Andrea's expressions thickens the air between us. His nostrils flaring, he fists his hands, looking at me with hunger.

"You had quite an entrance," he says.

"You saw me?" I smile, breathless. God, he looks good in his tux.

"I also saw that old fart ogling you," Andrea growls in a low voice that sends shivers down my spine.

There is something seriously wrong with me, because those shivers are only partially caused by fear.

Andrea grabs my wrist and pulls me back behind the row of large potted plants.

He presses his body against mine, making it impossible to move. Not that I'm planning to go anywhere.

He lowers his forehead against mine, daggers shooting from his eyes. "I miss you."

"You saw me yesterday."

"I was excited to see you tonight, but this is harder than I thought. I don't want anyone looking at you." His voice is a rumble that reverberates through me like a symphony, weakening my knees.

"I'm yours," I whimper.

He crushes his lips against mine, and with his kiss all the anxiety of the past few hours evaporates, eaten away by the intensity of this man.

We've spent all possible hours in the past few weeks together. It's not enough, and it's so much at the same time. Andrea has been painting, and I've been there, observing his mastery.

Outside his studio, we can't keep our hands off each other. Days at school have been the hardest. Seeing him and pretending we are strangers grows harder every day. And yet I'm inspired, alive, the happiest I've ever been.

Andrea squats and grips the hem of my gown. Bringing it back up, the fabric floats around, still covering me but giving him easier access. His hand slides to my core. "Is my girl wet for me? Missing me?"

He cups my sex and I tremble, grabbing his shoulders for balance.

He hums that guttural, deep sound of approval. "Let me make sure that every man here tonight knows who you belong to." He takes my earlobe into his mouth and sucks. "I wish I could mark this beautiful neck of yours, but I don't want you to get into trouble with your parents. I'll at least make sure you smell like me and your arousal drips down your thighs as you walk around, vixen."

Oh, what his words do to me.

"Andrea," I breathe as he pushes my panties to the side and shoves two fingers into my channel. "We can't..." My words die on a moan I barely stifle.

"My sweet girl, you need to be quiet," he whispers, working me hard, while his thumb rubs my sensitive bud.

I come so fast and unexpectedly that he has to hold me upright. My skirt floats back down and, as he wanted, my arousal trickles down my legs.

Andrea wipes his fingers with his silver pocket square. He puts it to his nose, inhaling deeply, and returns it to his breast pocket. "Now everyone will smell you on me all night, Vivid." He squeezes my jaw and crushes his lips against mine. "Behave, vixen, and remember I'm watching you."

He kisses my forehead gently before he leaves. The bastard.

My bastard.

I lean against the wall for several moments, waiting to regain the strength in my legs. Or a functioning brain.

I venture from behind the plants with a renewed spring in my step. With my hand I dust my skirt, enjoying the soft fabric. This dress is actually fabulous. Leaving the spot of my little rebellion, I'm smiling as I return to face my parents.

* * *

Dinner lasts for years. My father is brooding, barely answering with more than one word. My mother is excelling at a pissing contest with a wife of another guest at our table whose name I don't remember, mostly one-upping each other with vicious gossip.

I use all my energy not to gawk over at the Cassinettis' table. By the end of this evening, I'll be able to get a job as a spy.

I dust Mother's sleeve to glance at them over her shoulder.

I hold my glass to my lips for longer than necessary, looking at them through my lashes.

I go to use the restroom about two more times than is reasonable.

They seem in an excellent mood, talking, laughing, having a great night. Such a difference compared to our table. They are all beautiful, successful people. I wish Julianna was here, so she could tell me who is who.

A woman leans over and whispers something to Andrea, and he rolls his eyes, laughing. A pang of jealousy zips through me. She's holding the hand of a very fit and extremely attractive man, but I wish I was sitting in her chair.

There are two men at the table who must be Andrea's brothers. I wonder if he will ever introduce me.

As I'm returning from yet another bathroom run, my eyes meet with Andrea's. He's relaxed, leaning back and owning the room just by existing.

His gaze roams freely down my body in such a possessive way that my heartbeat stutters, heat pooling in my core.

The man beside him leans in and whispers something. Andrea nods and stands up, never once breaking our connection. I'm frozen to the spot.

People are again up and about, mingling, so my state isn't obvious. Or so I hope.

Andrea and, I guess, his two brothers head in my direction.

"Excuse me," the tallest and largest one says with a smile, and I step to the side, bumping into a chair.

The second man nods and moves past me. When Andrea reaches me, he slides his fingers into my palm briefly. "I hate that dress," he says and moves along, leaving me breathless and annoyed.

I return to my table, determined not to look his way.

"I heard Ernest's mother isn't very pleased with the match," Mother whispers to me. "I'd say you should visit her, but I doubt you can inspire a different opinion. Perhaps go and talk to London Lowe, so the old hag hears through the grapevine you're well connected."

I sigh. "Mommy, I don't think she cares. Why wouldn't she like me? She doesn't even know me. And I don't really know London."

"Have I taught you nothing? At least perform at these events. Chérie, we give you a lot of freedom, and you need to show us your appreciation. Appearances and contacts are the currency at these events." Mother speaks with sugar on her tongue, beaming while she spits the words at me.

I look around the room and find London in what looks like a heated conversation with Andrea. "She's busy."

"Mingle and get her attention. Go. Now."

Sighing, I stand up.

At the bar, London is pointing her finger at Andrea's chest, saying something, and then she storms away. He drags his hand down his face and gestures for the bartender.

Oh, no. I make my way to him. He sits on the high stool with one foot on the ground, staring at the display of bottles.

I squeeze around a small group beside him, grateful they block me from the rest of the prying eyes.

"Why do you hate the dress?" Redirecting my mother's destructive thoughts usually works, so in the absence of any better idea, I hope I can steer his attention from the bottles.

"What? Daddy dearest let the leash loose?" he snarls, swirling a glass with transparent liquid and ice in his hand.

"Don't be an asshole." I grab the glass from him and take a sip. It's sparkling water. I push the glass back to him.

"Checking up on me?"

He's upset about something. Completely out of his comfort zone. I've seen him like this. His typical playing ground for overall assholeness. I won't let him lead this conversation.

"Either tell me why you hate my dress or why

London pissed you off," I say with more confidence than I feel.

"Or what?" He turns to face me and pins me with a look that sears my underwear and sets my heart into overdrive. It's the look of a hunter, of dominance, letting me know who is in charge here.

"I'll fuck the first man who looks my way tonight." I cross my arms over my chest, my chin high. I won't, and we both know it, but it gets his attention.

The war doesn't just brew behind his eyes, it's raging, devastating, destroying. If he clenches his jaw any tighter, he'll dislocate it.

I touch his elbow. It's almost a phantom connection, but it stills him. He looks down at my hand and exhales what feels like an eternity's worth of tension.

He opens his mouth, but London's voice cuts through the room. Andrea sighs and grabs my hand. We stand beside each other, our touch hidden from the world by my gown. Luckily, the group in front of us stays to listen to London's speech.

"I won't keep you long. I wanted to thank you for all your generosity. The silent auction is going splendidly. Now, my assistants tell me that the most sought-after item is a collection of drawings. So far, the bid there is higher than the diamond necklace or the yacht vacation in the Mediterranean. Since the drawings grabbed your attention like this, I have a little secret to share."

Andrea almost crushes my bones, squeezing my hand. I look at him, not caring if someone picks up on our interaction. He turns his head and bores his eyes into me, his face rigid.

"I played you a bit by withholding the artist's name," London continues, while Andrea pleads with me. I'm not sure what is about to go down, and if it's anxiety or anger or something else on his face, but the way he's squeezing my hand, I know he needs me.

"These drawings have been in my possession for so long, I didn't even know if anyone would care to have them. But an outstanding talent can't be cheated of the credit it deserves, and your bids prove that his talent is timeless, even though the pieces are his debuts."

Oh my God. He told me about his feud with London and how they reconciled after I met her leaving his place.

I can't find words and I can't hug him, so I try to show all my support with my eyes. His chest is heaving, his fingers like a vice crushing my hand.

"Now you know what your pledges can do. You know how important this cause is. So, ladies and gentlemen, pull out your checkbooks, because you have a unique opportunity to save lives while you acquire an original Andrea Cassinetti drawing."

For the longest second of silence, everything goes still. Andrea closes his eyes. Several people move toward the corner where the silent auction is happening. Then the room erupts in applause and more people move.

I feel eyes on us. Well, probably on him, but right at this moment I feel like an extension of him, like our connection is a question of survival. He exhales and looks at me, shaking his head.

"Everyone is staring at you," are the first words he utters, whispering to me.

"I'm pretty sure it's you they're staring at."

He drops my hand and turns his back to the room, playing with his soda water. "That's why I hate the dress. You're ravishing in it, and everybody is stealing glances at you."

I let out a surprised gasp. In the midst of fighting a very public outburst of attention while unable to drink, he focuses on me. Or perhaps I have truly become his coping mechanism.

In the absence of alcohol, I'm there while he works, and I'm here while he struggles with notoriety.

That much responsibility might be too much. I'm not sure what to do with that realization, so I focus on something I might be able to control.

"Let them look. None of them is leaving with me

today. If we leave now, you can take the dress off, and I'll be back home before my parents realize."

"Oh, I'll be ripping the dress off, don't worry, Vivid." He smirks.

I grin, wishing we were out of here already, and regretting it won't happen with my parents here.

"Thank you," he whispers.

"Well, you might hate the attention, but those drawings are fucking amazing."

He whips his head around to face me. "Ms. Harrington, did you just cuss?"

I clasp a hand over my mouth. "I did. You're a terrible influence."

"I hope so. I surely hope so."

We grin at each other for a heated moment. God, I wish I was here with him.

"Andrea." A woman shows up from somewhere and we jerk away as if she caught us kissing.

I turn to the bar and wave at the server.

"Violet." Andrea doesn't even try to hide his annoyance.

I can't get the server's attention, so I decide to disappear, but as I turn, the woman smiles at me. The gallery owner.

"Well, hello. Nice to see you again. I don't know if you remember me, I'm Violet Mathison." She extends her hand.

She's wearing a beautiful light blue gown and has diamonds dangling from her ears, her neck, her wrist. She's so classy, and I feel like an elephant standing in a china bowl, intimidated by her presence.

"Ivory Harrington. Nice to see you again."

"What a small world," Andrea sneers. "Ivory is a student."

Violet darts her eyes between the two of us. The tender connection between us disappears into the fraught air between us. He's upset and I'm not sure why, but clearly his wrath or whatever he's feeling right now doesn't exclude me.

He's aloof and annoyed. I have whiplash. Whatever is going on, I'm caught in the crossfire.

I don't deserve this.

It's like he draws energy from me and then stomps all over it. We never have to face the world, and living in our own cocoon is much easier. Would we ever be able to enjoy our relationship out in the open? Will I be able to deal with his behavior, his moods, when faced with it every time something happens that riles him up?

"And a fan." Violet smiles. "I don't mean to interrupt, but can we talk?"

Andrea shrugs. "Go ahead."

Violet hesitates.

"What is it, Vi? You want me alone so you can

bully me into another show?" He taps his fingers on his thighs, but otherwise he seems composed. Not composed, ready for a fight.

"I'll leave you to it." I make a move, but he stops me with a bark.

"Stay."

Heat rises to my cheeks as I look at him, shocked.

"Please," he adds. We stare at each other for a moment. I sense Violet fidgeting a bit, but she doesn't leave.

I also want to slap Andrea.

So this is what he means about sabotaging everything good in his life? I stand by him while he's having his moment of whatever that was just before, and now he snaps at me.

Like my father.

Using me.

Needing me as his outlet.

The masochist in me wins my internal conundrum and I stay, glaring at him while my heart is breaking. I should bolt right now, but that would require courage. One thing that never shows up for me when I need it the most.

"Well, I didn't think this was a good idea here and now, but after London's clever little stunt, I thought I'd seize the opportunity. Let's work together again."

Andrea's jaw ticks. "I'm not interested."

"Do you have other offers? Andrea, we had our differences, but you must admit the last show was a great success."

"I don't have plans to sell my art anymore. Maybe you should tell that to London. It will increase the value of the last Cassinetti pieces still available for sale."

Violet raises her eyebrows. "Well, I see you're in a fabulous mood, so let's talk another time. Come by again, Ivory. You have a keen eye. Have a lovely evening." She turns and leaves.

Only then do I notice the man who stood behind her. He glowers at Andrea and takes her hand and kisses it. Violet beams at him and leans into him as he leads her away.

I look at the brooding man beside me.

"Stay?" I snap. "I'm not your dog." My chest heaves as I try to control the whirl of emotions within me.

He lowers his head, not looking at me. "I can't deal with this shit."

"Neither can I. Nor should I. You were right," I hiss, my chest cracking like fragile ice. "Your madness *will* drive me away. And I *do* deserve better."

"Vivid—"

I march out of the room, blinking my tears away. My heart is breaking into pieces too small to recover.

Chapter 25

Andrea

She is sitting on the floor with that little girl again, drawing. They laughed just now, and the sound hit me right in the chest. It's spreading there like a drug. I need another hit, but it's un-fucking-available.

It's been more than a week since the gala and Vivid has been avoiding me.

Can I blame her? No.

Do I miss her? Like I've cut off my own limb.

Should I force her to forgive my behavior? Probably not. She deserves better.

Does it matter? Fuck no.

She is mine, and I'll make her listen.

I glare at her over the heads of other students and kids. She hasn't once looked at me in all the days we keep running into each other. Some determination she has.

I'm practically chasing her around, waiting for the opportunity to accost her and fuck the stubbornness out of her.

It hasn't helped that Wiggins is dead set on working me to the ground, tasking me with all these extracurricular honors. She's probably just trying to keep me distracted enough not to get involved with a student.

It's not working. Fuck. I'm going to talk to Vivid. It's not like she can refuse a word with me among all the other students.

I push off the wall and then slump back when my colleague hands me a coffee.

"Are you sick again?" Fox frowns at me.

I have half a mind to tell her I was never sick, but I rein myself in. For Vivid's sake. She doesn't need the rumors. "I'm fine," I bark instead.

"Okay." She smirks. "You know, staring at her won't get you out of the gutter with Wiggins."

"I don't know what you're talking about." My retort is too fast. Even I can hear the bullshit.

"As you wish. But just like me, nobody is blind here. Let the girl be, Andrea."

I lock eyes with her, trying to scare her away, but Fox withstands my wrath with a smile.

"Thank you for the coffee." I storm out.

When I reach the hallway, I'm unsure where I'm going. Just away. Away from prying eyes. From all the students. From my esteemed colleagues. Away from this soulless job that I've been half-assing, anyway.

The cold air hits my lungs when I get to the arched walkway in the courtyard. I lean against a post and breathe.

With Vivid gone from my life, I lost my art as well. I haven't been in the studio since she left. My therapist would be pleased because I've been doing a pretty good job avoiding other vices. I ordered a few bottles, but had the presence of mind to call Gio before the delivery arrived.

I wanted to get hammered to forget the void she left behind, but I couldn't do it, because that would mean accepting that I've lost her.

I also didn't want to disappoint Vivid. As if she cared. Fucking catch-22. God, I need a drink. No. I need *her*.

Children's laughter echoes through the courtyard. The creative workshops are over. I should be there to supervise the clean-up, but I don't move.

The grass is still green, glittering with last night's rain. The drops shine in a kaleidoscope of shades, reflecting the light. I fist my hand, aching for a brush.

In my mind, the first strokes of a new painting take root.

I shake my head, but the imagery only grows. It's like forbidden fruit. Or just observing Vivid for half an hour sparks enough confidence in my creativity. I need her back. Things felt doable when she was around.

"Sorry, I don't think I'll go tonight. I have an exam to study for."

I almost stop breathing when Vivid's voice floats through the air.

"Come on, Ivory, just for a bit. You haven't hung out with us in weeks. Where have you been hiding?"

Fucking Varsity boy.

"Tim, maybe next time, okay?" Her stern tone ends on a quivering note. What the hell?

"Ivory, baby, you still owe me that date," the fucker drawls.

"Let go of me."

Enough. I dash from my spot, a hot surge of anger bubbling up inside my chest. I immediately spy his back, crowding her. I only glimpse Vivid's sneakers before I grab his collar.

I whip him around. Red sears through me as my fist connects with his jaw with a satisfying thud.

He stumbles back, covering his face. "What the fuck?"

I grip his throat and push him against the pillar. I

register Vivid's purple T-shirt, but I'm blinded by unmanageable emotions, seeing only the fucker who touched her.

"Don't you ever get within five feet of her, or you lose that grabby hand of yours," I snarl.

He stares at me, disoriented, before he finds his brain, and his pride probably. "What the hell is wrong with you?"

"What's wrong with you, you little piece of shit? Repeat after me, dickhead. No means no."

When he says nothing, just stares at me confused, I push harder against his Adam's apple.

He makes a gurgling sound and I release the pressure. I raise my eyebrows, and he gets the message.

"No means no," he rasps.

I let go of him and he stumbles away to gain some distance, spitting. "You'll pay for this," he slurs.

"You're delusional. Get the fuck out of here before I drag you to the dean's office."

Tim scurries away, and only then do I notice several students gawking at us. By sheer luck, none of them pulled out their phones. I was in the right here, but I doubt Wiggins would see it that way.

"The show is over." I dismiss the spectators.

When we're alone, I finally turn to face her. Vivid has her hand clasped over her mouth, looking at me wide-eyed.

"Are you okay?" I want to hug her, and I would. Fuck the stupid consequences. I don't care about who can see us.

But I'm not sure she's ready to take me back. Not that she has a choice.

And some code of decency I didn't even know I have stops me, because she was just assaulted and witnessed my attack.

She doesn't answer, just nods. Our eyes lock. There are a couple of feet between us, and yet the scent of jasmine envelops me with recognition and peace.

The torture of being this close, and also so far, makes me regret all my life choices. In no uncertain terms, I realize I'd do anything to be with this woman.

She calms me. She inspires me. She awakens a beast in me that is stronger than the demons and monsters I have been fighting all my life.

She is my lifeline.

"I'm not your father, Vivid. I was struggling with London's well-meant unveiling, and you helped me through it. And then when Violet came, I needed you there. I should have asked you, but..."

I rake my hair with my fingers. She dropped her hand from her face, but I can't decipher what my words are causing. If they are landing in her heart and soaring with acceptance, or burying me deeper in a place where rotten people like her father reside.

I sigh. "I sabotage all the good in my life. It's not an excuse, just an explanation. But I don't want to be that man anymore, Vivid. Not with you around. I'm not your father. I see you. I respect you. I..."

I lower my head. *I love you.* I can't watch losing her. It's ripping my chest into pieces as it is, I don't need a front-row seat. With closed eyes, I wait for the sound of retreating steps.

The world goes completely silent. In my head, life loudly ticks off the moments of my dismay. Tick. Tick. Tick. Tick.

"You should ice your hand." Her voice caresses my wounded heart. The words make no sense, but these are the first words she has said to me in over a week, and they sound like soothing music, a lullaby to my frail brain.

I look at my hand, my knuckles swelling already, but that pain is inconsequential. It's nothing compared to the agony inside me.

"It's okay. Are you all right?" I step closer, approaching her with caution.

"I know you're not like my father, but you often sound like him. I want to stand by you, but you need to treat me like you want it too."

"I do… I want you by my side more than anything. More than anyone."

She observes me for a long, endless moment. Or maybe only for a brief second. I don't breathe, don't flinch. I let her find what she's looking for, because I'm completely at her mercy.

"I want to show you something," she says, and starts toward the annex without waiting.

She doesn't need to wait, of course I'll follow her.

We get to one of the workshops and she stops by a table, wringing her hands in front of her, suddenly looking even younger than she is.

Her sculpture.

"You finished it," I croak.

"Being mad at you helped."

I close my eyes, exhaling. Fuck.

"Andrea, look at me please. You hurt me, but deep down I know you didn't want to. Channeling my hurt into this"—she nods toward her artwork—"it helped me understand your process a bit. It helped me understand how heightened emotions drive your inspiration and creativity. Maybe that internal doubt is the only way you can create the magic. But it doesn't have to be self-destructive."

I let out another long breath. Not the conversation I was hoping for, but I'll take anything. Anything to be in her vicinity. "It has been for me."

"But that's happening after you finish your work. You can't face the attention, the judgment, or even the praise. When I imagine someone looking at this, I feel physically sick."

"You get me." God, I need to hug her. Connect with her beyond words.

"And you get me." She smiles sadly, and the heavy stone that has been pressing at my chest drops.

We stare at each other. The freckles, the golden eyes, the crazy hair and the soft smile I missed so much. It's all at my fingertips. Beautiful. Vivid. Mine.

"Let's go home." It's a plea and a command, and I hope I won't have to throw her over my shoulder.

She raises her eyebrows and I add, "Please."

"I'll meet you at your place. We shouldn't leave together."

I groan and look behind to make sure we're alone. I step closer, not touching her, just absorbing her heat with my body. She shudders from this slight contact. I lower my head and inhale her perfume and the scent that is purely her.

"Okay, Vivid, see you at home. But hurry, because I need to sink my cock into your sweet pussy."

She moans. "I missed you."

"What was this supposed to be?" Vivid tilts her head.

She's wearing my shirt and that just-fucked expression. I enjoy her the most like this.

"After I left rehab I tried to paint one day, but I ended up just splashing the paint on the canvas. I'll paint over it eventually." I mix colors on a small plastic plate I'm using as my palette.

She drags the gigantic frame to the middle of the room and drops it.

"What are you doing?"

"Maybe we should finish it now. Together." She snatches a can of paint from the shelves and saunters to the workbench by the window.

All swaying hips and seductive smile.

Putting down my brush and the palette, I fold my arms over my chest and admire the view. This playful vixen is something else, as my cock can attest, straining against the zipper of my jeans.

Vivid pries the can open. Barefoot, she walks to the middle of the canvas and starts dripping the color down, dancing. The previous stains are red, and she is infusing them with dark blue splotches.

"Care to join me? We might create a masterpiece." Shimmying, she dips her hips and wiggles her ass in my direction.

"It won't hold my weight, but do continue, vixen." I laugh.

"Then let's break it." She pirouettes, making a wide circle with paint, laughing.

The feeling swelling in my chest is threatening, and welcome at the same time. I pull down my jeans and join her in her madness. I reach for the paint, but she snatches it closer.

"Get your own." She continues dancing to her imaginary music, making a mess of my studio.

I love it.

I love her.

I love my life when she's here.

Getting yellow from the shelf, I return and start splashing around. The canvas is almost covered now. With red, blue, yellow and our footsteps.

"Oh, no," Vivid purses her lips and flips the can upside down. "I'm out."

Her innocence crashes with her wanton abandon. She is my virgin and my little whore in one. I drop the paint. It splashes both of us.

Vivid gasps when I pounce.

We fall down and roll in the paint, kissing and laughing. She ends up under me, breathless and beautiful. I lower my forehead to hers, supporting myself on one elbow, while I free my cock with the other.

Her breath is intoxicating on my skin as she stares at me, quivering. I slide in and we both still, the intimacy of the moment saturating the air around us.

Vivid grinds her hips and I hiss, sinking deeper. Unlike any other times before, I move slowly, with reverence, and in awe of everything this girl is to me. I don't know if she feels it too, but her eyes mirror the chaos inside me.

Something is ripping me apart and mending me together. The sheer intensity of emotions within and the feel of her... It squeezes at my chest and helps to birth a new person.

It's like painting—the beauty is happening.

You can't command it. You can't force it. It just is.

"Andrea," she breathes, and her walls squeeze around me. We come together, hard.

I collapse and roll off her, squeezing her hand, trying to catch my breath. And some sense of reality.

"You were quiet," she whispers.

I turn my head and we grin at each other. "You make me speechless."

"I like your filthy mouth." She reaches out, her finger tracing around my face. "I wish I could draw like you. I would like to capture you the way I see you. Beautiful and raw."

I enjoy the lines she traces on my skin, appreciating the peacefulness of the moment. I could stay like this forever and wouldn't miss anything.

Here with my muse.

My love.

My life.

Her smile widens and I grab her hand, kissing her palm. It's yellow and blue. "Did you just paint my face?"

She bites her lip. "It's only fair. I'm sure my ass is encrusted in acrylic." Her eyes widen. "Oh my God, is the paint toxic?"

I laugh. "That would explain why I'm an addict."

Vivid's gape turns into a grin. Beaming, she rolls on me and pushes up, straddling me. "A former addict. The only vice you're allowed"—she drops for a kiss—"is my sweet pussy."

I cup her face, moving her hair out of the way. "Picking up on my dirty talk?"

"It's growing on me." She crushes her lips against mine.

"Let's get showered to mitigate the contamination," I say when we come up for air.

"Wait? Is it really poisonous?" She tenses.

"I don't know. It will be fun to explain at the hospital, though."

"Stop it." She swats me.

Laughing, I help her stand and immediately lift her into my arms. As I carry her downstairs, she sucks on my neck and then bites it gently.

"You know I'll get you back for that."

"So you can mark my body as yours, but I can't?"

I lower her to the floor when we enter the bathroom.

"Oh, I'm yours, Vivid. I'm yours, and I really hope you understand the burden."

* * *

"Why don't you believe in love?" I drop the question casually while we eat our dinner.

Vivid stills with her fork halfway to her mouth. "Do you believe in love?"

Ah, we're back to a conversation filled with questions and no answers. "I do. Yes." I don't tell her it's because of her. I want to approach this carefully.

She sighs and fidgets for a moment, playing with her food as if rearranging the peas into a certain sector of her plate was the most important thing. Then she takes a sip of water and starts moving around the rice.

I wait patiently while she goes through her process. Her breathing gets louder. She might draw blood if she doesn't stop biting her lip.

I assumed it was a loaded question, but I didn't expect this level of reluctance. Forcing myself to remain composed, I drum my fingers on my thigh instead of the counter.

I swear I see my life flickering in front of me. It's

not that my life depends on her answer, but it sure feels like it.

"Are you going to answer?" I ask instead of barking a demand at her.

"What was the question?" she asks innocently, mirth on her face.

It won't work on me. I'm getting to the bottom of this. I launch around the island and grab the back of her neck, kissing her roughly. Her arms flail up and she squeals, but I eat the sound with my mouth.

"I thought I was the old one in this relationship, and you forgot the question I asked two minutes to two hours ago?"

"I was hoping, in your old age, you'd forget you asked." She grips my hips with her legs and tries to distract me with more kissing.

I squeeze her ass. "Why don't you believe in love?"

She exhales. "Because my mother loves my father."

I expected a sappy story about first love or some feminist stand on things, but this hits me right in the stomach, immediately boiling my blood.

"Elaborate," I grit out.

"Not when you're this hostile." She glares.

I pull her into an embrace. "Sorry, Vivid. Your parents inspire my disgust."

She sighs. "My father doesn't love her back, but he still remains the sole source of her happiness. He mistreats her, cheats on her, manipulates her, and she still loves him. She gave him her life, her heart, her dignity. Love is blind, they say, but to me love is binding, and painful."

I cup her face, at a loss for words. I don't know shit about love, but I know the example she got at home isn't right. How can I make her see that? What do I have to offer when I'm still fighting my own demons?

I draw deep from the feeling she evokes in me. "It can also be freeing."

Now I only hope I can show her.

Chapter 26

Ivory

The dining room bustles with chatter, laughter, teasing and great vibes. The Cassinetti-Lowe family is large, and not even everyone is here today.

Andrea's mother, Bianca, welcomed me with open arms and a dash of suspicion in her eyes, but the rest of the family is just so... amicable, and informal.

The Thanksgiving dinner is a decadent affair prepared by a hired chef. There are servers doting on every detail.

It's different from the homemade cooking and atmosphere at the Biachis', but in many ways the same. These people are as rich, and more, as us, and yet...

This certainly isn't the empty, cavernous home I grew up in. Mother can summon her hostess talents for important people who my father wants to impress. But the rest of the household has been run by Martha.

I doubt Bianca Cassinetti does chores, but this house is clearly bent to her will. And she's done an amazing job of creating a warm home.

Andrea sits across from me—the seating plan freaked me out—and watches me through hooded eyes, a smile lingering on his lips.

"So, how did you two meet?" asks Massi, a famous chef and restaurant investor who sits to my right.

"At my exhibition," Andrea answers for me. And it would be annoying, but I'm so freaked out about meeting his family I'll take any help I can.

Meeting the family is stressful as it is, but given our age difference, I feel like we should have eased everyone into the idea. Instead, Andrea surprised me with this get-together.

He didn't tell me where we were going until we arrived, and by then I couldn't run away because Bianca was already beaming at the landing of her impressive house.

There is something seriously wrong with me, because he blindsided me and I'm pleased. Well, not with the blindsiding, but butterflies flutter in my chest around the idea of Andrea taking this step.

It's a significant step in our relationship, isn't it? I

texted Julianna from the bathroom, and the love and smiling emoticons she responded with made me feel better about meeting these people.

"That was a memorable evening." Mila, who is engaged to Andrea's brother Gio, giggles, and her fiancé groans.

My eyes widen when the recognition sinks in. She's the woman Andrea kissed the night we met. A wave of discomfort spreads through me with irrational jealousy. Jesus.

Mila pats Gio's hand. "Don't worry, Ivory, that kiss was the worst experience in my life," she deadpans, and now Andrea groans.

"What kiss?" Gina, Massi's wife, who is nursing a baby beside Andrea, asks.

"It's nothing," Andrea snaps, his gaze locked on me. It's like he's trying to X-ray my head to assess the damage. He leans back in his chair, distancing himself from the conversation physically. But with a family of this size, he can't live this down.

"Now I need to know," London says.

"Shut up," Gio snarls.

Mila laughs and Andrea fidgets in his chair. I can't help it and chuckle. My reaction smooths his features, the relief on his face is palpable.

"Children, let's focus on the reason we're here."

Bianca draws everyone's attention away from the embarrassing topic.

By the casual way Mila is entertained by the events of that night, I decide to let it go. Whatever the reason he kissed her, clearly it had nothing to do with here and now.

"Let me, darling," Bianca's husband Micah says from the other side of the table, smiling at his wife. Her eyes soften under his gaze.

I lower my head, blinking away tears. Witnessing such a tender affection between the two of them is overwhelming. I haven't seen this even at the Biachis', probably because Julianna's father is never around when I'm there.

"I'm grateful for having another lovely meal with all of you. I'm grateful for my reasonable health, and for the beautiful woman who took a chance on me and my girls all those years ago," Micah says, and the whole table sighs.

Bianca bursts up and rushes around the long table to hug her husband. I glance at Andrea, feeling like I'm intruding on a private moment of these strangers who make me feel more welcome than my family ever has.

Andrea winks at me with a smirk and I almost yelp when I feel his—I hope—foot stroking my ankle. Oh, how I wish we were sitting next to each other.

"I'm grateful for all these beautiful moments we create together." Bianca squeezes Micah's shoulder and looks around the table.

Massi, Gina, and their son Sebastien say their thanks, followed by Sydney and her fiancé Hunter, who I saw on TV. London says something funny, and her handsome boyfriend Dominic retorts with sarcasm. They kiss, clearly grateful for each other.

I don't hear half of the words, because the idea of me saying anything in front of these people is a tad intimidating. And if I'm honest, I'm most worried about what Andrea might say. What is the right thing to say here?

I can't declare I'm thankful for him. That's embarrassing. Too soon. And not in front of this audience. But I can't not mention him at all. He's the only thing I'm thankful for, anyway.

After Mila and Gio say something, everyone looks at me. I lick my lips, my eyes darting around the table. Andrea's foot glides higher, rubbing between my knees. I wring my hands in my lap, heat burning my face.

"I'm grateful for being here today," I whisper, my eyes finding the only intended recipient of my words.

His smile is wicked, and I know he understands all the meaning behind my words. I would relax now if it wasn't for his foot pressing against my skin. Thank

God this table is too wide for him to reach further. My pussy disagrees strongly, wetness pooling in my underwear.

Andrea bores his eyes into me with an intensity that might just set me on fire. "I'm grateful I found my muse. To keep me away from my demons. To show me that beauty doesn't have to be born from pain."

I swallow my gasp, his words sprouting goosebumps all over my skin. Ignoring the rest of his family, Andrea practically fucks me with his eyes. I can't catch my breath, but I don't want to pant here.

"Wow, who knew you were talented with words as well, bro," London says.

"Excuse me." I push the chair back, my napkin falling to the floor. "I need to use the bathroom."

I rush from the room.

Overwhelmed. Scared. Thrilled.

All at the same time. His words play in my mind on a loop. This can't be happening. He didn't say he loved me. He doesn't. Yet, those were the most beautiful words anyone has ever said to me.

He declared without declaring, in the most devastating way.

I run cold water over my wrists, trying to calm down.

And his eyes. Jesus. I can throw out my underwear.

In the mirror, I catch myself smiling. This might be a grin that not even my parents could wipe away.

I open the door and collide with the solid wall. Andrea's strong hands help me regain balance as he holds me close to him.

"Are you okay? You ran away like a spooked rabbit." His eyes on me have a direct line to my heart. It paces around my chest like a caged animal.

I wrap my arms around him and capture his lips. Catching him unprepared, we stumble, but he finds purchase against the wall. I devour him with my lips, trying to tell him everything I'm too scared to say with words.

How much it means to me that he brought me here. That he supported my sculpting. Showed me how beautiful I am. Pointed out that my parents don't deserve the excuses I've been making for them. Allowed me to inspire him. Fucked me and made love to me.

How much I adore him.

"Hmmm, Vivid, if I knew introducing you to my family would get you this horny, I'd have dragged you here sooner." He hums against my lips, squeezing my ass. His erection digs into my hips.

"Idiot." I giggle.

"Definitely, but all yours." He bites my lower lip.

"Shall we go home and take care of that pool in your underwear?"

I gasp. "Never mind my underwear, your cock will rip through your zipper."

"My vixen is learning fast. This is the first time you said cock. And yes, my cock needs you as much as your pussy needs me."

I melt into his arms, but I'm not ready to leave. I roll my lips.

"What is it?" He picks up on my hesitation immediately.

"Can we stay a little longer?"

He groans, but smiles. "Of course, but within limits. My family needs to be enjoyed in moderation."

I kiss him again. "Thank you."

"Let me take care of my problem and I'll join you in a minute." He adjusts his crotch and I return to his family, giggling.

This man is tilting my world on its axis.

"I enjoyed meeting your family." I lean against the doorway of his bathroom. Naked. It's funny how comfortable I am in my own skin when I'm here.

"Yeah?" He stretches his jaw to the side, running the electric razor around his neck.

"It's just amazing how you're all supportive of each other, and successful," I muse, watching the beautiful man in front of me.

He taps the shaver on the sink and washes his face. "Today we were all on our best behavior. But I haven't spoken to London in years."

"I can hardly imagine that." I step closer and trace my fingers around his shoulders. He shudders and our eyes meet in the mirror. My breath hitches. Our bodies are so attuned to each other, I wonder if I'm becoming an addict here.

Is this how my mother used to feel? Was she this dependent on my father's touch? Did that obsession drive her to madness? Somehow, I can't imagine my parents ever having this kind of closeness. This consuming, but magical, reliance on giving and taking.

My parents' relationship isn't a fair game. My father has always had the upper hand. But am I an equal partner here?

Completely exposed to Andrea's moods, to his fierce need for my presence. To his possessiveness. It all makes me feel powerful and vulnerable at the same time.

What if I'm like my mother and I'd let him strip me of all reason? Just like right now, his one penetrating look shatters all my defenses.

"Vivid?"

His husky voice sounds like a warning. I snap my eyes back to his in the mirror. He steps aside and looks at me.

"Let me fuck those thoughts out of you."

I blink a few times, completely disoriented by his yearning and my reverent pondering. Shocked by his crassness and strangely pleased by it.

I snort.

His eyes darken. I'm powerless against this look. I swear I could orgasm from that gaze alone.

"Hands on the vanity." He pushes my shoulders and I gasp. It's a mix of surprise and hot pleasure spreading through me. "You need to watch me fuck you, so you understand—"

He steps behind me, and with his hand between my shoulder blades nudges me forward. I land on my elbows.

"Eyes on me, vixen," he commands, and I snap my gaze to the mirror.

Andrea traces his fingers down my spine. The reverence in his eyes is akin to the look on his face when he paints. Like discovering beauty between the blind strokes of his brush, he could just as easily be seeing me naked for the first time.

He leans in and scoops my leg under my knee, pulling it up and against the vanity, spreading me wide open for him. I tremble on one leg, but I know there is no way he'll let me collapse.

I'm naked, completely at his mercy with my ass jutting up, pushing against his erection, but I trust him wholly.

He slides his hands from my ass to my clit and hums his approval. "Wet and hot for me already, my sweet little slut."

I lower my head, fighting the avalanche of sensations his one touch unleashes.

His slap shocks me. "Eyes on me," he growls.

I look up again and meet his gaze in the mirror. "You're going to watch the whole time. You're going to see what you do to me. Understood?"

I nod, but there is a part of me that wants to shut my eyes, because the intensity of him, of my thoughts, my doubts are too much. Too destructive. And yet very honest.

But I obey and watch. He murmurs his dirty words of praise as he plays with my clit, and then fills me with his hardness.

Moaning, gasping, sighing, I don't once disconnect our gaze. Andrea fucks me slowly at first, worshiping me with his attention, but slowly he loses control and sets a punishing tempo.

My hips will be bruised from hitting the marble counter, my core will be sore from the savage attack.

But my soul, my heart, seem to grow wholesome, consumed by the sight of the man behind me completely unraveling.

An orgasm swipes through me in a violent wave. I drop my forehead to the cold surface. Andrea fists my hair and pulls me back roughly, making sure I continue watching.

And what a sight it is, when this beautiful man scrunches his face and lets go with abandon, spilling himself inside me and filling me with his cum and so much more.

Still jerking inside me, he leans down, covering my sweaty back. He kisses my shoulder, panting.

"Did you watch the whole time?" His voice is gruff.

"I had no other choice," I almost chuckle, but I'm too spent to fully form it.

"Good. Now remember it every time that you doubt who has power in this relationship. It's you, Vivid."

His words break me and build me up again, but before I have time to fully comprehend the depth of his statement, Andrea withdraws, wipes me with a hand towel and scoops me into his arms.

"Next round is in the bed," he says darkly.

I laugh. "No one can ever accuse you of lacking stamina."

He drops me to the bed and launches at me,

covering me with his solid body. "Lucky you." He smirks, and before I know it he flips me around and plunges into me.

Two more orgasms later, we lie tangled between the sweaty sheets, completely spent and utterly blissed out. I know I am.

"I think I'll call Violet Mathison in the morning," he murmurs into my hair.

I smile. "You want to have a show?"

"We can have a show together." He whispers into my ear, nuzzling my neck. But no amount of caressing can distract me from that suggestion.

I sit up so fast my head spins. "What are you talking about?"

"Why not?" He puts his hands behind his head, amusement playing across his face.

I count on my fingers. "For one, I'm not an artist. Nor do I have any art to display."

He shrugs, unimpressed. "Meh."

"Meh?" I jump to my knees, punching him in his shoulder.

"Hey." He grabs me and tackles me, rolling me on top of him while wrapping his legs and arms around me, caging me in an embrace. "No need for violence."

"I'm not ready for..." I shake my head, as if that could help me find reason or comprehension of his ludicrous idea. Or keep the anxiety at bay. "That." I don't find a better word.

"Stop fidgeting, Vivid, my cock can't get hurt. We both need the fucker." He winks. "From my own experience I can tell you that you will never be ready."

"Andrea, please, I don't want to. I can't." Jesus. Has he lost his mind?

He kisses my forehead. "I disagree. You can. But I accept that you don't want to."

I exhale with relief and put my head down on his shoulder.

"For now," he adds, and I groan. The bastard laughs.

We lie in silence for a beat before I ask, "What made you change your mind?"

"You."

While I don't understand what he means by that, my heart picks up its beat. I don't know if I can take on such a responsibility. At the same time, the idea thrills me. Jesus. I'm such a mess around him.

I look up, frowning.

He gives me a sad smile. "You told me my doubt doesn't come from my work, but from the attention and public display and all that shit that comes after I complete a painting."

"So you're going to fight fire with fire?" Immediately my mind goes to his addiction, and I almost want to talk him out of it.

"No, I'm too broken for such an experiment. I'm going to put on an anonymous show."

* * *

The Thanksgiving weekend carries on in a lazy, languid, love-making atmosphere. As I shower in the evening, I'm sad I can't stay here longer. Somehow we created this cocoon of our own world, and the idea of returning to reality is depressing.

I dry myself, get dressed and join Andrea in the sitting room.

With his feet on the coffee table, he lounges in his underwear. How in the world did I land the sexiest man alive?

He pats the seat next to him and I join him. He kisses the crown of my head. The intimacy between us is so effortless and natural, my gloominess soars. How can I go to my parents after this?

"I wish I could stay." I sigh.

He pulls me into his lap and kisses me roughly. "I'm going to resign."

"What?" Where is this coming from?

"If I'm going to put on a show, I need time to paint. And I don't want to sneak around anymore. We don't have to go public until you choose to, but I don't want to be your professor when we do."

I smile. "That feels like a sacrifice I can't accept."

He chuckles and kisses me again. "Vixen, I'll let you in on a secret. I hate that job."

I gasp and study him to uncover the truth, but he's serious. "Wow, your female students will be devastated."

He cups the back of my neck. "The one female student that matters has unlimited access to me."

My smile grows so wide that my jaw might crack, but it's what soars in my heart that scares me and delights me at the same time.

Andrea's phone interrupts us. Swearing, he slides me down next to him and grabs his phone from the coffee table. "Mother." He shrugs and almost declines the call.

"Answer her." I poke him with my elbow, and he sighs but takes the call.

"Mom." He smiles at me and rakes his hair with his fingers. I don't make out the words, but Bianca is talking fast, and Andrea frowns and shakes his head. "I've never been better. What's going on?"

I have no idea what news his mother shares, but he flips his eyes to me, narrowing them at the edges. His face goes rigid as he clenches his jaw. The darkness that takes him over is threatening.

And the worst part is, the utter disdain is aimed at me.

It's so strong I slide backward on the sofa. Andrea reassures his mother he'll be fine, but that's a lie. He hangs up and closes his eyes.

"What happened?" My voice dies on the wave of worry sweeping over me.

"Who the fuck is Ernest Cornfield?" Glaring at me, he stands up, his hands shaking.

"Ernie?" I'm stunned, unable to connect the dots. Why would his mother call him about Ernie.

He flinches. The hurt in his eyes mixes with disbelief, and I can almost see him retreating into a world I have no access to.

"Ernie? So you know him?" He snorts. "Get out, Ivory."

A slap would have been a gentle caress compared to that. "What?"

"Get the fuck out before I do something we'll both regret." He hurls his phone across the room. It lands with a thud.

I jump up and walk backward. "How do you know about Ernie?" The chaos ripping through me is physically painful. How did a peaceful weekend go up in flames this fast?

He turns his back to me and walks to the window.

"I bare my soul to you. I trust you with my inner

struggles, and you're fucking engaged!" He shakes his head, his voice is laced with contempt. "Check the society pages. Apparently you're to wed *Ernie*."

I gasp. "Andrea." His name on my lips is a plea. I want to explain, but I don't even know what I'm explaining. And the worst part is, I don't think he'd listen.

"Just go."

Chapter 27

Ivory

The door hits me in the back as I rush outside. There is no point reasoning with him now. Especially since I have no idea what the heck happened.

But how did we go from domestic bliss to this? How could he turn off his emotions in one single second? Tears stream down my face, flooding out my frustration and hurt.

Hurt. His. Mine. Ours.

It seems to be the primary glue of our relationship.

And its principal ruin.

With shaking hands, I type my name and Ernie's into the search bar, then I stumble down the steps and start running down the sidewalk. The trimmed hedges lining the pavement scratch my arm as I scroll and run.

Half a block away from Andrea's house, I open the first announcement loaded on the search page.

I stop and tilt my head back to scream at the sky.

When I look down again, I meet the bewildered stare of an elderly lady who pushes her walker, taking a wide berth around me.

"I'm sorry," I apologize, wiping my tears.

The lady smiles, I think. My vision is blurry. Still, I can see her smile is pitying, sympathetic. Or maybe she wants to call the cops.

My mind offers glimpses of disconnected thoughts only.

Who announced the engagement?

The hurt on Andrea's face.

Why didn't Ernie warn me?

Andrea's refusal to hear me out.

What am I going to do now?

The ground is swirling. Should I go to Ernie? Home? To Julianna? I groan in frustration, because only one stubborn answer keeps marring my thoughts. I want to go to the house half a block behind me.

I'm not wanted there. Damn him with his temper and insecurities. How could he just throw me out? And it was his mother who called and told him. How embarrassing.

A yellow cab approaches and I flail my arm. This might be the first time I've hailed a taxi in Manhattan on the first try. As the car pulls to the curb, Andrea's voice slices through the air.

"Vivid."

He's on the street, barefoot, but when he jogs in my direction, I jump in the cab. "Brooklyn Heights. Go," I urge.

I turn and see him running, and then he stops, his hands in his hair. A strange sense of déjà vu consumes me. The theme of our relationship: me running away and him chasing me.

I'll deal with this later. First, I have to figure out what's going on.

No, first I have to pack up and leave my parents. They can't do this to me. Where can I go?

My leg jumps up and down of its own accord. I'm tapping my phone on my thigh. Leaning forward, I hug my knees and try to breathe to tame my nerves into submission. It doesn't work, and my heart hammers against my temple at what I assume is less than a healthy rate.

I'll have to quit school and start working. Perhaps I can crash at the Biachis' for a few days.

Until I figure out what's next. My phone rings in my hand. My head almost hits the roof as I jump, dropping the phone.

"Are you okay?" The driver eyes me in the rearview mirror with suspicion.

I bend over to search for my phone that is blaring from under the seat. "I'm not," I sob. "But I will be."

The driver widens his eyes and lets out a long breath.

I finally fish my phone out and sit back. Andrea's name lights up the screen. I can't talk to him now. His ballistic reaction in this situation was unwarranted, hurtful, and selfish.

He snapped out of it quickly, guessing by his bare-foot chase, but still. Let him stew in this a bit.

I decline the call and make another one instead.

"What the heck, Ernie?" My voice comes out like a squeal.

He yawns. "What's up your ass?"

"Are you high right now?" I want to tear my hair out and he's lounging somewhere, unaffected.

"Yeah, you should try it. You're too uptight, Ivory."

Liquid splashes, ice clinks and a female voice plays in the background, and it hits me. He doesn't know.

"Well, this might sober you up. Our engagement has been announced. It's trending on society pages."

Saying the words out loud isn't worse than Andrea's dismissal, but it's right there with it, trying to give me a heart attack. Or a panic attack. Or any other attack that my body must suffer through to cope with all these feelings.

"What the actual fuck? I haven't even bought the ring." High as a kite. Jesus.

"Focus, Ernie. I guess our parents decided you getting on one knee is an unnecessary nuisance."

My phone beeps with another incoming call. Andrea won't stop until I talk to him. He should have thought about that when he threw me out. Asshole.

"I can't marry you." Finally, Ernie sounds as freaked-out as the situation warrants. It doesn't solve much, but somehow it makes me feel better. Like I'm not alone anymore.

"Really?" In the face of this messed-up situation I find sarcasm. Not helpful. "And I was hoping to become Mrs. Cornfield."

He groans and yells something. I imagine to the sky like I did earlier. "Fuck, Ivory, let me fix this."

"What do you plan—"

The line goes dead.

For the rest of the ride, I keep declining Andrea's calls and planning my conversation with my parents. I'm failing miserably.

He keeps calling, and I can't think of one useful thing to tell my father.

Maybe I'll just go upstairs, pack a few things and then go to Julianna's.

CASSI

Vivid, please, answer me. I'm sorry.
Let's talk.

CASSI

Tell me what to do? I overreacted.
Who the fuck is he, anyway?

CASSI

Vixen, please, talk to me.

CASSI

I'm fucking sorry, Vivid. Talk to me.

I turn off my phone because I need to stand up for myself before I lose myself in his arms.

After I pay for the cab, I trudge toward my house. Father's voice catches me before I reach the front entrance. It thunders with an intensity that stops me in my tracks.

Actually, as I strain to comprehend the meaning, I realize it's not the intensity, it's the tone.

It's not his usual self-confident, narcissistic manner. There is something broken in his shouting.

"We're ruined. Ruined." It's the first thing I hear clearly when I finally open the door.

"Darling, please, calm down." My mother's voice joins in from the dining room.

"I need this alliance, stupid woman!" My father's voice breaks.

I step into the double door opening, sensing

Martha's presence in the background on the other side of the foyer by the kitchen's entrance. I glance at her. Her hands are clasped over her chest.

She gives me a sad smile, shaking her head. I'm not even sure what she's trying to communicate to me. Support? Compassion? Dismay? Warning? All of them, perhaps.

I turn to face the situation in the dining room. My father is slouched in a chair and Mother pats his shoulders, probably driving him mad more than comforting him.

"Ah, here you are." He narrows his eyes on me and perks up, as if my presence has given him a jolt of energy. An evil one, I suppose. "Where have you been all weekend?" Father stands up, but Mother pushes him to sit down again. "Leave me alone." He swats her away and stands again, this time squeezing by her, almost tripping her. "I have had enough of this fucking shit." He storms out.

They know I wasn't with Ernie? What's going on here?

Martha makes a cross in front of her. In vain, because no God can save this family. Father grabs his car keys and slams the door to the garage, shaking the house.

Mother sighs and collapses into the chair he vacated, covering her face in her hands. "Oh, chérie, what an embarrassment. I'll never live this down with the ladies at the club."

Okay, now I'm properly confused. The opinion of the club members is the last thing on my mind. "What happened?"

"Ernest broke off the engagement. He got some floozy pregnant, and he's going to do the honorable thing and marry her." She sneers the word "honorable."

So Ernie did take care of everything. A boulder drops from my shoulders, and I finally inhale with some sort of freedom.

Freedom?

Oddly, my mind offers the first clear thought since the paradise of the past weekend went up in flames with the engagement announcement. Not a thought, really, a picture. An image of my sculpture flickers through my head.

Freedom.

"We weren't engaged." I sigh.

"Oh, I wish I didn't call the papers." Mother shakes her head, whimpering.

She did this? "How could you?" At this point I'm not even upset with her. She's been serving me doses of disappointment all my life. I guess I've grown immune to it.

"I wanted to help things out a bit. To push you and Ernest in the right direction. Oh my God, now I have to request a retraction everywhere." With her fingers, she massages her temples.

"Why?"

I'm not even sure what I want to know. Why she betrayed me? Why she jumped ahead and announced something that wasn't true? Why she's failed me all my life? Why I care? Why I still wish she was my Mommy?

"What do you mean why? I'm not going to explain to everyone the engagement is not happening. They can read about it." She stands up. "I have a headache." She leaves me standing there.

Weariness squeezes at my bones as I head to my room. I fall into bed and close my eyes. In the morning, I'll figure out what to do.

* * *

The light is too bright as my mind returns to reality. I don't open my eyes because I don't want to wake up yet. It doesn't matter, anyway. I will still be in a room next to my mother's. My father will still be disappointed in me.

I need to patch things up with Andrea. I groan at the thought. I'm not ready to forgive him. The thought makes me sad. If he feels half as bad as me—

I sit up. What if he started drinking last night?

What if he did something to jeopardize his recovery? The idea squeezes at my heart. He said I keep his demons away, but that's a responsibility I can't take on. Can I?

I'm already taking on so much with the woman who should be my parent.

If he goes off the rails because of our argument, it's on him. And while the rationale might be sound in my head, my heart bleeds with worry.

My mother's moans reverberate through the hallway outside my door. Here we go again. I swing my legs over the edge of my bed. I'm still wearing yesterday's clothes.

I open the door and find my mother standing in the doorway of her bedroom, her forearm dramatically flailed over her eyes.

She peeks at me. "Oh, chérie, you're home. Would you please find Martha and get me some of her tea?"

I move on autopilot like a million times before, but then I stop and turn to the banister overlooking the foyer. "Martha," I yell at the top of my lungs.

My mother gasps behind me. "Ivory, I told you my head hurts."

Martha almost slips as she rushes from the kitchen and looks up, wide-eyed.

"Would you be so kind as to get Mother tea for her

headache? Thank you." I start back for my room, my mother gaping at me.

I'm proud of myself, but it's not as liberating as I thought. It's just sad how dysfunctional my family is.

After I take a shower and realize I slept through most of my classes today, I pack up a few things and decide to go to Julianna's.

I leave a note for Mother with Martha who is coming upstairs with the tray. She looks at me in awe. It's the first thing that's made me smile today.

"Have a nice day, Martha."

* * *

"Are you sure you don't want a cookie?" Agatha has been doting on me since I arrived, because I burst into tears the minute she opened the door.

"Okay, I'll have one," I sob.

Julianna hasn't come home from school yet, so I've been sitting in their cozy kitchen. Lost.

Agatha puts a plate of macadamia nut cookies on the table and sits down. "Is it your parents?"

She doesn't know the full extent of our family drama, but she's gathered enough over the years to get the picture. And she's an intuitive woman, so she might be more clued in than I think.

Exhausted, I tell her the tale of my engagement

fiasco, including my boyfriend's reaction—obviously she has no idea who I'm talking about.

"Your parents have had a lot of issues, and you've always been caught in the crossfire. But you should be proud of yourself, Ivory."

My hand freezes halfway through a bite, and the cookie hangs from my mouth as I frown at her.

She pats my other hand. "You have always shown them love. You've always shown up, trying to be what they wanted you to be because you cared. And that's commendable behavior. One they didn't deserve." She shrugs and makes a disgusted face. "But one that makes you a better person. They could have poisoned you, but look at you. You're a passionate and caring woman."

A sob rips through me and I almost choke on the cookie. Agatha holds me in her arms through my meltdown while I stain her blouse with wet crumbs, tears and snot. When I finally compose myself she hands me another cookie, and I sniffle loudly.

How many more of my breakdowns will this woman witness? It's embarrassing.

"And that boy of yours," she starts, and I chuckle at her calling Andrea a boy. If she only knew.

"He hurt you, but when you decide if you're going to forgive him, recognize where that hurt came from. I'm not condoning his behavior. Sometimes people hurt others for their own personal gain, selfishly. But often they hurt to cope with their own hurt, to numb their own pain."

I pay the cab fare and get out of the car. Dread immediately washes over me. I rushed out of the Biachis' as soon as Julianna came in and told me Andrea didn't come to school today.

In the cab, I finally turned on my phone. The number of missed calls and messages made me want to kick myself. He really tried to reach out and I made him suffer. He deserved it, but as I stand in front of his house, I regret my stubbornness. I'm too late.

A group of people is scattered all over the few steps to his front door, smoking, drinking, kissing, and one couple is... Jesus. I look away and push through, trying not to step on anyone, half expecting police sirens to blare behind me.

The door almost doesn't budge because someone inside is leaning against it. The stench of alcohol, smoke and human sweat hits my stomach as I finally shove in, bumping into people.

There are bodies everywhere—standing in the hall-way, sitting room and the kitchen, draped over almost every piece of furniture, lying on the stairs.

Conversations, laughter, moans and strangely inviting lounge music mingle in the air. I snatch a candle that falls onto the carpet as I enter the living room. Jeez. Everyone is moving in slow motion, weed playing the key role.

My eyes dart around, but I don't see Andrea. Someone wraps their arms around my shoulders and puts a bottle of beer into my hands. "Hey, sweetheart, what's your name?"

I shake off the person and push through to get to the kitchen. A young man is telling some tale, and everyone watches him with reverence. Anarchy, regime, and freedom are a few words that register.

When I don't see Andrea, I drop the bottle at the counter and make my way upstairs, tripping and stumbling as I try to avoid limbs.

Moans are louder here because people are fucking everywhere. My heart hammers and I stop dead, oddly fascinated by women and men bending, lying or kneeling in all possible sexual positions.

I should move, but I can't take my eyes off the hallway orgy. To be honest, a part of me doesn't want to move, because I was ready to find Andrea drunk or high, but this...

An unknown feeling of possessiveness grips me and propels me forward. He isn't in any of the guest bedrooms. I barge into his bedroom at last.

A male silhouette is in shadows against the light coming from the window and I gasp. Oh my God. I catch sight of the woman in the mirror in the corner as he fucks her from behind.

"You like to watch, darling?" The man's question floats through the air, and I exhale in relief. I don't recognize the voice.

I rush to the bathroom, and when I find it empty I shut the door behind me and lean my back against it, trying to catch my breath.

He isn't here, having sex. My relief is short-lived when I realize he *isn't* here. Where the heck is he? I rush up the stairs. These aren't as crowded. Only three people crouching around a tablet, watching something.

I push the handle of the studio, but the door doesn't budge.

"Don't you even try," the guy with the tablet says. "Whatever is in that room, entrance has always been banned. Andrea forgot to lock it once and, man, he lost his shit when someone got in there."

"Do you know where he is?" The urgency in my voice makes them all look up and stare at me.

The tablet guy shrugs. "The last I saw he was going out to the patio with some chick."

I shudder, but a morbid sense of self-suffering kicks in and I make my way down, my heart breaking.

Chapter 28

Andrea

I always thought this would be the tree where they would bury me after I joined the twenty-eight club. I'm thirty-one, so I guess the plan failed. The tree, however, still provides solace.

In the noise of my life.

In the absence of her.

The ground is cold, my ass freezing through my damp jeans. The bark digs into my skin through my T-shirt. I welcome any discomfort or pain that will make my mind stop swirling in self-loathing.

With my eyes closed, I let the sounds coming from my house wash over me. People—my friends?—were thrilled I was throwing one of my famous parties. They are having a great time. I should probably go inside.

I sense someone approaching, light on their feet.

"I told you I'm not interested..." I start, believing

it's the girl who has been trying to get me into the bedroom all night, but the scent of jasmine wipes my mind blank.

"Vivid," I rasp, and before I think I'm reaching for her and wrapping her in my embrace. I hold on to her, worried she might disappear again.

She snakes her arms around my shoulders and matches my fierce hold. Fuck, she's back. She's here.

"You came," I whisper into her hair. I grip her head and angle her, so I can look at her.

"Why aren't you partying?"

I snort. Of course she would lead with a question. "No amount of noise can fill the void left by you."

She sighs and jumps on me, wrapping her legs around my waist. She buries her face into the crook of my neck, and I laugh out of sheer relief. Stumbling, I half fall and half stand against the tree and find her lips.

Kissing this woman is the new mission in my life. Fuck everything else, as long as I get to do this. Her soft moan into my mouth makes me want to drag her to a chapel and marry her right now.

When we come up for air, she lowers her head against mine and we stare at each other, the need for words non-existent.

"I faked my admission tests," I blurt.

"What?" She jerks her head back.

I lower her to the ground and put a finger on her mouth. "Let me finish."

For whatever reason, I need to tell her everything, strip down to the foundation of my monsters. The need to do it is so overwhelming that I pace to gather my thoughts.

"I was so scared I wouldn't make it to the L'ecole des Arts in Paris that I paid someone to prepare my portfolio. I had the money, he had the talent, and... Well, I got admitted, but for the three years there, I felt like a fraud. I've been feeling like one ever since. After my graduation, I couldn't disappear from Paris fast enough. And then my degree—the fake fucking degree —got me my first exhibition, and London, in her twisted charity attempt, bought out everything anonymously."

I stop and find her eyes. Feeling lighter of my burden, I expect to meet disappointment and disapproval, but what I find is... a neutral expression, I think. She must be in shock.

"My entire career has been a fraud. I could never allow anyone close enough because they would find out. But you... I want you as close as possible, so I'm telling you. No one knows."

She wrings her hands in front of her for a moment, or the entire night, and finally she pounces on me for the second time. This time, I catch her without faltering.

"Your career is not a fraud, you stupid man. Okay, you cheated to get into that school, but while you were there, who studied? Who followed through with the assignments, whose work was evaluated to get you the diploma? You're the most talented artist I know, and you need to forgive yourself for the mistake you made when you were eighteen. Accept your gift."

She runs her fingers across my forehead, the touch light and burning. It's not lost on me that this young woman is wise beyond her years, and I have her shitty parents to thank for that, probably.

They might not love her the way she deserves, but they forced her to mature before she had to.

I don't point out she's preaching the acceptance of my talent while she still stubbornly refuses to accept hers. There is a more pressing matter we still need to address.

"Thank you," I croak and kiss her. "I'm sorry, Vivid. I drove you away because I was an asshole."

"You hurt me."

I hold her tighter and speak into her hair. "I fucked up. I'm sorry, vixen. The worst part is, I'm not sure it won't happen again."

"It probably will. The running after me barefoot is getting old." She smirks. "I'll put up with your bullshit for a moment longer. Just like you fight my insecurities."

Fuck. I'm on probation, but I couldn't be happier. "Thank you."

"As long as I don't have to wander through the bodies in your house. I almost died expecting to find you with someone else."

I let her slide down my body, my cock already at half-mast. I cup her face. "There isn't anyone else who can do this to me." I point to the tent in my pants.

She shakes her head, half chuckling, half sighing. "I was worried about you."

"And still you didn't answer my calls."

"You hurt me. I'm glad you're sober, though. But..." She licks her lips and shudders with a sigh.

My world tilts, not yet collapsing, but crumbling slowly. She came to check I'm sober, and now she's going to leave. Fuck. I clench my fists.

"I can't take responsibility for your actions. You're teetering at the edge, and you can fall anytime, but I can't be responsible for that. I don't want to tiptoe around you. You matter to me. You matter to me very much, but—"

I yank her to me, relieved even though her body remains rigid. "Hush, Vivid, I understand. I don't want you to be burdened with my shit, but I can't turn it off on demand. It will take some time. Let me try to do better next time. Lashing out and sabotaging has been my coping mechanism. Please let me do better by you. Let me try."

She lets out a loaded sigh and melts against me. We stand there for a moment before she shivers. "We'll catch pneumonia."

I laugh. "Let's go inside then."

"Yeah, well, there are people fucking everywhere, including your bed." She makes a gagging gesture.

"Fuck. You got a glimpse of my past. Now let's focus on the future." I take her hand. "I'm booking a hotel."

* * *

I look down at her teary eyes and almost explode in her mouth.

It took us almost an hour to get rid of everyone, and then another hour until we finally ended up in a suite at a swanky boutique hotel. It's near the school, ironically.

We were both exhausted to the bone, but we couldn't keep our hands off each other, and then Vivid shocked me when she dropped to her knees.

"Teach me," she said, and fuck, this girl will be the death of me.

She is a vision, utterly beautiful as she tries to take me down her throat.

"Look at you, vixen, getting on your knees and wrapping those luscious lips around me," I hiss as she continues with eagerness. "Touch yourself," I command.

Her eyes widen, and then she drops one hand between her thighs and moans around me.

"Fuck, baby. I'm close. Come on, ride your hand for me while you milk me dry."

And my beautiful vixen does as she is told.

"Good girl, swallow every drop."

A wave crashes over us both at the same time. Vivid swallows, and then collapses to the floor. I follow her, gathering her into an embrace, kissing her. Tasting myself on her is my new favorite food group.

"I'm not marrying Ernie," she says when she comes down.

"Thank God for that. Fuck." I slap her gently. I forgot about the reason for our brief breakup. "Why would you mention him now? Vivid, I swear to God, don't ever talk about another man while you're in bed with me."

She giggles. "We're not in bed," she quips. "Our parents wanted us to get married and we were playing along, pretending to get them off our backs. Ernie is marrying a girl he's been dating. She is pregnant."

I push up onto my elbow and swipe the hair from her face. "What the fuck? The announcement—"

"My dearest mother. She wanted to help move things forward. My parents believed I was with Ernie all weekend. That was the official version because he went to the Caribbean with his girlfriend. My parents thought the invitation to his yacht meant he was going to pop the question."

"And they didn't wait for it to actually happen?"

She shakes her head. Spread on the carpet, her long limbs and dark hair, and really everything about her feels like peace. Like home.

"I would have never thought that even a fuck-up like me is an upgrade compared to them."

She chuckles humorlessly. "Don't pat your own back too much. My father didn't set the bar very high. He completely lost it when he found out, yelling that we are ruined." She rolls her eyes.

Feeling like a failure has been the soundtrack of my life, but failing her in this situation, not being there for her, opens a fresh wound in my chest.

And oddly it empowers me, because in this moment, here and now, I know beyond any doubt that I'd do anything to right things for her. To never disappoint or abandon her.

"I'm sorry about everything. You needed me by your side—"

She puts her finger over my lips. "We'll both do better next time." She kisses me.

I lift her and carry her to the bed, gathering her in my arms.

After she falls asleep, I take my phone to the bathroom.

"What's wrong?" Gio answers.

"Calm down, nothing is wrong. And hello to you too." I snort.

"Hello? It's almost midnight," he growls.

Shit. "Sorry, I didn't realize."

"Give me a moment," he whispers. I hear the door click and then he comes back. "Where are you? Are you okay? Mila told me about the engagement. What's going on?"

I drag my hand down my face, sighing. "Her parents announced it, but it's not true."

"What the fuck? That makes no sense."

"Exactly. Listen, Ivy mentioned a few things here and there, but I wonder if her father is trying to marry her off because of his financial problems."

"That's all sorts of fucked up. How can I help?"

"Can you look into his financials? Cecil Harrington."

"I've heard of him."

"Can you check him out?"

"That's not so simple." Water runs and I hear his gulps.

"Isn't that what you do? Sniff out financial problems so you can swoop in and make money out of them?"

For a moment I think he hung up, but then he says, "Okay, I'll see what I can find out. But, bro, what will you do with that information?"

"I don't know." I really don't. "Pay his debt, I guess."

Gio whistles. "That's crazy."

"If it sets her free."

* * *

"Wake up, sleepyhead, I got us breakfast." I kiss Vivid's forehead. "We need to get to school in an hour."

She pulls the covers over her head, groaning. Sliding my hand underneath, I pinch her nipple and she moans, peeking up at me.

"Good morning," she says sleepily.

I kiss her. "Come eat. I got you a toothbrush as well."

She clasps her hand over her mouth, wide-eyed, and I laugh.

"Bastard." She kicks me and I grab her leg, dragging her out of the bed.

I push her out of the bedroom, slapping her ass. Her hair is in disarray as she saunters naked to sit at the table set with room service. She lifts the cover and laughs. "Did you order everything on the menu?"

"What did you expect? A bag of chips? Besides, you need all your energy, because right after school we're coming back here to test the rest of the surfaces."

She takes a bite of her toast, her eyes twinkling with mischief. "Sex slavery is a criminal offense."

I snort. "So now you're a lawyer?" I sit down and sip on my coffee.

She attacks her eggs and pancakes, stuffing everything into her mouth like she hasn't eaten for days. Shit, she probably hasn't eaten since I threw her out of my place two nights ago.

It's the first time I've seen her not being graceful, and my shoulders heave with suppressed laughter.

"What?"

"Nothing." I grin. That grin will dislocate my jaw, but I can't help it when I watch her.

"Stop staring at me." She throws a strawberry across the table.

I catch it and pop it into my mouth. "I want to meet your parents."

She freezes and narrows her eyes. "No."

"What do you mean, no?" I put my cup down.

"Why do you want to meet them?" She pushes her plate away.

"To stop their matchmaking. They need to meet me, so they're comfortable with our relationship. Besides, you met my family."

She swallows and lowers her eyes. She plays with the toast. For fuck's sake, what is there to think about?

"Vivid, I told you I'm resigning. We're going public. I'm not hiding with you anymore." I try to temper my annoyance.

She drops the toast and slouches in her chair. "I... I..."

"Spill it, vixen. What's the problem?" I tap my fingers on the table. To say I'm not pleased with this conversation would be an understatement.

"It's just happening so fast, and things at home are shitty right now—"

"Things at home have always been shitty, and they won't get resolved. I want to meet your parents. The sooner the better."

"I'll think about it." She takes another bite of her toast, but the hungry enthusiasm is gone.

"No." I stand up, the dishes clanking.

"Why are you pushing it? After you resign, we can be together. You don't need to meet my parents."

"Vivid, for fuck's sake, don't be ridiculous. We're together, and there is no guarantee your parents won't announce another engagement. From everything you told me, that house is toxic. I want to meet them, and then you can stay with me. You're an adult, you don't need their permission."

She huffs and marches to the bedroom. "I'm going to take a shower."

I dash after her. Grabbing her arm, I whip her around. "Not until we finish this conversation."

"I have nothing else to say." She jerks her arm away from me, but loses balance. I catch her, her body crashing into me. She stiffens, but then sighs and relaxes into me. "Okay. But I'm not moving in with you. I'll find a job and somewhere else to live."

Her need for independence pisses me off, but even a bastard like me knows I need to indulge it. Fuck, doing the right thing is exhausting.

"Okay." I kiss her.

"Okay?"

"Yes. I don't like it, but I understand." Our eyes lock, and I may spook her completely, but I can't shut up anymore. I wrap my hand at the back of her neck, the need to own her stronger than ever. "I love you, Vivid."

Her eyes flash wide, and her pulse speeds up under my fingertips. I kiss her roughly and she doesn't necessarily participate, but doesn't recoil either.

"Calm down. I know you don't believe in love. You don't need to say it back," I say against her lips.

Her heartbeat goes haywire as she pants against me.

"Will you let me love you?"

She stares at me as the moment stretches, the silence deafening in my head.

"Will you let me love you, Ivory?"

The burden of my life drops, setting me free when she nods finally.

Chapter 29

Ivory

"Well, hello, nun. What have you done to my girlfriend?" Andrea looks me up and down, smirking.

I'm wearing a conservative gray dress, suitable for a person several decades older. Nothing like he's seen me in before.

I briefly considered getting an outfit from my closet at Julianna's, but I want my parents to be as pleased with me as possible.

So I look like a convent student.

"Stop it. Mother bought me the dress. I want everything to go smoothly."

He snakes his arm around my waist and jerks me to him, nuzzling my neck. His earthy scent carries me back to the first time when he landed on top of me at the gallery and I relax slightly.

We've gotten this far from that moment—we can survive one meal with my parents.

The thought doesn't provide the confidence boost I need though.

"I find the dress sexy as hell. I can't wait for you to wear it when you drop to your knees and wrap that pretty little mouth around my cock." His dark whisper sends my heart into a wild gallop. Now I'll have to sit through dinner with wet underwear.

I whimper. "Please behave."

He laughs, straightens up and kisses my hand. "My lady."

He smirks to mock me with his proper behavior, but I don't get a chance to berate him again because Father clears his throat.

I jump away from Andrea like he's just burned me. The way my face ignites, he might as well have.

My parents are standing at the base of the staircase across the hallway. My stomach constricts when I imagine how much of our exchange they witnessed.

I've been out of my mind since this morning. Julianna had to practically resuscitate me over the phone several times. I don't know why I care about this meeting so much. It doesn't matter if they accept him or not. It won't change anything.

As if sensing my internal breakdown, Andrea

slides his fingers through mine and squeezes. The gesture spreads some peace through me.

He pulls me toward my parents, and I follow like this isn't my house, my hostess duties completely forgotten in the fog of this situation.

My dark manor existence is colliding with my rogue life outside of here, and a sense of premonition crawls up my nape.

"Mrs. Harrington, I can see where Ivory's beauty comes from." Andrea kisses Mother's hand and gives her the flowers he brought.

His words are perfectly suave, the flowers are expensive enough to her liking, the compliment makes her giggle. Okay, maybe I should give Andrea more credit. I might be a mess, but he can handle this for both of us.

"Pleased to meet you, and call me Eden." Mother attempts to smile, but she had her Botox injection yesterday, so it's just a stiff movement of her facial muscles.

"Cecil Harrington." My father extends his hand. "You can call me Mr. Harrington." He gives Mother a vicious glance to remind her how her friendliness toward our guest displeases him.

Andrea flashes him a cocky smile. "Mr. Harrington, nice to meet you."

We move to the dining room. Father takes his seat at the head of the table, Mother is beside him, and our seats are set across from her.

Andrea moves the second chair for me, planning to sit beside my father, but I rush around and take that seat. Andrea snorts at my childish attempt to protect him. We all sit down, and Martha comes in with the appetizers, serving us in complete silence.

How different from the Cassinettis' home where I was seated across from Andrea, and I felt safer than here in my own house.

Under the table, he puts his hand on my thigh and I relax slightly. Mother is looking like a doll on a cake, melting with a slightly deformed expression.

Father stares into his plate and I berate myself for freaking out all day instead of preparing conversation topics.

"So, you're my daughter's professor." Father spears a shrimp with his fork.

"I resigned my position at the Institute, and technically, while I still taught there, Ivory was never in my classes." His answer is level, but I can see his jaw ticking. He squeezes my thigh.

Talking about me as Ivory feels so foreign, but welcome at the same time. It's like he is infiltrating my family life and I finally have an ally here.

"Ivory went to that school for a year only." Mother takes a sip of water.

"Silly idea, studying art," Father says.

I put my hand over Andrea's, hoping to stop him from responding. I fail.

"I respectfully disagree. Ivory is very talented. It'd be great if she pursued a more artistic curriculum than the theoretical one." There is nothing respectful in his tone.

My father snorts and I squeeze Andrea's hand again, pleading with my eyes. His nostrils flare, but he follows my lead.

"Ivory was accepted to several prestigious universities and she'll major from economics at Columbia. We consider the Institute as something she needs to get out of her system," Father says.

"I enjoy my studies." My voice comes out almost inaudible.

I thought I could speak up for myself, stand up for myself, but here in this house I lose my voice, no matter what strength I find outside.

Here, I've always been the girl who desperately seeks her parents' approval. The behavior is unhealthy, but too ingrained.

Andrea removes his hand, leaving me desperate and a bit wild with frustration. He taps his quad with his fingers now. He's so wound up, I think even I might explode. The loss of his touch hits me hard.

How are we going to survive this stupid dinner?

I don't care anymore how it ends, as long as it's over. I'm just going to sit here, and Andrea can handle himself. After all, he was the one insisting on this lovely introduction.

"When Ivory returns to Columbia, she'll meet the right people. Set herself up for a successful, comfortable life." Mother puts her cutlery down.

"You mean find herself a well-off husband?" Andrea mirrors her move, leaving his shrimp salad untouched.

"And what is it you have to offer her?" my father challenges.

"You mean besides loving her, supporting her in all her dreams, believing in her, taking care of her and standing by her, so she can grow in whatever way she needs and wants?"

His words should make me feel better. They should make me feel heard and understood, but my mind stubbornly hangs on to the fact that he got me into this utterly uncomfortable situation.

I can cope with my parents fine by myself. But sitting under their attack when someone else is caught in the crossfire—someone I care about—that's something I'm not equipped to stomach.

Especially since he's an equal instigator. Well-meant. Much better intended than my parents, but still pouring oil onto this fire that he ignited.

Mother clasps her chest and Father huffs. "Some romantic notions of an artist are not what we expect for our daughter. What we brought her up to achieve."

"I don't care about your aspirations for her." Andrea throws the linen napkin on the table.

Now my mother gasps. I slouch into my chair, hating all three of them for talking about me as if they had the license to know better. As if I wasn't here.

"Andrea, please, you need to understand we want only the best for our daughter." Mother puts her hand on my father's, and he doesn't recoil.

Look at that, they found their common ground. Dictating my future.

"Ivory was brought up to expect a certain standard of life," Mother continues.

Andrea laughs. "I'm not claiming my net worth is comparable to the Cornfields, though it probably is, but money doesn't matter much to me."

Mother chokes and Father scoffs.

I want to disappear. Run upstairs, let them have their pissing contest and hide. Like forever.

I'm exhausted. Disappointed. Deflated.

There is no chance they would ever accept him. I'd remain between two spots forever.

Andrea continues, "But my finances are certainly in much, much better shape than yours."

Mother makes another strangled sound. I look wide-eyed at Andrea.

"How dare you!" My father stands up, his chair flying back.

Martha enters with a soup bowl and stops in her tracks.

"Leave," Father demands.

I'm not sure if he's addressing Andrea or our house-keeper, but Martha turns to leave. Then she halts, pivots back and drops the dish on the table.

The broth sloshes to the tablecloth.

The linen absorbs the greasy stain, quickly spreading through the white threads.

I focus on that, tuning out the shouting match.

"All I'm saying is, I can and intend to provide for your daughter better than a man who mortgaged his house three times over already." Andrea is standing now as well.

And I join him. "Stop haggling over me like I'm a piece of meat." I look up as if I haven't learned yet that no help comes from there.

The oxygen feels like a rare commodity as I take a breath. Blinking away tears—I don't even know what they are for—I turn to my father. "Is it true, Papa?"

"Who is he to poke into our affairs? That's unheard of." Father's face is red, large veins marring his forehead. Mother jumps up and tries to calm him.

"Is it true?" I search for the answer with Andrea.

He nods.

"Is that the reason for your urgency to marry me off?" I look at my mother. "Why didn't you say something, I could have helped. Use Granny's trust."

My father laughs bitterly. "It's all gone. Why do you think I allowed you to drop your studies, you stupid girl?"

"Don't fucking talk to her like that." Andrea launches at my father but stops himself. Vibrating with energy, he growls, raking his hair.

"Don't *you* talk to me like that in my own—" Father gasps and stumbles, clutching his chest.

"Cecil," Mother screams.

"Papa?" We both rush to his side.

"I can't breathe." He jerks his tie. I loosen it for him and try to unbutton his shirt, but the stupid button slips from my fingers.

"Cecil, Cecil, what's going on?" Mother squeals as my father collapses.

I close my eyes, leaning against the cold wall behind the plastic chair in the waiting room. Andrea has been holding my hand for hours now, but I wish he wouldn't.

Through that touch I sense his worry, his anxiety, his frustration, his regret, and it messes with the roller coaster of my own emotions. I need to process, grieve, worry, focus on myself.

His presence right now confuses me. But I hold his hand for dear life. Because it also gives me a sense of belonging, safety. It empowers me.

The worst part about the dreadful situation is that I can't fully lean into my anguish because I'm worried Andrea would fall off the wagon.

It's exhausting. I'm exhausted. I hate the stupid woolen dress that scratches me everywhere. I hate Mother's silent sobs in the corner. I worry that we might be homeless.

I'm concerned about my father. He's been in surgery for two hours now. He might not deserve my worry, but he doesn't deserve to die either.

I should have never agreed to the stupid dinner.

My two worlds clashed, and now we all face consequences more severe than I could have ever imagined.

"Can I get you anything?"

These are the first words Andrea has said to me

since dinner. He's been providing silent support, but mostly been the worst distraction.

I need to sleep and think and breathe. But none of it is possible under the circumstances. Or with his looming presence.

I shake my head.

The swinging door opens and a surgeon marches out, making eye contact with Mother. We all jump up and hang on to his expression.

"He's out of the surgery, and stable."

Several sobs slice through the air and I realize one of them is mine. How strange life is. The man who never showed me love still resides in my heart.

The doctor's words wash over me, not making much sense. Coronary. Bypass. Recovery. ICU.

"Thank you. Can we see him?" Mother asks.

"Only the immediate family. For a few minutes." The surgeon nods and points to the door behind him.

Mother rushes forward.

"I'll be right there," I call after her, and she nods at me over her shoulder.

I don't look at Andrea, I don't move. I stare at the small blue hair line pattern of the linoleum.

It's like standing at a fork in the road. Both destinations carry importance, but both seem like an uphill battle, an exhausting, thorny path.

When his presence becomes too unbearable, I turn to Andrea. "You should go."

"I'm not leaving you here." He shakes his head and takes my hand, but I recoil.

He flinches and it breaks my heart, but I need to think about myself. For once in my life, I need to make my own mistakes.

"Andrea, don't make this harder for me." I sniffle. "I appreciate everything you've done for me. You helped me find myself."

He frowns. "What are you saying?"

"That you should go." I swallow around the lump in my throat.

"Vivid—" The hurt in his eyes sears me like the sharpest blade.

"I told you I can't take the responsibility. I wanted to. I tried. But my family needs me right now, and the only thing I'm thinking about is that if I stay with them, you won't paint and you might reach for your usual vices."

"Vivid—" he warns. "You're choosing them?" The disbelief in his voice robs me of oxygen. "Vixen, don't. I love you. I need you." A shadow passes through his face, like he realizes that was the wrong choice of words right now.

"Exactly. But what about what I need? I... I'm twenty-one. I can't be there for so many people." I flail my arm in the direction where my mother and father are. "They are shitty parents, but they are the only ones I have."

He studies me with an expression that breaks my heart, and then his eyes darken. He sets his jaw and nods.

I watch him leave without a word. And with him leaves a piece of me I didn't know he already owned.

Chapter 30

Ivory

I thought one dies when their heart breaks. No such luck. I'm very much alive. Existing. From one day to another.

It's been two months since my father's heart attack. Two months of absolute agony.

I sit up in bed and scratch my head. My hair could do with a good wash and a treatment, but I can do that tomorrow or the day after. It doesn't matter. The days blend into a colorless blur anyway.

I brush my teeth, tame my mane into some sort of bun and give up on the loose strands sticking around.

I head downstairs and hope to leave unnoticed. Mother coos in the dining room, and Father is complaining about her fussing around him.

This is one of the strange outcomes his heart attack

caused—my parents, amidst a life-and-death experience, somehow found their way to each other.

Or Father is still too tired to chase business and other women. I don't know, but seeing Mother this happy is slightly nauseating. Could be I'm just jealous.

I glance at the breakfast table and catch him smiling at her like they were meant for each other.

"Chérie, come and have breakfast with us." Mother pushes out a chair for me.

"I'm not hungry." I pour myself a cup of coffee, but no amount of java has helped me to feel less tired.

"You should eat something. You're getting awfully skinny. Men don't like that." She spreads butter on toast and puts it on my father's plate like he's a real invalid.

Her lack of compassion for my broken heart makes me want to flip her off.

"I need to go to school."

I still have time, but talking to them is exhausting. Any conversation is exhausting when your heart bleeds.

"About that," Father starts, "you should look at other options. You're a smart girl. A business major would suit you."

A few months ago, I'd have latched onto the smart girl compliment and tried to please him more. Today I see his compliment for what it is, a honey trap to get me to do what he thinks is right.

"I'll continue my art degree, Papa." My gaze doesn't waver. Neither does his. His jaw is rigid, and I can almost see the argument playing out in his head, but in the end he just nods and returns to his toast.

While they still try to control my life and my choices, they know they've lost all power. As of six weeks ago, this house belongs to me.

Cassinetti Holding, which I researched and found out to be Gio's company, bought my father's company with all its debts. The contract had a condition. The title to the family house—now mortgage-free thanks to the holding company—had to be transferred to me.

Andrea gifted me the house and took care of my parents' financial problems. It makes his absence from my life so much worse.

"Are you sure you don't want to take something with you, chérie?" Mother chirps.

"I'm good. See you tonight." I turn and almost collide with Martha.

"I guess he ran out of flowers." Martha shrugs and pushes a potted cactus at me.

I have been receiving a bouquet every day for weeks now. Every day a new color, a different type of flower. Some of them so exotic I don't know where the heck they came from. Though I know who they came from.

I grab the pot, and a smile spreads across my face.

"The most beautiful, expensive arrangements delivered every day, and the girl smiles at a cactus," Martha mutters and shuffles away.

Did he finally remember my *favorite* plant, or is today somehow special? It's a small plant, and there are no messages. I lift it, but the bottom of the pot is just plain. Oh, the time I spent searching the vases for some sort of message.

Deflated, but still more excited than I've been in weeks, I place the cactus on a console table by the entrance and go outside.

"Good morning, Ivy." Oliver opens the car door with a smile.

"Morning."

I raise my eyebrows like every morning. I don't need to ask the question anymore. It's been the same for weeks. Has he seen his employer? He shakes his head, and I sigh, blinking away my tears.

Oliver waited for me several days after Father's collapse. He was also hired by Cassinetti Holding, but everything has been done over the phone through some concierge service.

I slide into the back seat where a small bag waits with my lunch.

I've been showered with luxuries, gifts and basic needs—my meals and the roof over my head—for almost two months.

Two months of longing.

Two months of sadness.

Two months of emptiness.

The benefactor of my current lifestyle has disappeared from the face of the earth. His phone is disconnected, he's gone from school.

I went to his house several times, but by the mounting fliers in his mailbox, he hasn't been there.

Why did I send him away? Where is he? I considered visiting Bianca Cassinetti, but I haven't mustered the courage yet.

If her son ended up drunk somewhere after I pushed him away, I wouldn't be able to look her in the eyes.

I wrote him a letter, explaining how my choosing my parents was born from that dreadful moment of seeing my father's eyes drifting away.

I told him how I hope he understands I wasn't only choosing them, I was choosing him as well. Giving him the opportunity to find himself. To stand on his own two legs.

I doubt he read the letter, given the overflowing mailbox at his house.

It hurts so much. I don't want him to stand on his

own two legs. I want to be there for him. It seems like the only way I can breathe is when he is around.

But where the heck is he? Every morning when the flowers arrive, when I greet Oliver and find my lunch bag in the car, hope blooms inside my chest.

Every evening when I stare at the ceiling, I wonder if he set all of it in motion to take care of me, but has no intention of returning to my life.

Isn't that what I asked of him? To leave? I only have myself to blame.

"We're here, Ivy." Oliver gets out and opens the door for me.

"Thank you. I'm going to study at a coffee shop with Julianna after school. I'll call you when we're done."

"Are you sure you don't want me to drive you?"

"No, it's just around the corner from here. I'll see you later."

The idea of setting foot in the cafe where he pulled me to the bathroom to help me with my self-image has my heart hammering. What if he's there... Stupid hope.

* * *

"I ran into Tim yesterday." Julianna tackles me from behind and shuffles us behind a pillar in the outer path of the courtyard.

My jacket is in the classroom, and I shiver. "Julianna, I'm freezing. Let's go to class."

"I have to go to the annex. He was all sheepish about his disappearance." Her eyes are so wide that her eyebrows might reach their hairline.

"He hardly disappeared. He decided to study elsewhere." I shake my head.

Though Tim's switching schools in the middle of the school year shortly after my father's accident shocked us, I forgot about him pretty quickly. It's not like my mind can keep hold of any information.

"Well, he didn't want to tell me much, but he hinted it wasn't *his* choice."

I rub my arms. "I'm freezing. And frankly, I don't care why he left. It has nothing to do with me."

"Doesn't it?" She narrows her eyes.

I sigh.

"Ivy, the flowers, your lunches, the driver..." She counts on her fingers.

Julianna doesn't know about the debts and the house. That's so weird and weirdly generous I'm afraid to say it out loud, even to my best friend, because it would force me to think about it. Decide if I'm willing to accept it. Not that I have much choice in the matter.

She continues, "After what Tim did to you, maybe Cassi made him leave. To keep you safe."

"Don't be ridiculous. I have to go. See you after class." I rush away, my heart pounding.

Could she be right? Could removing Tim from my life be Andrea's doing? I'm not sure if I'm pleased or disturbed by it.

What's his game? Whatever it is, I don't want to play it. If he wants to stay away, he should just stay away. Oh God, please no.

I hear nothing Professor Fox says during class, my mind on overdrive.

School has been the only place where I could, for a few moments here and there, focus on something other than the man missing from my life. Missing, but still very present.

I've been sculpting, experimenting with materials and techniques until my fingers practically bleed. Only then does my pain find purchase, a release, an escape.

Today, however, Fox could talk about the garbage removal schedule and I wouldn't notice.

Why did he send the cactus today? Why do I hang on to that gesture with such hope?

"Ivory." Fox stops me after she dismisses the class.

"Yes?" I look at my exiting classmates as if they might save me. Not that I'm in trouble, am I?

"Is all your work ready for evaluation?"

What? I frown.

"Your sculptures? The faculty accepted your application to switch majors, but it's conditional on the evaluation of your portfolio."

I blink a few times, her words registering in slow motion. "My application?"

She smiles. "You have nothing to worry about. Most of us saw your *secret* artwork in the annex, but you need to officially present it. Is it all ready, or do you need more time?"

"I'm switching majors?" My incredulity doesn't affect her at all.

"Well, yes, congratulations. My colleagues and I are very impressed with what you've been sculpting. You're very talented. Let's make it official. Let's say tomorrow morning at eight?"

I nod and keep nodding, as if the slight shake of my head could rearrange all the information and make sense out of it. It doesn't, but since I'm speechless, I can't even investigate more.

"Good then. I'll let my colleagues know that your presentation is in the morning." She pats my shoulder and leaves me there, crumbling into pieces.

In the doorway, she turns and smiles. "It's good Professor Cassinetti noticed what you've been doing. Keep up the great work."

Tears roll down my cheeks as I stand there, rooted to the ground.

"Where have you been?" Julianna pokes her head

through the doorway. "What the hell happened, Ivy?" She rushes in and hugs me.

"I got accepted to the fine arts program." I sob, and with all the tears I've uttered in the past weeks, these might be my only tears of joy. Tentatively. My heart still bleeds.

"Bitch, that's awesome. You didn't tell me you applied." She fake-glares at me.

"I didn't." Another sob pushes through the tears and a smile.

"Well then, how?"

"Andrea—" I breathe his name and my chest squeezes. I haven't said his name out loud for two months.

"Cassi did it? That's awesome. I'd like to have a boyfriend who solves all my problems and rearranges the world to make my life easier." She sighs.

"Only he's not my boyfriend." I grab my backpack. "Let's go." We leave the classroom. "He sent me a cactus today."

"That's the least romantic gesture, if you ask me." Julianna slides her arm through mine and squeezes.

"It has meaning for the two of us, but I still don't know what the message is." I stop, exhausted from the ordeal. "Julianna, what if this is it? He made sure I study what I secretly wanted, that I pursue my talent. He took care of everything for me. All the shadows of my past have been addressed, so now he can leave me to live my life. Without him. Because I asked him to."

My friend's face loses its typical carefree expression. Even the eternally joyous Julianna understands what I've lost.

* * *

"Ivory, I think I speak for all my colleagues when I say you impressed us." Fox looks around the room, and three other faculty members nod. "We look forward to helping you develop your talent starting next year. There are some credits you need to catch up on before the end of the school year, so please sort that out with the admissions office. Congratulations." She shakes my hand.

They all follow, praising my talent and dedication, congratulating me.

Finally I'm left alone, and I take a moment to admire all my sculptures. I can't help but smile. I've come a long way. I wish I could thank the one person who encouraged it all. Who inspired most of it.

When I look up, a gasp rips through me. My heart hammers against my ribcage, all oxygen disappears, and tears threaten again.

But my focus is completely consumed by him, casually leaning in the doorway.

Andrea pushes off and saunters forward, his gaze glued to me. God, I forgot how magnetic his presence is.

It feels like a lifetime has passed since I saw him at the hospital, and at the same time not a minute has existed between then and now.

"Vivid," he rasps, and I start shaking.

The relief, joy, anger and resentment swirl through me. "Where have you been?" I snap, gasp, accuse and welcome. All at the same time.

He smirks. The bastard smirks. "I missed your questions."

He says it with such a reverence that I gasp again. My body quivers with recognition. His voice. His eyes. His long fingers wrapped around a small pot.

He follows my hand and gives me the cactus. "For you."

"I already got one." This conversation is moving in a weird direction.

"Since they are your favorite," he quips, "I thought I might do a repeat. Also, I'm fucking running out of the world's flower supply."

I snort, shaking my head. He puts the cactus on the table and takes one more step. His scent strips me of my defenses. Every fiber in me is drawn to him, but I refuse to take the last step.

He rakes his hooded gaze down my body, devouring me with his eyes. God help me.

"You think it takes only a few flowers to get into my pants?" I raise my chin, hoping he won't see that it would take way less. Also, I'm terrified to address the real issues in the room, so I'd rather dance around it.

"Thousands of flowers, a house, a completely bankrupt business, a car and a driver..." He takes another step. "Worth every penny."

"Stop," I cry, not sure if I mean his words or his steps. "You didn't get me the one thing I wanted the most."

He frowns, tilting his head.

"You," I whisper, and step back.

Andrea sighs and closes his eyes for a moment. When he looks back at me, the intensity of his gaze hits me, shaking me to the core.

This man owns me. My soul, my heart, my body.

We stare at each other silently, searching for words that could build a bridge for us to continue, or start anew. Or at least move from out of this self-inflicted purgatory.

He looks so much better than I remember. The haunted look is gone from his face, not completely, but he looks much healthier.

While I was withering, he was clearly thriving.

Suddenly, my two months of suffering bubbles to the surface.

"So where did you go? You just disappeared? I didn't know where you were. If you were still alive. I was worried. I wanted to talk to you. I needed to talk to you. I lost my soul mate, my lover, my friend. I went to your house. I kept calling. Where did you go? Did you have fun?"

I spit the words with contempt, but it doesn't match what I feel. Nor does it make me feel better.

He looks at me unimpressed. "Don't be a brat, Vivid."

I chuckle humorlessly. "Bastard."

"You asked me to leave." He delivers the accusation, and I turn because I can't face him. I wipe away the stupid tears.

"Don't you dare turn your back on me. I did what you asked. I did it because I understood you needed space. I gave you time, and God help me I wanted to give you more." He sighs. "Look at me."

My shoulders shake with suppressed sobs.

"Look at me, Vivid," he growls, and I turn halfway, because what little maturity I possess stayed at home today.

He launches at me and grabs my shoulders, forcing me to face him.

"Do you think I wanted to stay away? I stayed

away because I wanted to find myself. To give you a better, stronger version of me."

My breath hitches and I sag in his hold, unable to command my legs anymore.

"Remember how here, in this same room, I told you I believe in your talent, your passion, your spirit? How I want to see you fly? I meant every word, and that's why I stayed away. You told me how your father is the only source of happiness for your mother. I couldn't have you accepting the same burden."

My vision blurs and I whimper, his words feeding my insecurities, mending my wounds and soothing the hurt. Not yet rejoicing, but feeling slightly hopeful.

"I stayed away, got my shit together, spent my days in therapy and in my studio, forcing myself to paint without you around. All the while the thought of you has never left my mind.

"I stayed away to prove to you that I won't make your life more difficult. I live and breathe to make it easier for you. But at the end of the day, Vivid, I failed. I fucking failed."

I shake my head because I fear the next words. I don't want to talk anymore. I don't care about the explanation. I just want all of this to pass.

"I failed because *you are* the source of my happiness. Perhaps not the only source, but certainly the most important one. Because I can live without all my vices, without my art, but I can't live without you. I know you deserve better than this broken, fucked-up man, but you're it for me, Vivid. And you can send me away all you want, but I'm fucking staying. I asked you to let me love you. Well, tough shit, I'm not asking anymore. You will let me love you."

I pounce. Wrapping my arms and legs around him, I plaster my mouth all over him, kissing him while crying and hitting him with one fist at the same time.

"Fuck, I missed you." He stumbles blindly until my back hits the wall.

We channel everything into the kiss. The vengeance, the pain, the longing, the frustration, the weeks of separation, the lost memories and the found closeness.

"Fuck, Vivid, I need you."

"I'm playing hooky today. Take me home."

Chapter 31

Andrea

"See you next week, man," Matt, my sponsor, shakes my hand and walks away. I sit in the coffee shop for another half an hour before Vivid's classes are over.

The last two weeks have been... well, spent mostly in bed. And on other surfaces of my house because we couldn't get enough of each other. After months of pining after her, I couldn't hold back.

I don't deserve her, but she still wants me. That hope kept me going in those longest months when I stayed away from her. It was for the best. For her and for me, but it was fucking hard.

That's when Matt came into my life and has been, quite frankly, the solid support I needed. Instead of trying to fight my own battles, I leaned into the support system my therapist has been advocating all along.

I tap my fingers on the table in front of me, running the itinerary through my head. I'm surprising Vivid with our first official date.

I considered flying her to Europe, but she has classes, so we need to stay more local. I scratched all my big ideas, because at the end of the day it came down to two things: I want to spend time with her, and I want everyone to see that she is mine.

I'm not even kidding. If she wouldn't freak out, I'd have bought a billboard on Times Square to advertise my claim on her. Perhaps I still will.

I check my watch and make my way out of the coffee shop. Walking toward the school, I can't wipe the stupid smile off my face.

She comes out chatting with Julianna Biachi. When she notices me, she frowns and smiles at the same time and walks to me gingerly.

"What are you doing here?" She looks back.

"Waiting for my girlfriend." I pull her to me and capture her lips. She gasps and her friend cheers from across the street. I flip her off and she laughs.

Vivid, on the other hand, is frozen. "What's going on?" I look at her.

She's stunning. No make-up. No frills. Just the wild curls, the mesmerizing eyes, and those swollen caramel lips.

"Everyone saw us."

I step back. "Are you ashamed of me?" I mock my offense.

She laughs and wraps her arms around my neck. "So, we're like official now?"

I kiss her forehead. "We've been official for a while. Now we're public, vixen."

She hums and takes my hand, leaning into me. "I like that."

I walk, enjoying her body close to mine. "The car is around the corner."

"Where are we going?" She squeezes my hand.

Holding hands. Have I ever done that? The contact is so natural, I don't want to ever walk without it.

"Shopping." I kiss her temple, ushering her down the street.

"Shopping? What do you need?"

"I have everything I need right here." I bring her knuckles to my lips. "We're getting you a new wardrobe."

"What?" She stops.

"Move. We have a dinner reservation, and a private tour of MoMa after they close. No time to shuffle around." I grin and keep dragging her behind me.

Oliver greets us and we get inside the car, all the while Vivid glaring at me. I pull her into my lap. "Unleash the questions, woman."

"Why do I need a new wardrobe?" She fidgets and

my cock stirs. Fuck. We might end up going back home.

"Stop fidgeting, because I'll have to walk with a boner all afternoon and people will think you don't know how to take care of me." I kiss her roughly and she glances toward Oliver, wide-eyed.

I laugh. "Oliver, can you hear us?"

Oliver rolls his eyes. "Of course not, Mr. Cassinetti."

"See." I shrug. "I want you to have your clothes at my place. You said you have some at Julianna's. Given I'm higher on your friends list, I demand you have clothes at my place as well."

"You demand? That might just knock you down a few points on that friends list." She glowers at me, but a smile is ghosting her face. "What about the MoMa?"

"I booked us for a private tour, but we'll have dinner first. At a Michelin-starred restaurant." It's handy to have a brother who is a famous chef.

"Why are we doing all of this crazy stuff?"

"To get you dressed, fed, culturally satisfied and..." I get closer and whisper in her ear, "and thoroughly fucked at the end."

She glances at Oliver again, who to his credit doesn't move a muscle on his face. I run my hand under Vivid's skirt, and on second thoughts, we should get a different car.

"I meant why have you planned all of this? We have never been—"

"On a date." I finish the sentence, and the smile that spreads on her face is like a shot directly into my vein. The best fucking high.

"It's our first date." She beams. It doesn't matter what I planned, what we do, how much it costs or where it happens.

As long as we're together, I'm invincible.

* * *

I had a few boutiques closed for us and the stubborn woman keeps haggling with me to buy less for her.

"I really don't need so much. I don't want you to buy all these things for me."

"Jesus, woman, shut up, I'm buying them for myself."

"Well, you already bought my house and my father's company—"

I shut her up, seizing her lips. "I can assure you that Gio is turning the company around at a profit. Let me buy you shit. It makes me happy, and if you continue fussing, Vivid, I swear to God I will bend you over my knee right here and you won't be able to sit for a week."

Oh, that eyes-wide-open gaping expression is my

new favorite source of entertainment. She huffs and stomps her foot. With her arms folded across her chest, she glowers while they run my card.

At Cassa Cassi, my brother prepares us a three-course meal that is almost as decadent and delicious as my company. Vivid starts to relax, and I love how she gets more and more animated as our conversation flows smoothly through the evening.

"So, how do you feel about your new exhibition?" She takes a bite from her chocolate dessert, licking the spoon. Little vixen. She doesn't even know what she does to me.

"For now, indifferent. I've been preoccupied with more fulfilling endeavors." I find her hand on the table.

"I'm an endeavor?" She chuckles.

"Why would you think I'm talking about you?" I tease.

"Oh, it's all the other women. Sorry I assumed."

"Assume away, vixen, but there will never be another woman. You're it. And you're mine. So there won't be any other man for you," I say darkly.

"Don't threaten me." She licks the spoon again, playing with me.

"I would never. But the threat remains for any man who touches you." I'm not even half-kidding.

Her eyes widen and sparkle at the same time. She swallows, licks her lips, and takes another bite.

"So what about your exhibition?"

"What about it?" I stroke her hand with my fingers.

"You showed me the pieces and they are fabulous, so what's next?"

"Are you ready to put your sculptures out there?" I lean into my chair, perfectly content to watch her. Even though right now she's squirming and frowning.

"What does that have to do with anything? I'm a student. I'm not having a show. You are."

"I was hoping you'd join me."

She drops her spoon, glaring. "Stop it. I'm not ready."

I shrug. "Whatever you say."

She looks down, and for a moment I fear I spoiled the pleasant atmosphere.

"Vivid, I'm not ready either. And there is no rush. I don't want to be a slave to my work. It needs to bring me joy. Besides, my current endeavor is taking up all my energy."

"You're horrible."

"You're incredible."

Watching her at MoMa, my love and pride swell. As an art history student, she's eager to ask and discuss things with our guide. I'm staying behind, just soaking in her passion.

I've done a lot of shit in my life, but kissing my brother's fiancée and earning myself a well-deserved punch might have been the best fuck-up of them all. It landed me on top of the girl who stole my heart and scared away my monsters.

Though I guess if I didn't take that teaching job I wouldn't have run into her again, and God knows where I would be now. Sometimes a shitty decision can lead to the best outcome.

"This was wonderful. Thank you." She beams as we say goodbye.

The air is infused with spring and peace. That's how I've been feeling. New beginnings that bring only peace.

I wrap my arms around her and kiss her deeply. "You're beautiful," I whisper, and she shivers.

"Those were the first words you ever said to me." She smiles against my lips.

"Never have I spoken a deeper truth. Well, until I said I love you." I play with the hair that is framing her face. I could touch her for the rest of my days and not tire of it.

She steps back and studies me. "I have to tell you something." She wrings her hands in front of her.

Fuck. "You're scaring me."

She smiles, looking at me through her lashes. She bites her lip and exhales a long puff of air.

My heart thumps in my temple. What has her so worked up after what I felt was a great evening?

"I was wrong." She raises her chin, owning the statement while I have no idea what she's saying.

"About?" I give her a lopsided smile.

"About love. What my parents have isn't love. Love isn't a sacrifice. It's the simple joys to share with another person. When the two come in equally, it's the most wonderful feeling in life. Fulfilling. Satisfying. Comforting and inspiring."

Her words spread through me like a drug. Have I really showed her a different love than the one she grew up with? Me? With no prior experience, I fell for this girl, and perhaps she can reciprocate one day.

I open my mouth, but she stops me with her outstretched arm.

She wets her lips. "Andrea, you're in this wholly, unconditionally. And I don't want to let you love me." She frowns and shakes her head. "What I mean to say is that I want to love you back. I mean, I do. I love you."

I yank her to me, her body bouncing off my solid frame, and I hold her so tight I doubt she can take a breath, but I can't help it. When the avalanche of emotions passes through and I can finally breathe, I pull away and smile at her.

"Say it again."

She giggles. "I love you."

My face might never find its way back into decent composure as I grin at her. "Again."

Amidst all the luxuries tonight, her laugh is the most decadent thing. "I love you, Andrea Cassinetti."

I seize her lips, my heart swelling. "Again."

She pushes me away, swatting at me with a laugh. "Stop being so demanding." She turns and runs from me, hopping down the steps in front of the museum.

I chase after her, but she stops in the middle of the staircase, spreads her arms and yells at the top of her lungs, "I love Andrea Cassinetti."

Epilogue

Ivory

A jolt of pleasure rakes through my body, jerking me out of my sleep. Heavy hands pin my hips to the mattress. My mind lingers between the fog of slumber and something else. Lust. Joy. Arousal.

Andrea's talented tongue between my thighs has become my daily wake-up call. I arch my back, moaning. I don't even open my eyes, just let the ripples of sensation destroy my body in the best possible way.

I come, crying out his name, and he drags himself up my body, resting on his elbows beside my head. His face glistens after I came all over it, and he wears that cocky grin that makes me giggle.

"Good morning, Vivid." He kisses me deeply, letting me taste myself, and my legs wrap around his waist of their own accord. "How is my favorite sex slave this morning?" He wiggles his hips, his cock pressing against my soaked folds.

I frown. "Your favorite? Do you have others?"

His eyes darken. "Would you be jealous?"

I raise my eyebrows, probably failing to look stern or offended or whatever because I'm just wonderfully blissed out. "I would cut your balls off."

The bastard laughs. "That would be your loss, vixen."

"It looks like before you feasted on me you had some breakfast already." I kick him lightly with my heel.

He cocks his head.

"Well, it wasn't humble pie." I bite my lip, trying to stifle my laugh. "More like an ego-boosting yogurt? Narcissistic toast. Cocky cookie. Overconfident—"

He eats my words with his mouth, kissing me like it's the first time all over again. With the passion and dedication he gives freely to everything he loves.

This is what I've been waking up to for months now—to being cherished, devoured, taken care of in more ways than I thought possible.

All I need to do is accept. Allow. Take. And Andrea gives generously.

I moved in with him last month. His sister Sydney gave me a part-time job, supervising art classes for children with learning challenges at her center. It's a modest income for the few hours I can pick up helping there, but it gives me a bit of independence.

I received a scholarship to cover the tuition and study materials at the Institute, which I'm pretty sure was influenced by Andrea.

There is a part of me that rebels against this dependency—questioning if going from my father to my lover is the smartest thing in my life. But the way Andrea makes me feel—needy, but also needed—settles that battle every time.

He looks down between us and tuts. "You made a big mess, Vivid. We need to get you nice and clean. Shower, now."

"I made a mess? If you kept to your side of the bed—"

"Careful how you finish that sentence." He rolls off me and pushes me gently off the bed, following me.

On the way to the bathroom, he stops me in front of a large mirror that he had installed across from our bed. Not only because the man loves watching us fuck, but because spending a few moments here every morning has become a ritual.

He stands behind me, holding my shoulders, and I look at myself, feeling his hungry gaze roaming my body in the reflection.

"Number one," he whispers into my ear.

I swallow, grazing my body and fighting the urge to close my eyes. "I love my shoulders."

He nips me gently there, while his eyes remain glued to me. The reverence I see in them gives me confidence.

"Two." He nuzzles his head at my nape, inhaling deeply.

"My eyes?" It comes out as a squeal. Some mornings are easier than others. Sometimes I fake it for him, and sometimes I truly find things to love about myself.

"Was that a question?" He pinches my nipple so unexpectedly I jump, but he wraps his arms around me, holding my jaw from behind. "Try again."

I roll my eyes and he bites my shoulder, this time for real. I groan. "I love my eyes."

"Good girl." He holds me tighter, his erection jerking between us. "Number three."

"Hmm..." I bite my lip, smiling. "I love the monkey hanging on me."

He flashes his eyes to me, a wicked grin on his face. He releases me, his eyes darkening. "Run."

Delicious shivers cover my body as I bolt, rushing from the room. We run around the house naked like a pair of lunatics, until we topple onto the sofa in the sitting room.

Andrea flips me onto my hands and knees and punishes me. Just as I had hoped.

* * *

"Are you nervous?" I squeeze his hand. He's been bouncing his leg since we got into the car.

Oliver is driving us to SoHo, but the traffic is moving super slowly. We upgraded to a custom-made Escalade with a partition because poor Oliver needed some privacy. Well, we did.

Locking his eyes with mine, Andrea brings my hand to his mouth and brushes my knuckles with his lips. "I'm okay."

"You look nervous." I slide closer to him and cup his face. "You don't have to be. You're just a guest." I kiss him gently.

He nods and exhales. I guess his first anonymous exhibition is as nerve-wracking as any other before.

"So, who is the other artist?" I ask to distract him.

Stupid traffic. I wish we were out of this car. It really feels claustrophobic with all this nervous energy.

Tonight, Violet Mathison is introducing a new artist who works under a simple name: Andy. It's a joined exhibition with another first-timer.

Preparing for it, Andrea/"Andy" enjoyed the artistic freedom, and tonight people will see pieces that differ from his previous work.

Without the usual pressure to live up to his hype,

he allowed himself to enjoy the creativity. I'm not a collector, but I think this is his best work yet.

He wraps his arm around my shoulder and kisses the crown of my head. "You'll see."

Well, I guess there won't be any distracting conversation. I put my head against his chest and he stops bouncing, and instead starts tapping on my back. If I can absorb some of his anxiety this way, I'm happy to do it.

We finally arrive and get out of the car, and I stop in my tracks. "What is Mother doing here?"

"I invited her." Andrea snakes his fingers through my hand.

"Chérie. We've just arrived." Mother kisses me on both cheeks. Behind her, Archie nods his greeting.

The reason I was finally able to move out from my parent's—technically my—house is Archibald Grimwald III.

During Father's recovery, Mother discovered the reason for our poor financial situation. Gambling, multiple long-term lovers, and a few failed investments.

The last one she was willing to oversee, the second one she'd chosen to ignore for years, though learning the extent of my father's betrayal broke her. The gambling was the cherry on top of it all.

Mother went into therapy and then ran into Archie at the club my boyfriend had been paying dues on because she couldn't live without it. Archie worships the earth she walks on, and it feeds her ego with the right amount of attention she's been craving for years.

She's divorcing my father and living with Archie already. And she's become slightly better at parenting, adoring Andrea. Or the expensive presents he keeps giving her.

I don't think he does it to please her or win her over as much as he's making sure she's placated enough to be nice to me.

"We're so proud of you, chérie." Mother shrugs in glee.

"Okay?" I blink a few times, watching her loop her arms with Archie as they enter the gallery. "What was that about?"

Andrea grips my neck and yanks me to his mouth, kissing me breathless.

"You'll be fine. If they hate it, you can laugh in their faces. You enjoyed the process, and that's what matters," I whisper against his lips.

He stiffens a bit and pulls me into a hug. We stand there as people pass around us.

"Vivid, your life might change tonight. In fact, it will change for sure, and I want you to know that I'll be there every step of the way. Enjoy every minute."

His words set me on high alert. "What are you talking about?"

He points to the poster in the window and the hammering in my chest goes wild. Before I can react or run away, Andrea squeezes my hand and drags me inside. For the opening night of *The Chains: A Joint Exhibit of Andy and Vivid.*

* * *

"Are you mad at me?" He snakes his arms around my waist.

"Very." I lean into him, a smile playing at my lips.

The exhibition has been a phenomenal success. Most of Andrea's paintings sold out already, and someone bought three of my pieces. Andrea stood in the shadows, letting everyone talk to me.

Violet introduced me to everyone, and I gave three interviews.

"I will make it up to you," he whispers darkly. "On your back, on your knees, begging me for more. I promise."

I laugh. "You could have skipped this one." I point to the wall in front of me. "It's kind of personal."

The gigantic canvas with splatters of colors and prints of our body parts hangs alone on the back wall of the gallery.

"The idea of someone hanging our fuckfest and

admiring it every day was just too tempting." He smirks.

"You're such an asshole."

"Proudly so, vixen." He kisses my cheek, holding me tightly.

I turn to face him, grinning. "Thank you."

Frankly, I would have never agreed to exhibit my work, but he knew it, and he didn't let my insecurities stop me.

"Thank *you*, Vivid. You keep bringing colors into my life."

I kiss him, the murmur around us dissipating. "I love you, Andrea."

"I love you too, vixen. Now let's go home. I need you naked already."

Paris

Back in late August

I tap my foot, assessing people in the coffee shop. The adrenaline rushing through my veins is addictive. That must be the reason I keep doing this. Why else?

When I first snatched someone else's coffee, I truly intended it to be just that—a one-time item off my bucket list. It was the first thing on my adventure list, to challenge myself to live on the edge a bit.

That first time when I casually picked up someone's coffee as soon as their name was announced, a jolt of excitement rushed through me before I even reached the door. I ran with that coffee like a madwoman, laughing.

I ended up giving it to a homeless person, and that felt doubly good. I was like the Robin Hood of coffee. Okay, not really, but still, the exhilaration came with a side dish of craving.

The second time, I surprised myself. I didn't plan on doing it.

But as soon as a caramel latte for someone named John—and really, if you come up with such an unimaginative Starbucks name, you don't deserve your fancy coffee—landed on the counter, I couldn't help myself. I snatched it.

And the rest is history. I'm not completely reckless, I always sweep the place to make sure there isn't anyone who knows me.

Just like today. It's raining and the coffee shop is too full to execute a swift exit. I check my watch. I should pack and move my shit to Andrea's to get settled. He's returning from rehab in a week.

I might be stuck—voluntarily—with him for a few

days to aid his recovery, so I better enjoy my little rebellion.

And this… it infuses some relaxation into my life. Twisted? Perhaps. Cathartic? Definitely.

When the line finally clears I assess the people inside, position myself between the counter and the door.

"Double shot vanilla iced latte for Finn," the barista announces.

"I'll take it," I say casually, and dash for the exit.

"Hey."

The voice comes too clear, as if already from the outside. I don't look back, but I pick up my pace, crossing the street.

Screeching brakes make me turn around as I reach the curb on the other side.

Tall, broad shoulders, expensive suit, the man curses at the driver who almost rammed into him.

My heart hammers in my chest. I should run, but I'm glued to the spot. Who would chase after their coffee and almost get run over by a car?

I look at the cup in my hand. Finn. That's who. Idiot. I roll my eyes, and that's when he meets my gaze.

The busy Manhattan street continues flowing in its usual rhythm while I go still.

His eyes are the deepest green. His light brown hair falls into his face as he finally reaches me.

If I knew my victim—Finn—needed his caffeine this badly today, I wouldn't have chased my thrill at his expense. He looks like he's been partying all night.

Or something terrible happened to him. Aside from having his coffee stolen, or being almost smashed by a car.

His jaw is set rigid, but it's not just anger that oozes from him. It's pure testosterone and, oh my God help me, my ovaries scream for attention.

He narrows his eyes at me, and I want—should—turn and leave as quickly as possible.

To my side a shopping cart full of garbage or something rolls past. I glance at the owner, a scrawny-looking lady, and shove Finn's coffee into her hand.

"Enjoy," I squeal, and wish I could give her a twenty-dollar bill, but there is no way I can rummage through my bag before Finn—at least his Starbucks name is cool—kills me.

"Well, thank you, darling." The lady beams.

Finn gapes after her for enough time for me to disappear, but for some outlandish reason I stay rooted to the ground.

The expanse of his shoulders is unreal. The man must lift several times a day.

"What the fuck?" he snarls.

I swallow, thinking about some sort of witty, original, sarcastic, or really just English words to say.

He narrows his eyes and smirks. "London?"

I was expecting anything but this. He knows my twin sister. Fuck.

"Oh, sweetheart, this is rich. You stealing coffees." He steps closer, and his masculine scent envelops me with some strange hormones that wipe my ability to think. His eyes go from angry to hungry, and my center clenches.

Holy shit.

"You'll have to make this up to me," he says suggestively, and it should appall me, but it doesn't. And then I remember.

A one-night stand.

The item on my bucket list I haven't been able to cross because I'm not that kind of a girl.

But London could be.

"Well, let me buy you another drink, then." I smile seductively. A jolt of thrill sweeps through me when his eyes darken. He wets his lip and, Christ, I think I just poked the bear.

Well, London did.

Seriously, Paris? What a meet-cute!
*While you're waiting for Paris and Finn in **Reckless Bond**, read how Violet Mathison, the gallery owner, found her happily ever after in **Chosen by the Billionaire**.*

In this enemies to lovers romance, the socially awkward hacker brings trouble to Vi's steps, but their love story is **"an excellent read from beginning to the end"**, *according to a reader's review.*

Ivy and Andrea travel to Paris and she surprises him in the most wonderful way. Read all about it in the bonus scene here: www.maxinehenri.com/hunger or scan:

If you loved this book, please spread the word and leave a review. One sentence is enough to help other readers and make me very happy.

Also by Maxine Henri

Untamed Billionaires Series

Tempted by the Billionaire (A Fake Relationship Romance)

Chosen by The Billionaire (An Enemies to Lovers Romance)

Chased by the Billionaire (An Age gap/Innocent Heroine Romance)

Stolen by the Billionaire (A Forbidden Love Romance)

Reckless Billionaires Series

Reckless Fate (A Second Chance Romance)

Reckless Desire (A Single Dad Romance)

Reckless Dare (A Fake Relationship Romance)

Reckless Deal (A Grumpy/Sunshine Bosshole Romance)

Reckless Hunger (An Age Gap Romance)

Reckless Bond (An Accidental Pregnancy Romance)

Author's Note

If you read my other books, you know I like to flirt with arts—tango, flamingo, visual arts, design.

Maybe it's the shadow artist in me, never fully ready to explore my creativity. Or it can be just my honest admiration.

In all the previous books where I toyed with the theme, I didn't really dive deeper into the artist's soul.

The tortured process of creating, the constant self-doubt, the highs and the lows. I'm very familiar with all of them as a writer and I tried to voice them through Andrea and Ivy.

Yes, their love story is beautiful, if somewhat forbidden, but it was their personal struggles and self-doubt that I enjoyed putting on paper. And struggled to write:-).

I hope you enjoyed reading their story and perhaps

found inspiration in it to get out there and truly believe in yourself.

Now, no doubt, Andrea is one of my darker heroes, but I love him. He's so dominant, yet so scared of life. I love his polarity.

I truly hope you fell in love with him and Ivy as well.

Love,

Maxine

About the Author

Maxine Henri is a contemporary romance author who infuses her stories with steamy passion and complex characters. When she's not crafting stories that will have you swooning, she can usually be found sipping on a cup of black tea while reading a good book. Or traveling to new destinations.

Maxine believes that stories matter. They facilitate emotional journeys, inspire and entertain. And when it comes to books and fiction, stories are a great escape and probably the most beneficial addiction on this planet.

Her billionaire romances are the perfect escape, offering a taste of luxury and adventure. Maxine introduces heroes who may have a dark past, but are always balanced by a lighter side. And her leading ladies? They're strong, independent women who may be a little broken, but always find their way in life.

You can connect with her on any of these platforms:

facebook.com/maxinehenriromance

instagram.com/maxinehenriromance

bookbub.com/profile/maxine-henri

amazon.com/author/maxinehenri